# He Would Never Know How He Had Hurt Her!

"Why are you so afraid?" he murmured against the warm moistness of her parted mouth.

His kiss moved to her ear, and his tongue drew loving patterns on the side of her neck. "Has someone hurt you, Leigh? *I* won't hurt you."

She battled up from the depths of submission like a drowning person crazed for air. Wouldn't hurt her? He had nearly killed her, and she was playing into his hands, letting him do it again.

Her eyes flared wide and locked with his. "Leave me alone, Padgett Williams! Don't try to understand me. Don't try to save me from myself. Just leave me alone."

**LINDA SHAW**
is the mother of three children and enjoys her life in Keene, Texas, which she shares with her husband. When Linda isn't writing romantic novels, she's practicing or teaching the piano, violin or viola.

Dear Reader:

Romance readers have been enthusiastic about Silhouette Special Editions for years. And that's not by accident: Special Editions were the first of their kind and continue to feature realistic stories with heightened romantic tension.

The longer stories, sophisticated style, greater sensual detail and variety that made Special Editions popular are the same elements that will make you want to read book after book.

We hope that you enjoy this Special Edition today, and will enjoy many more.

The Editors at Silhouette Books

# LINDA SHAW
# December's Wine

Silhouette Special Edition

Published by Silhouette Books New York

America's Publisher of Contemporary Romance

**Other Silhouette Books by Linda Shaw**

*All She Ever Wanted*
*After the Rain*
*Way of the Willow*

SILHOUETTE BOOKS, a Division of Simon & Schuster, Inc.
1230 Avenue of the Americas, New York, N.Y. 10020

To my children—Randy, Shelley and Tim.

# December's Wine

# Chapter One

Slamming doors was not a habit of Leigh Vincent. When she did it now, jarring the water decanters on two desks and shaking the fronds of a fern potted nearby, Becky Fisk turned her head to gape at her superior.

Leigh dropped a smart leather attaché case to a chair and removed a wide-brimmed hat, placing it on top. She was tall and slender, and her oval face, instead of wearing a scowl, sparkled. Pleased with herself, Leigh leaned against the dark wood door, green eyes laughing, looking like an exquisite ebony-haired cameo caught in relief.

"You look as if you ate the canary, cage and all," observed Becky, her plain features crinkling. From habit she moved toward the coffee maker to pour a generous amount into Leigh's hand-painted coffee cup. "What happened?"

Leigh ignored the tiny run creeping up her stocking and bent one trim knee to the carpet before her desk. Opening a drawer containing dozens of files, she removed a dog-eared one labeled PETER JOSHUA. With a limber movement she rose and brandished the client's file at Becky as if it were a sword.

"This," she answered. "I just had brunch with the producer of International Films, Limited. I persuaded him to raise the bid on Pete to twenty thousand dollars an episode. Padgett Williams will *not* get Peter Joshua for Everest Productions, Becky, not while I'm the agent."

Before Becky could lift her eyebrows at Leigh's habitual—and unexplainable—aversion to producer Padgett Williams, the shrill buzz of the telephone interrupted them.

Pushing a button and covering the mouthpiece with the same hand, Becky whispered to Leigh: "It's probably Penelope. She's called three times this morning. Frantic, as usual."

Leigh braced her hips against the top of her desk and, keeping the connection broken with a forefinger, waited for Becky to finish the amenities with a distraught Penelope Frame. The sultry brunette had filmed two commercials for a nationally known shampoo and was already hassling with the company.

"Yes, Penny?" Leigh said, patiently listening to the new complaint over the shampoo contract. Unconsciously she toyed with a long gold chain hanging around her neck.

"They told me I had four spots, Miss Vincent," wailed the frustrated actress. "And I've only done two. They've already gotten a girl for the airport take."

"Now, don't get upset yet, Penny," soothed Leigh. "Let me talk to Mel. I'm sure he plans to use you on two more. Why wouldn't he? You do excellent work. He may want to have a few months lapse with a new face, that's all."

"He loved what I did. He said so! Oh, they're all liars, every last one of them. *Why would he do this to me?*"

Twisting her face into a grimace, truly sympathizing with the girl, thinking there was some truth to what she said, Leigh held the telephone four inches from her ear.

"They always have reasons, darling, even if they're bad ones. Let me see what I can do. Go to a movie or something. If I miss you, I'll put a message on your answering service. Don't cry all day and mess up that lovely face, do you hear me?"

Sniffing, Penelope groaned her agreement. "Oh, okay. But, damnit, if that little witch Karen has put out and Mel's taken her over me . . . I'll . . . I'll sue the monster. I swear I will!"

Leigh's soft laughter had the effect of soothing oil on turbulent waters. "You know I'm with you. And I won't make a move without you. Now go do something. Except eat. I'll get back to you."

Thoughtfully replacing the receiver, making a mental note to herself, Leigh rose to spread the Joshua file out on her desk.

"She'll be all right," the secretary predicted and placed the brimming coffee cup upon Leigh's desk.

"I know. But I'd like to slap both of Mel's faces."

"Do you think Everest Productions will make a counterbid on Pete?" Becky asked. She set a small stack of messages beside Leigh's phone. "Mr. Williams probably thinks the LEV Agency is the kiss of death by now."

Smiling, Leigh paused to remove the jacket of a two-piece linen suit the color of rich moss. As she draped it over the back of her swivel chair she shook her head.

"That's okay with me. And no, I don't think Everest will bid again. They don't spend that kind of money for a television series, for one thing. Besides, Peter isn't worth more than twenty thousand an episode."

Leigh bent over her desk, scanning through the Joshua file, flipping through photographs of a stunningly handsome man in his early twenties—blond, ruggedly muscled, typical beefcake material. Looking over her shoulder, Becky heaved a long, honest sigh.

"He's hardly worth that, more's the pity."

Sheets of correspondence rustled through the quiet of the eighth-floor office as Leigh searched for one letter in particular. Withdrawing it, she thoughtfully placed it beside the hefty Los Angeles telephone directory. Then she ran a well-kept nail down a list of numbers taped to her desktop.

"With *that* face," Leigh said, dialing, then gesturing to a group of contracts representing a dozen western-wear television commercials Peter Joshua had filmed, "who needs talent?"

Lowering herself to her chair, Leigh reached for her third cup of the day. Sunlight, filtering through a window which shut out the clamor of the city below, reflected off a gold bracelet circling her wrist. Already she was tired, she thought. And her day would not end before eight o'clock in the evening. There were times when she would gladly walk away from it all.

She had opened this small dramatic agency when she was only twenty-three, fresh out of a state university attended the hard way—nights—and armored with a shield of stubborn desperation. The two women had worked together for five years now. It seemed a lifetime.

Leigh wondered at her secretary's tact. The woman couldn't help but think her attitude toward Everest Productions was mysterious—excessive, to say the least. But no matter how curious Becky grew, she never pressed the issue. When Leigh had explained that she simply did not like Padgett Williams as a producer, Becky accepted it at face value, though the excuse was pathetic, ridiculous.

Padgett Williams had the reputation of being the finest producer in Everest history, perhaps the entire industry. A genius, some critics called him; a throwback to the Golden Age of films; a miracle worker on film.

Yet, as an agent, she had not only refused to seek Everest's business, she had gone out of her way to get counterbids against them. Not one of the LEV Agency's clients, if offered a contract to work with Everest, had ever signed.

"Mr. Radnor?" Leigh now spoke into the telephone with the correct amount of distance in her voice, a skill she had perfected. "This is the LEV Agency."

"I've been expecting your call," said the aloof Everest attorney with a skill *he* had perfected.

"We have a counterbid on your offer to Peter Joshua, Mr. Radnor. The insurance-investigator series, you remember."

The attorney muttered something totally unintelligible. Leigh arched her dark eyebrows at her secretary as if to say, Padgett William's man is losing his cool already.

"May I ask who made the counteroffer, darling?" he asked, his tone laced with intimate suggestiveness.

The expression on Leigh's face remained serenely pleasant. She smoothed back her simple black chignon with a steady hand, but her tone was firm. Mr. Radnor was foolish to think she was susceptible to a thrown-out endearment and a bit of flattering innuendo.

"Now, Mr. Radnor, you know I can't tell you that, not at this stage of negotiations. But if you wish to make another offer, I will gladly relay it to my client."

"For a beautiful woman, Miss Vincent, you have the mercy of a black widow spider," retorted the legal adviser to Everest Productions. "When will you contact Joshua?"

"This afternoon."

"Could you hold off on that? At least until three o'clock?"

Pinching the receiver between her jaw and shoulder, Leigh scribbled some notes on a pad before her. "Certainly, Mr. Radnor."

"Before you hang up, dear," the man inquired with more caution than before, "tell me, is Everest bidding against just one studio?"

"You're correct on that score," she told him. "Now, I'll hold off contacting my client until three o'clock. If I haven't heard from you by then, my advice will be to accept the other offer."

The attorney took a breath which sounded to Leigh as if he would like to have called her an obscene name. His invitation for cocktails surprised her.

"Oh, I am sorry, Mr. Radnor," she replied evasively. "My afternoon is a disaster as it is."

His laugh was forced and only a hairsbreadth from mockery. "You're a tough lady, just as they say, aren't you, Miss Vincent?"

Leigh's fingers tightened about the receiver until her knuckles turned white. Her smooth skin tensed over the high aristocratic cheekbones, and she cautioned herself about losing her temper. "Well, we won't go into what *they* say, Mr. Radnor. I'm sure it makes for very boring conversation. Around three o'clock, then?"

"Three o'clock," agreed the disappointed attorney. "Mr. Padgett wants this young man." With a brief goodbye, Leigh quietly replaced the receiver.

When the two women's eyes met, Leigh's hardening with a glittering affront she could not disguise, Becky unconsciously touched her lips with her fingertips. But the secretary said nothing. She watched her superior sweep across the room to a small cubicle which they used as a makeshift dressing room. For a moment the only sound was Leigh washing her face and repairing her makeup.

Being a dramatic agent was not easy these days, Leigh reflected. Actors were in depressing abundance, not only out of work but with little prospects of getting any. Talent was not an issue. anymore; economy was. Placing a mediocre actor such as Peter Joshua had been almost like asking someone to sign a contract for the moon. But Leigh's instincts had proved true. Miraculously enough, the public had warmed to the sweet innocence of Pete's handsome face. Directors appeared willing to exert the extra effort to make up for his lack of talent. If the cameras rolled too long and tempers raged white hot, bank accounts remained in the black anyway.

Presently Leigh stepped into the open doorway, repinning her chignon with absent ease. Once again, she felt in control.

"Tell me, Becky," she said slowly, pausing, leaning a slender shoulder against the facing, "just how much gossip do you hear about me? What do other secretaries say about me on their coffee breaks?"

Leigh knew by the way Becky shifted her eyes that the woman would rather have been asked any question than that particular one. Yet Becky was a loyal and faithful friend; if she said something, a person could stake her reputation on it.

"You could guess what they say, Leigh," she hedged, "and not be too far wrong."

"I know they think I'm hard-nosed. That's no secret to anyone," mused Leigh, her eyes distant, as if she remembered things she would rather have left buried in the past. "What else? Don't spare my feelings."

"Are you sure?"

"I asked, didn't I?"

"Well," admitted Becky, "some . . . think you have a lover."

"A lover!?" Leigh exclaimed, halfway between laughter and disbelief. "Who, for heaven's sake?"

Becky shrugged. "The name changes every time you take on a male client. At the present, it's Peter Joshua."

Leigh's shoulders drooped and her hands stilled at the injustice of such vicious tongues. For several moments she said nothing, frowning at the run in her stocking, as if she were considering repairing it.

"I'm sorry, Becky," she said. "Once all that talk

died down about Margie, I thought people would grow tired of speculating about me. Some people can lead absolutely scandalous lives, and no one says anything. I have a daughter and no husband, and I've been the favorite topic over drinks for years. Why?"

The toothy smile curving Becky's mouth was the only outstanding feature in a plain, comfortable face.

"Leigh, if you were fat and ugly no one would say anything. If you had a face like mine, people would say you were lucky. You just can't keep a low enough profile, not in the work you do. And you're too smart. People resent that, especially men. What can you expect?"

The smile Leigh sent her was small and slightly defeated. She switched off the light in the cubicle as if gossip didn't matter. Gathering up her handbag, pausing to search for her car keys, she studied them for a moment without seeing.

"I think I should give you a raise for all the extra garbage of this job," she told Becky.

"I'm satisfied, Leigh. I always have been. Where shall I say you're going, if anyone calls?"

Scooping up her jacket and draping it across her arm with a bleak, negligent grace, Leigh settled her hat on her head. The brim dipped low, obscuring the directness of her eyes, giving her the faintest glimmer of mystery.

"School gets out early today. I'll pick up Margie and drop her off with Mother. But I'll be back before the Ellery Queen of Everest Productions returns his call."

Becky laughed softly.

After Leigh had pulled the door shut behind her,

she paused in the long hallway. For once it was empty, and the elevator stood open, staring at her with its square, unblinking eye.

Eighteen years old, she thought, her eyes vacant. She had been only eighteen years old when she had conceived Margie. She had broken her father's heart. Well, even in this liberated age, one still paid for one's mistakes, didn't one? If she had been a man, the single male parent, everyone would have smiled and cooed their sympathies: *You poor dear, how noble, being a mother and father to such an adorable child.* But no one said such things to her. They looked at her with blame in the angles of their chins and said, *Oh.*

Ah, well, she admitted she was bitter. But she didn't imagine the surprise whenever she said her name: Miss Vincent. *I see,* they said, smiling politely, when they were blinded to what she was, when they couldn't possibly see.

Spring days, Leigh decided as she weaved her small tan Buick through the honking frenzy of Los Angeles traffic, could actually be a turning point in her life if she let them. Beyond her, clear California skies spread forever. Flowers thrust themselves upward everywhere she looked, perfuming the air so that one smelled something besides fast-food exhaust and diesel fumes. Her mother's jonquils and narcissus overflowed the beds at home, and the trees were covered with new foliage. Los Angeles had gotten a face-lift. And what was wrong with a face-lift? Her life could use one.

Leigh knew she would arrive at Margie's school too early, but moments alone were hard to come by. She craved a quiet time to lean her head against the steering wheel—to wait, to slow down, to think, to rest.

Parking outside a tall chain-link fence facing an ostentatious sign which read New Coventry School for Girls, she watched the bright colors of shirts and skirts flit across the playground like runaway scraps of yarn. As she flicked off the ignition and slumped in her seat a dozen fourth-grade girls soared in the swings and swooped down a slide, screeching at the top of their lungs.

Play period was Margie's last activity of the day and Leigh spotted her immediately. She waved, and Margie, screwing up her impish face, dipped in a ridiculous curtsy. Then she bobbed off with a friend. Leigh took off her hat and pressed her temples.

How like her father she was, except for the eyes. Margie had inherited Leigh's own clear green eyes, but that was all. No judge or jury in the country would deny Padgett Williams's claim of paternity if Padgett knew that Margie was his daughter—which he did not know—which he would never know.

Oh, Lord! she mourned, slumping forward with a heavy sigh. It never failed, did it? She never heard Padgett's name or saw one of his productions without being reminded of that American Legion dance ten years ago. She had thought time would heal the cutting edge of the memory, but it hadn't. She was beginning to despair that anything could.

"You mean you've never drunk champagne before?" her friend Marty had teased as she placed the second glass into Leigh's protesting hand.

The dance floor, having taken all day to decorate, was filled with graduating seniors and their friends. Even among all those spiraling, clamorous people, it had taken her the space of one minute to spot him.

She viewed him from a distance and wondered what he was doing there—a tall, supple figure with watchful, brooding eyes. He had come searching for a friend, one of the teachers, but she saw only the Marine uniform which marked him as solitary, different.

When Marty forced the glass of champagne into her hand, his gaze captured hers and held, as if he chided her. He arched one dark brow in a sober-faced salute, then lifted his beer in a toast across the room. His smile flashed across his face with the startling clarity of sunlight through menacing thunderheads. "Some enchanted evening, you will see a stranger . . ."

Not exactly like that, Leigh remembered grimly, forcing a smile as Margie opened the car door and tumbled onto the seat.

"I would like a hamburger on the way home, please," Margie chirped sweetly and immediately flattened her upturned nose against the window to wave goodbye to someone.

After much repetition, their afterschool routine was a familiar, comfortable game. Sometimes it took the form of a gentle contest, a bright daughter outwitting a dull, naive mother. Today Margie was a regal princess, throwing out her demands with a glib confidence that all would be granted because she was Marjorie Vincent, nine-year-old darling of Leigh Vincent.

"Would you, now?" Leigh came back with exaggerated firmness as Margie's buoyancy decreased a small amount. "And what if I'm broke? Penniless? A pauper?"

Her daughter considered this possibility for a moment as Leigh veered off onto a highway exit which would quickly take them out of city bustle.

"Then Grandma would have to take on more piano students," she decided, solving her problem with practical childishness. "And I would just order French fries."

Laughing, Leigh settled back in her seat. The glance she tossed her brown-haired daughter was warmly affectionate. "Your sense of self-sacrifice is so uncomplicated, my dear. What did you do today? Anything interesting?"

"Jenny McKinney told Miss Scolby she looked like Captain Kangaroo," Margie confided with a perfectly straight face.

"Oh-ho. I suppose Miss Scolby hit the ceiling."

Margie giggled. "She pushed her glasses up on her nose and said, *'Miss McKinney!'*"

"Is that all?"

"Well"—Margie turned up a realistic palm—"she really does look like Captain Kangaroo." Her girlish mirth rippled, and she twisted in her seat to peer at the car following them.

Here, Leigh considered, was where she should be able to muse that Margie got that gay little laugh from her father. Although Leigh didn't know precisely what Margie had gotten from her father except most of his physical characteristics. His voice? His disposition? His inclinations?

Padgett's laugh . . . As the senior-class party had broken up into small private groups and migrated into homes of people she had never seen before, it had been a rich, delightful sound. She had walked beside him on the beach—a naive innocent—holding his hand, dizzy from too much champagne and the powerful intoxication of his chiseled virility.

Yet it had been his silences that had unraveled her. Those long, wordless lulls when he stopped walking and tipped up her chin with a strong finger and probed his way into her mind, as if he wondered if she were real. His eyes were so gray and honest, yet they brimmed with memories of war she sensed he had never shared with anyone. His breathing was as torn as hers, and her senses began to blur, her knees to weaken, and the crash of her own pulse deafened her.

"Leigh, sweet Leigh," he said hoarsely and with some effort, "this is insane. Why am I hurting so badly for you?"

The hard circle of his arms drew her into another world, where she kept stumbling over the unexpected masculine smell of him, the hypnotizing roar of the surf. She pleaded with wide, yearning eyes, begging to be taken.

"I don't know," she whispered and slipped her hands beneath his shirt, pressing with her palms to show him the burning which consumed her. "I can't think. I—I can't . . ."

"I should be shot for this," he muttered as he drew her downward to the sand, as he groped for the eagerness of her mouth with his, as he became her first—and only—lover. . . .

The Buick left a dusty film hovering in the long driveway which drifted behind them like sheer powdery sugar. The old pillared house stood like some sentinel against the gentle, undulating California hills beyond it. Deep in the shadows of trees the color changed from the pale blue glint of open sky to a deep lilac laced with silver green which was perpetually cool.

Vincents had lived in the house for four generations, which was not all that impressive a history, Leigh thought. She pressed her foot to the brake before a double-doored brick garage. Now, two single women and one small child rattled about in these high-ceilinged rooms, requiring little of one part-time maid and a man who came twice a week during the summers to help with the grounds.

Leigh glanced at the sleek silver car sharing the drive with them. "I see Mother hasn't finished with her pupils."

Scooping up her bag, she strolled across the clipped lawn as Margie dashed ahead. When the door opened, the faint sound of a Bach invention drifted from a wing facing the east. Elizabeth Vincent had three pianos in this house. Leigh had cut her teeth on piano concertos, the opera, and orchestral concerts.

After a moment of prowling in the refrigerator for a snack, Margie planted a hasty kiss on her mother's cheek and skittered up the stairs for a frivolous afternoon of cartoons.

"It's a holiday, Mother," she called back as an excuse before Leigh could protest.

Hating to interrupt a student's lesson, Leigh nonetheless made her way toward the studio and rapped gently on the door. Immediately the sound of voices and music hushed. A tall, graceful woman opened the door and smiled. She wore her hair parted in the center and pulled straight back to bring into prominence the same striking cheekbones Leigh had inherited.

"Come in, Leigh, it's all right. You remember Stanley Gibbs, don't you? He came within a hair of winning the Van Cliburn competition last year."

Leigh smiled at the angular face behind thick horn-rimmed glasses. "I only came to tell you I have to go back to the office, Mother. I've deposited Margie. She's in her room."

"I'll see to her. Faith said she would put on a bite of dinner before she left. You will come home to eat, won't you?"

"Probably not." A glance at her wristwatch sent her moving toward the door. Placing a fond kiss on the smoothness of her mother's cheek, Leigh inhaled the delicate fragrance. Always, that marvelous smell. "I really have to dash back to L.A. It's good to see you again, Stanley."

If Stanley acknowledged her, Leigh failed to hear it. She ambled toward the front door through the dark, early-century rooms with somber, heavily grained wood and glass, and burgundy velvet and brown silk the color of rich earth.

She had been born in this house. Her father had stood before that very mantel when she told them she had seen a doctor, that she was two months pregnant. He had braced one elbow on the mantel and buried his graying head in his hand. No one had said very much. But she had heard them talking, arguing, and the weeping of her mother late at night because Leigh had refused to tell them who the father was.

It had all been properly dignified. None of the family had condemned her or suggested she go away for a while. But her father had died two years later. She would never know if she had hastened his premature death. Just now, remembering him, Leigh could not bear to look backward as she pulled the heavy door shut behind her.

At precisely fifteen minutes before three o'clock Leigh rushed into her office, glanced at Becky's lengthening list of phone calls, and placed a paper bag in the center of her desk.

"Again?" Becky's protective disapproval did not perturb Leigh in the slightest. "You've lost too much weight to keep doing that, Leigh."

"I'm sure I'll live." Leigh disregarded the advice.

She shrugged out of her jacket, not bothering to tuck in the soft folds of the silk blouse which persisted in slithering from the waistband of her skirt. Fishing around in the sack for a piece of grilled cheese sandwich, she took a bite and moved to pour herself a cup of black coffee. Soft wisps of hair had fallen free of her chignon and began to curl artlessly about the oval of her face. Meaning to repair her dishabille the moment she finished eating, she jotted hurried notes.

Without lifting her head she said, "I can handle the rest, Becky. You've had a big day already. Go home."

Becky actually had put in a rigorous day, but she hesitated. She made no secret of believing Leigh was a compulsive worker who would someday collapse on the spot.

"I could come back in later, Leigh. Why don't I do that? Then you could have a clear desk tomorrow."

"Nonsense," disagreed Leigh, her mouth full.

She rose to brush the crumbs of her lunch into a napkin, thinking she had just enough time to repair herself by the time Everest's Mr. Radnor returned his call. The paper bag made a noisy crumpling as she threw it into the wastebasket.

"Go on home, Becky," she called over her shoulder on her way to the dressing room. "I will see your smiling face tomorrow."

As she removed the pins from her hair, holding them between her teeth to brush out the long silky swirls, she was only half aware of a commotion outside. With a few deft strokes she twisted the tresses into a bun and began pinning it into place.

The voices were raised in heated discussion. Who in the world? she wondered, stepping from the anteroom, both hands lifted to the back of her head, her mouth filled with hairpins.

The two men were both tall, and though one had his back to her, she recognized his voice immediately as that of Hugh Radnor. She stiffened when, with a ruthless lack of warning, her eyes collided with the hostile ones of Padgett Williams.

Coming face to face with Marjorie's father was a tableau she had fantasized hundreds of times. She had pictured herself as the wronged champion of virtue, the outraged victim who rushed forward and screamed, *I will never forgive you! You have ruined my life!*

But now she was helplessly frozen, incapable of moving, of speaking, of even thinking coherently. Somewhere in the murky vagueness of her shock, Leigh realized they were all staring at her. They expected her to do or say something appropriate. She thought she was less capable of civilities than she had been of prudence ten years earlier.

Without the slightest flicker of recognition, Padgett moved toward her, assurance in his lithe build, arrogance in the saunter of his steps. He was more slender now. At forty, the handsomeness of his face had grown more sharply delineated. The silver of his hair, in dramatic contrast with the black of a soft turtleneck sweater, was stunning. The curve of his lips—she couldn't call it a real smile—assaulted her senses.

Like some windup doll running down, Leigh slowly removed the pins from her mouth. One slender hand dropped to rest upon her breasts, which rose and fell with panic. She was positive he did not miss that fluttering gesture, yet it was not for the reason he thought. She felt abysmally trapped.

"May I do somethi—"

"Oh, I do hope so, Miss . . ." His interruption was rudely spoken, calculated to rattle her. "Miss, ah—"

"Miss Vincent," Hugh Radnor supplied, tonelessly efficient. Reaching inside his suit coat, the attorney consulted a small notebook, then flipped it shut.

"Oh, yes," Padgett agreed.

Her name, shockingly, seemed to have no effect on him whatsoever. That should not have surprised her, she thought. It had been too many years. Lifted out of an expected context, names often meant nothing and the mind played tricks.

"Miss Vincent," he went on smoothly, "the female paragon who dangles Peter Joshua beneath my nose, then snatches him away. The lady agent who enjoys teasing my attorney. That's not very nice, Miss . . ."

He hesitated, then grinned infuriatingly, like a boy planning a naughty prank.

*"Vin-cent."* She spat out the name between gritted teeth. "And I find I don't make as much money being nice, Mr. Williams."

He did not refute her observation, and she stepped briskly to her desk. Without lifting her eyes she knew he was measuring every step she took. He was a complex man, full of anger, curiosity, and amusement all at the same time.

To keep him from noticing that she was trembling, she opened a drawer and withdrew a pair of tortoiseshell eyeglasses. Putting them on, she felt, at least afforded her a modicum of disguise. She fumbled for her chair and sat before her knees betrayed her completely.

"Would you please be seated?" she invited with a

forced coolness. She gestured at several chairs positioned about her desk. "I was expecting Mr. Radnor to call."

For a full thirty seconds he did not speak. His intense gray eyes narrowed as he paused, and Leigh realized she was holding her breath.

"And then you wouldn't have had to hide behind those glasses, would you?" he asked solemnly.

Padgett did not sit, but his attorney lowered himself to a chair and balanced an attaché case upon his knees. He meticulously placed his notebook upon it and clicked his ball-point pen, readied.

Pressing her fingertips against her upper lip, Leigh decided that taking the offensive was all she had left. "Does your visit mean you're prepared to make a counterbid for Peter Joshua's contract, Mr. Williams?"

He appeared to be concentrating. When he aimed a lean forefinger at her face, Leigh unconsciously adjusted the glasses, then wished she hadn't. It was an exposing move.

"Every time we make an offer on an actor, Miss Vincent," he said, "he has the strangest way of escaping us. Do you have any comment upon that phenomenon?" She scribbled agitatedly on a pad as he talked. "First," he continued his list, "we lost Teresa Jessell. Then Neil Cord. I could name at least a half dozen more, Miss Vincent. Warner generally ends up with them. Or Columbia. I don't understand. Isn't Everest money good enough for you? We're solvent."

She took a long second to moisten her lips. Then she lifted her chin and struggled to look elegantly unruffled. "You're not making this easy, Mr. Williams."

The glasses, she found, did not shield her from his

scrutiny, and they shielded her even less when he stepped purposefully to the side of her desk. Catching one hip and thigh upon the edge as support, he placed the flat of his palm insolently over her notepad, trapping her hand with its fiercely gripped pen. Her eyes riveted to the tanned strength of his hand. Thinking that this could not be happening, she watched his denim jacket fall open to reveal the distinct trimness of his waist and the outline of his stomach, which was flat beneath finely cut pants.

"You're the one who's making it difficult, my dear," he countered logically. "Or is it all merely a matter of incompetence on your part?"

Wrenching her hand free, Leigh cradled it in her lap as if it were burned.

"Sir," she replied tightly, "in my work, the actor goes to the highest bidder of his choice. If you want Peter Joshua, you'll have to make a higher offer than your previous one. That's how it works."

An odd expression drifted across Padgett's face. He cocked his head, as if puzzled at her abrasive haughtiness. Leigh felt the sudden scald of her cheeks and knew the reaction did not escape him. Just how far did empathy go? He could not possibly guess how inseparably her life was joined to his in the creation of another human life. Could he?

As if he were dissatisfied with his own conclusions, Padgett slowly pulled himself upright and stood squarely. "Well, Miss Vincent. I think you come with a high price tag."

Her eyes wrenched upward to the angles of his features.

His voice deepened to a cryptic huskiness. "I'm not sure I can afford you."

This wasn't, Leigh figured, a cat-and-mouse game

with him. She could not imagine a man less inclined to play games. His reputation was one of ruthless pursuit to get exactly what he wanted. If she played games, she would surely lose.

Getting up from her desk, Leigh stepped forward. "Becky, I can handle this from here. Why don't you go home as we planned? I'll fill in the papers on Pete and leave them on your desk."

The smoothness of Padgett's voice behind her gave her a start. She spun about.

"Hugh," he said casually, as if he didn't notice, "why don't you just go on, too? I think Miss Vincent and I might as well thrash out this little problem over dinner."

"I beg your pardon," she began.

"You already have plans for dinner?"

"Why, no, but—"

"Good. I have reservations at Cardeau's. Hugh, on your way back to the office, could you tell them to expect two?"

Swiftly agreeing, as if this were all some carefully rehearsed script of Everest Productions, Hugh stepped through the office door into the hall. Without a second glance at the anxiety staining Becky's round face, he motioned to the secretary.

"After you, madam," he said with precise nineteenth-century deference.

Shrugging, as if to say she intensely disliked all of this, Becky sent Leigh a frowning message. Are you sure? she asked without any sound.

Leigh nodded to her secretary, motioning her out into the hall with Mr. Radnor. She didn't turn to face Padgett Williams then but stood watching the door close, much as if she were in court, rising to receive her sentence.

In less than ten minutes she and Margie's father were in her office, alone. She could picture him behind her now, lounging indolently against her desk. And she had no idea what to say to him, where to go from here. Veiling her eyes, setting her mouth with a certain blandness to disguise her dread, she spun about.

When she did, Padgett wasn't leaning against her desk at all. He stood directly behind her, looming above her. He could have touched her cheek. His inspection—appallingly thorough, capable of stripping away externals—was not very different from another inspection years before. For one mad instant she imagined he knew, that he felt . . .

She vowed she would not be intimidated; the man was a magnificently clever actor. He calculated everything—his moves, his timing, the innuendoes of his breathing. But he was only a man, and she would not make a second mistake with him.

Resenting his macho strategy, Leigh ignored his nearness and stepped to a chair where her hat lay with her jacket. She saw him move to assist her, but she didn't want him touching her. Shrugging into the jacket in a calculated effect of her own, she warned him with a gesture that she could not be taken in by his charisma.

As if her riposte were a literal one, bringing him to a halt with a bloodstain on his shirt, he paused. He thought a moment, then chuckled. He understood her message exactly.

"I don't know what your game is, Miss Vincent," he said softly, remaining where he was, one hand plunged deeply into a pocket while she gathered her handbag and attaché case. "But I swear to heaven, before this evening is over I *will* know."

Her green gaze locked with his. "Do you think so, Mr. Williams?" she came back. She reached for the doorknob and did not look at him again. "Many have said that to me before. None have ever known."

## Chapter Two

$\mathcal{L}$eigh stood several feet behind Padgett as he conferred with the headwaiter at Cardeau's. She rarely went anywhere with a man. Standing here now, on a step higher than he, confronted with the broad span of his shoulders in a tapered denim jacket, was more than a little disturbing.

During the half hour it had taken to drive, they had hardly spoken at all. The truth had deadened her tongue a half dozen times, yet she could not say it. How many opportunities had she missed the last five years? Hadn't she had a dozen chances to say, *Padgett Williams, you have a daughter?* And none so good as this. But no, she could not tell him who she was.

The evening would be intolerable.

With his arm filled with a number of leather-covered menus, the waiter stepped forward to lead them to a table. Before Leigh could take the last step, Padgett's fingers closed firmly about the bones of her wrist.

Her eyes flashed to his with the urgency of electricity. He warned her with a look: You are here with me, and even if you don't like this place, please me and be cordial.

So Leigh moved with him, hardly daring to enjoy the pleasant sensation of heads turning, nodding to her because she was with him. She drew back against him only once; it seemed wrong that he should touch her again. His fingers tightened upon her wrist. He is in control, she thought. Again, he is in control. Unwanted memories of a moonlit beach flashed through her mind.

Cardeau's was more famous for its clientele than for its cuisine, and Leigh admired the exquisite eclectic decor. Clusters of casually dressed intellectuals filled the cozy nooks and semiprivate crannies. Warmly paneled walls were cluttered with photographs and caricatures of actors and a few better-known writers.

As Padgett held her chair she took it gratefully, her poise nearly exhausted. Turning her palm toward the hum of conversation, she said, "Am I supposed to smoke extralong cigarettes and sip vintage wine and talk knowledgeably about Henry Thoreau?"

A surprisingly boyish smile teased one corner of his mouth. As the waiter scribbled on his flourished pad Padgett paused to order them a martini.

"You may smoke and sip anything you want," he replied dryly as the waiter moved away, "but for pity's sake don't discuss Thoreau."

She was desperate for something to say besides Where is all this going to end? I can't bear for you to hurt me again. "Don't you like Thoreau?" she blurted.

"I like the looks of Peter Joshua. Would you take off that hat?"

Involuntarily she placed both palms to the crown of her head, as if she weren't sure whether he hated the sight of it or planned to wrestle it off her.

"What's wrong with my hat?"

Padgett smiled at her feminine predictability and, without the least awkwardness, leaned forward. With his face tilted as it was, it nearly touched hers beneath the drooping brim. His look asked her how he had missed knowing her before now.

Leigh froze immediately, her eyes fixed on the smooth planes of his nose. The lingering fragrance of soap blended with his aftershave. After all these years it still affected her—the masculine smell of him, the driving force of him. For that one charm which had not changed she almost hated him.

"Not a thing," he said and watched the semblance of a smile stiffen on her lips.

She twisted her head away, then back, her lips parting. "But I—" she whispered and stopped, waiting.

Neither of them seemed to draw a breath.

Leigh thought, for that moment, that all life ceased everywhere. A spell spun out over the space between them—invisible, drugging them like some devilish witch's potion, pulling them together until his mouth nearly touched hers.

Somewhere the shattering of glass sent a gasp rustling through the room. Instantly the spell snapped. Blinking rapidly, Leigh suddenly came to herself in astonishment. Padgett made an oddly choked sound and drew back.

He wiped a hand across his mouth. "I want to see

who I talk to," he finally explained and settled into his chair.

She was too shaken to even reply. Ten years, and she was right back where she started from. Whatever had sparked between them once was certainly not incapable of exploding to life again. That chemistry, or whatever it was, had not disappeared with the passing of years. If anything, it had grown more volatile.

In the space of mere seconds Padgett's smile returned, as pleasant as before. It would be easy to believe it had been a fleeting illusion. Padgett, after all, had always sold himself well. His people adored him and probably broke their backs for him.

He was a dangerous man, she decided, letting out her breath. And she was much too bitter, too lonely. She removed her hat with hands which refused to stop trembling. Her words were remote and tight, unlike her own voice.

"I got the distinct impression you brought me here to lay down ultimatums, Mr. Williams. Not talk to me."

"First impressions are usually wrong. Shall we begin again?"

She wanted to say he could not possibly go back far enough to begin again with her, but the waiter interrupted to take their order. Grateful for the chance to observe Padgett without his knowing it, Leigh busily removed her glasses and placed them in her purse. She studied him through a thick frill of lowered lashes and thought, This is the father of my child.

Padgett's virility was not exactly understated; it was obvious in the carriage of his head, which could sometimes appear arrogant. The corded muscles of his neck, his narrow waist that could afford to be seen in hugging pants, and his lean, tight buttocks drew a woman's eye. He looked directly at the waiter when he spoke. She liked that; most people did not really notice whom they gave orders to.

She listened as Padgett ordered their dinner in French without first asking her what she wanted. His gestures when he talked were expressive and fluent. How egotistical of him! How conceited! But she didn't object. Whatever it was, she knew she would like it. That in itself was an uncanny familiarity. She wondered if he realized it.

When Padgett turned suddenly, she was unprepared for it. He had caught her in the act of spying.

"Some of my friends call me Paddy," he said easily, embarrassing her because his grin told her he had enjoyed being watched.

She did not reply.

"Are you going to tell me your first name?" he prodded, sipping his drink, then lacing his fingers together. He appeared to regret the bite of his sarcasm in her office. His appreciation of her sensitivity as a woman softened his eyes. "Are you afraid?"

Yes! She was terrified of the memories that hearing her name might trigger in him. She laughed lightly. "Don't be silly," she said. "My name is Leigh. *My* friends call me Leigh. You may call me Miss Vincent."

The rich depth of his own laughter did strange things to her. She smiled involuntarily.

"There's no need to be afraid," he said and noticed how the ebony color of her hair contrasted with the paleness of her face.

Trying to calm herself, Leigh glanced about the

room and listened to the rumble of many people talking, eating, the faint echo of Donna Summer over the silvery clink of flatware against glass. The line between Padgett's brows deepened. She could feel him grappling to figure her out. Things he did not understand were shifting in his head, a past which he could not pinpoint.

"There's something about you," he mused softly, then paused, shaking his head. It sent a lock of hair tumbling across his forehead. She wished he would brush it back; it made him look too much like the old Padgett she knew.

*"Déjà vu?"* she suggested, then forced a brilliant smile to divert his thoughts. "There are many things about me. My fortune is the believability of my face. I remind people of the girl next door. Isn't that who I remind you of, Mr. Will—"

He held up a cautioning finger.

"Padgett," she corrected herself, then grimaced, lowering her eyes. She was chattering; she despised hearing a woman chatter.

He balanced his jaw on his fist. "I believe you're giving me a performance," he said, amused. "But that's all right. My fortune is knowing a good performance when I see one."

Brilliant color washed up the sides of her neck. "I'm sorry. I shouldn't be giving a performance. Let's get down to business."

"Do you perform for all your clients?"

She averted her face, resenting the question. "Ordinarily I'm a very simple person. No, I do not perform. I like my work, and I'm good at it. I give people a service that's worthwhile. I can live with that."

Padgett lifted his shoulders. The corners of his lips

curled, and she found that alarmingly attractive. The waiter placed silver and napkins before them, and they continued talking around him.

"Is that all you want," he questioned, "to live with it? Why didn't you say that you love it, or that you're proud of it?"

She could have been eighteen years old again, unable to define herself. "How I look at myself is not the issue here. We came to talk about Peter Joshua."

As the waiter placed a crepe of Stroganoff and a salad before her, she had to lean around him. Rich red wine filled their glasses, and Padgett sipped before he spoke.

"Do you think it's selfish to want something solely for yourself, with no redeeming motive of being worthwhile, as you put it?" He threw out his hand with pretended dramatic flair. "Do you have visions of serving society?"

"You make films. Don't you have visions?"

"I make films for the money."

Leigh pursed her lips at him, thinking it was an extremely dispassionate view, especially for a man who didn't even need money.

"Ah, well, at least you haven't fallen into the trap of us mere mortals who console ourselves by believing we do something beneficial," she said.

Padgett touched his heart like a wounded Shakespearean Hamlet.

"And you're overacting," she added.

In spite of her banter, Leigh felt as if Padgett were slowly stalking her back against a wall where she would be trapped into saying something horribly incriminating. The last thing she wanted to do was join the ranks of his adoring public. She chewed her food without tasting.

Then, as if impulsively burning her last bridge, she dared to say: "I think you sound like a taker, Padgett, not a giver."

With a surprised arch of his brows, Padgett watched her green eyes challenge him. Most of the women he knew desired his approval so much that they said nothing of any consequence for fear of saying the wrong thing. But Leigh not only refused to coddle him, she openly disapproved of him. He grew absorbed in the pinkness of her mouth as she ate and let his own dinner sit untouched.

"In fact, Padgett," she went on, so caught up in her own boldness that she flirted with the chance of giving her secret away, "I think you've probably been a taker all your life. Am I wrong?"

Bracing his forearms on each side of his plate, he almost smiled at her. He lifted a finger to rub the space between his nose and his lip.

"Probably," he agreed, "but I've never had anyone say it to me, just like that."

"Perhaps it's time someone did," she said. She raised her glass at him, then sipped. "I think you're a selfish man, Mr. Williams. You never give, and you resent someone who does. You're a man of power. You make decisions which involve millions of dollars and people's whole lives. But you don't remember what it's like to be where I am."

Her color was intriguingly high. She was involved with making her point, and Padgett leaned back, fascinated.

"How old are you, Leigh?"

"I beg your pardon?"

"You heard me. How old are you?"

Leigh felt the wine rushing to her head, and she replaced the glass on the table with a harder thump than she intended.

"I'm twenty-eight years old. That's rather rude."

"Is asking a personal question rude? Why?"

A flushed confusion flitted across her face. She placed the tips of her fingers to one temple and pondered where his questions would lead.

"You've never married?" he asked with some hesitancy.

When Leigh's eyelids fluttered shut, Padgett hesitated to push her too far. But the compulsion to understand her made him lean forward and wait.

"How does this concern Peter Joshua?" Leigh replied without opening her eyes. "Do you wish to raise your offer, Mr. Williams?"

"Don't Mr. Williams me. Are you separated, Leigh? Are you divorced?"

How did he dare ask that question? How did he dare probe into an area which touched him so absolutely? She wanted to shriek at him that she knew all about him, how his name was linked to women who were glamorous and ruthlessly amoral. Many women and much gossip!

She leaned forward, her hand outstretched on the table, her lashes lowered to hide her irritation.

In her distraction her blouse fell gracefully open. It was such a natural movement—revealing the scanty sheerness of her bra, the whiteness of the tops of her breasts—that Padgett first flicked his eyes away in guilt. Then he grew powerfully, perilously aware of everything he had seen of her: the soft allure of her throat, her wrists, her ankles, her toes in sheer stockings and slender-heeled shoes.

His mouth compressed, and he grew achingly hungry to touch her. Unable to stop himself from staring, he wondered what she would look like without the blouse, or without anything at all.

Leigh was too absorbed in her own discomfort to notice how intently he watched her. Or the stiffness which seemed to spear through him.

"I don't like games," she said curtly. Drawing away, she touched the neck of her blouse with absent feminine grace. "I'm not married," she finished bluntly. "I've never been married. And I'm not starving for a man, if you suffer from that misconception."

Padgett's jaw knotted. "I don't think I have any misconceptions about you."

For a moment she looked as if she would leave the table. She seemed to freeze inside, to draw far into herself, until the color faded from her face. Turning her head so all he could see was the sloping curve of her cheek, she straightened her spine quite tall. Her words came unexpectedly, even to her, he guessed.

"My daughter is nine years old."

Leigh thought, amazed that she had told him this fact, that Padgett would at least catch a surprised breath. Most people required a few seconds to adapt to that piece of information, even in this liberal age—to blame her, or understand, or disregard it altogether.

Padgett did not pause. He spoke immediately, as if he genuinely wanted to know. "Has it been difficult raising a daughter alone?"

His question was honest, asked without malice. Yet a brilliance of fury washed through her. Her eyes glittered to life because *he* had asked it. How dare he, *he* who should have been there? *He* who should have stood beside her and faced Gentry Vincent as he leaned upon the mantel and buried his face in his hand? He should not have just disappeared from the face of the earth so she could not find him, even after weeks of desperate searching.

"You have no right!" she lashed out and bent, fumbling for her things.

Padgett, unused to a woman he could not figure out in a matter of minutes, ran his fingers through the silver-streaked locks of hair. Temper blunted his eloquent brows.

"No right?" he argued. "Right to what? All I said was—"

"I have to go," she said abruptly. But what she wanted to tell him was that he had no right to break down her defenses with a look, a tone of his voice. He had no right to make her want to tell him everything, even how she had lain awake nights despising him.

She rose without any pretenses of etiquette. She knew she was behaving like a madwoman. She didn't care.

Padgett's hand darted out, meaning to prevent her from leaving. But Leigh was too quick. Realizing that she was creating a small scene, she grabbed up her attaché case. Instinctively she hugged it to herself, as if a pain were passing through her body.

"Thirty thousand dollars for Peter Joshua, Mr. Williams," she said and turned.

"That's unethical," the producer accused hotly.

"The subject is closed then."

"No, damn it!" His palms struck the table, and then his head jerked aside as he, too, became aware that people were staring.

"Then call me at my office, Mr. Williams."

"I don't understand you."

"I'm sure you don't."

She tugged on her hat with miserably shaking hands, all the time thinking wildly, He looks at me and does not know! How? *How?* If it were me, *I* would know!

At her turning, Padgett was half out of his chair. An expression of bewildered defeat drew tight lines beside the edges of his mouth. He wasn't often defeated. And Leigh, comprehending, felt an honest sorrow for him. He was, in his man's way, quite as sensitive as she.

"Don't come after me." She shook her head, hardly getting out the words.

His hands supported half his weight as they gripped the edge of the table. "I will call you in the morning," he said, hardly aware of his words.

She was already moving away. "Yes. Do that. In the morning."

"I'll be damned," she heard him mutter as she slipped past.

# Chapter Three

𝒥f Leigh had not been ethically bound to attend the yacht party, hosted by Everest Productions to officially launch the filming of its new series starring Peter Joshua, she would have emphatically refused. Spending an entire evening cruising off San Francisco Bay, smiling artificially until her face threatened to crack, watching Padgett being openly courted by a battalion of actresses who hoped to land some insignificant bit part, was not her idea of fun.

"But I can't go without you, Leigh," Peter had said in his slow, demanding drawl. "I won't go without you. Take the commission you earned and buy yourself a party dress. And don't you dare wear your hair up."

"Leave my hair out of this, Peter," she jokingly

retorted. "I'm the agent. You're just the actor, remember?"

They both groaned at her pet peeve, her often violent peeve, of how little artistic control the actor wielded over the finished product of his work. By the time the director, the editor, and the producer finished with it, the clients often came to her, boiling mad, because they hardly recognized their original role.

Padgett, according to his habits which Leigh had made it a policy to learn years before, did not involve himself too much with television. He left that sibling child—budgetwise and timewise—to associate producers. The investigator series would undoubtedly be one of those.

But he did make certain his presiding presence was felt by everyone from the imperious director down to the humble script typist. Padgett was a noted tyrant for detail, and his directors were carefully selected men who knew how to work even when they were emotionally and physically exhausted.

Leigh had been surprised when Padgett negotiated Peter's contract the day after their confrontation at Cardeau's. Although, as she was leaving, he had said he would call, they had both been upset. As she recalled her own puzzling behavior, she expected the producer to logically write her off as a petty annoyance, a female who should be sharpening pencils in a safe office somewhere.

"I'm giving a party for the entire cast," Padgett had announced at the end of the negotiations. "You're invited."

The invitation caught her off balance. "Oh, Mr. Williams," she protested in a schoolgirl's high voice, "thank you, but—"

"Some of my guests are avid supporters of Thoreau," he teasingly reminded. "You should fit right in."

Leigh's reply came more stiffly. "That was just a chance remark."

"You can form a society: The Avid Supporters of Thoreau Club."

"Can we charge dues and have an exclusive membership, Mr. Williams?" she sneered caustically at his facetiousness.

"Certainly. May I join?"

"No!"

Padgett's laughter rumbled deep in his chest, a disturbing musical sound she remembered well. Covering her lips with the fingers of one hand, she imagined him leaning back at his desk, his feet propped up. Gossip said he often wore tennis shoes on the set, with no socks.

"Well," Padgett urged, as if he were enjoying this, "since you won't let me join the club, you must come to my party." She made a gritted protest. "I insist," he added with a sudden, intensely meaningful solemnity. "I want to see you."

"I don't want to see you."

"I don't believe you."

Leigh was as aware of her fragility as he seemed to be, and she wished she had the nerve to say a blistering oath right in his ear. "Do you take pleasure in embarrassing me, Mr. Williams?"

"No," he said soberly, his words low and husky. "For some weird reason, God only knows why, I just take pleasure in you. Please come."

His total lack of pretense almost angered her. As he waited for her reply, her temper was as capricious as a cloud. She groped in her head to find something abhorrent in all this to give her the impetus to refuse and be staunch about it. But her only excuse was a door to the past which she could not risk opening, and she could not tell him that.

So Leigh Vincent dismissed the distasteful vision of herself strolling about the deck of a yacht with a glass of sparkling white wine in her hand, becoming swallowed up in groups of women with extravagantly daring cleavages and men with smartly styled haircuts. It was all part of her job, especially if she wanted to continue representing Peter. She agreed to be there.

Shopping was never easy for Leigh. Her taste, unfortunately, was far too refined for the size of a working mother's bank account. Yet when she stood in the dressing room of a scandalously expensive boutique downtown, gazing at her provocative reflection in an Emmanuelle Khanh design, she knew this was one time she would be reckless.

The dress was the exact shade of her eyes, three-tiered and belted with a ribbon which streamed to her knees. Her neck and shoulders were beautifully displayed, yet the gauzy printed jacket lent it a gentle, Spanish effect. With the correct piece of jewelry it would be stunning. And if she curled her hair tightly to form a fluffy frame about her face, she would be in that small class of quietly glamorous women who managed to give the impression of hiding more charm than they showed.

But would *he* think she was glamorous? And was she ashamed for hoping he would? Using the overworked gambit of attracting Padgett's attention and then disdainfully ignoring him was beneath her, she admitted. But it was so tempting—a dangerously clever *coup de théâtre,* a finishing touch for exacting such a handsome percentage for Peter Joshua's series.

If only it could be the finishing theatrical stroke. Vengeance was an unending hunger, she had discovered, never really satisfying, demanding more, always more. Yet she could not seem to rid her life of the man. How could she? Every time she looked at Margie, Padgett smiled back at her.

The night of the cast party, after a discouraging week of struggling to concentrate on her work, finding it impossible to think about anything except how things might have been, Leigh stepped from her upstairs shower into a spacious bedroom. From a cedar-lined closet which spread the width of one entire wall, she removed the dress and carefully smoothed it across the foot of her bed.

After twenty minutes she finally had her makeup on. Pleased with the exact amount of green shadow on her eyelids, touched with a delicate highlight, Leigh moved back from the mirror with a sigh. She drew on a wisp of bikini panties and dropped the dress over her head to slither down like a cool spray of water on a hot summer evening, deliciously silky and luxurious.

She was attempting to clasp a single opal pendant about her neck when Margie's soft rapping interrupted her.

"Are you decent?" she piped.

"Never!" Leigh called back, cupping the jewel in her palm.

Entering the spacious room, Margie was followed by Elizabeth, who was cleaning her glasses with a tissue as she entered. Amazed, Margie halted abruptly in her tracks. With almost as much surprise as her granddaughter, Leigh's mother adjusted the spectacles upon her nose. Her expression was little less than shocked, as if she had witnessed the emergence of a splendid monarch butterfly from a very ordinary cocoon.

"I don't think I've ever seen you so lovely, dear," she complimented. "Isn't your mother just lovely, Margie?"

"Gee," whispered Marjorie, walking about the unfamiliar vision of her mother, one foot after another in a sober-faced circumference.

"Well, the way you two sound," wailed Leigh, "a person would think I made a habit of dressing in a potato sack. Goodness, Mother, I just bought a new dress. I haven't had one in ages. What's wrong with that?"

"Not one single thing, darling. Not one thing." Elizabeth, watching her daughter with the intuitive intimacy of a lifetime, saw the one emotion that Leigh's makeup did not camouflage—excitement. It flushed her cheeks the most delightful tint of pink and caressed the tips of her ears. "Here, now, let me fasten that," she offered.

Without giving Leigh the opportunity to refuse, Elizabeth caught the silver chain in two fingers and looped the smoky opal about the long column of her throat. "You have your father's hair," she reminisced, touching it lightly, smiling.

"Thank you, Mother." Leigh brushed her lips across her mother's cheek, and as she did Elizabeth captured her fingers, pressing them with an urgency Leigh seldom glimpsed.

"Please, Leigh. I want you to have a lovely time this evening. It's been so long since you've gone out."

"But it's business, you know that."

"It doesn't have to be *just* business, does it? Promise me you'll forget your job for one evening, and the responsibilities of this house. Forget Margie and me, too. . . ."

"Don't forget *me!*" objected Margie, and they both laughed at the comically forlorn face.

"You know what I meant," Elizabeth scolded, then directed her attention to Leigh. "Laugh a little, Leigh. And if someone asks to see you again, for goodness' sake don't say 'get lost' before you even consider it."

Leigh brushed the advice aside with a gay protest in order to conceal the surge of irritation spearing into her stomach. Tactfully she moved from her mother's fondness, which felt at the moment as if it would smother her. She knew Elizabeth only wanted her happiness. Still, the velvet rebuke was always there: the illegitimate child.

She leaned into the mirror to inspect the arch of a perfect eyebrow. The tip of a slender finger followed its curve, and Leigh said too casually, "My, if I didn't know better, I'd think you were pushing me into a relationship."

Elizabeth shrugged. "Would that be so bad?"

"You mean, because I'm twenty-eight years old and am still single?"

Leigh clamped her mouth shut just in time to stop herself from blurting some hideous remark about Margie's lack of paternity. The investment which the two women had made in shaping Margie's adjustment to that fact was a costly one. After much love and wise devotion, the girl accepted her lack of a father with the emotional strength with which most girls accepted having divorced parents.

How foolish they were to risk having one outburst wreck the delicate work of years, Leigh thought. She smiled stiffly.

"I plan to have a wonderful time tonight, you two. Don't wait up for me, okay?"

Recognizing that her well-meaning intentions had barely missed disaster, Elizabeth sighed. "I think it's about your bedtime, isn't it, little one?" she suggested.

Margie, for once, did not resist. Displaying an intuitive tact which wrenched Leigh's heart, the girl backed out of the room with the flair of a small court page leaving the presence of a queen. As her footsteps receded down the hallway Elizabeth paused in the doorway.

"I didn't mean to cause a crisis, dear. I only want you to have a few pleasures in life before it passes you by. And life does pass you by, Leigh. One day you look up and it's half gone."

Leigh not only loved her mother, she respected the gracious support she had been through the years. "I know, Mother," she said, staring at the bareness of her toes peeping from high-heeled sandals. "I'm sorry, too. Margie comes first, you know that."

It was so easy to burst a bubble, Leigh mused, her shoulders drooping with bleak discouragement, her eyes growing vacant with unfulfilled dreams. How many ways could she prove herself to be a fool? She couldn't hang fancy labels on what she had been doing. She had been anticipating this evening with Padgett; she had dressed for him; she had let her fantasies drift about him. Oh, God, how stupid! Again, how stupid!

Her jaw clenched hard as Elizabeth left. A stabbing pain pierced her temple. Not once did she glance back at the mockery of the mirror. Peeling off the gown as if it were a deadly leprous rag, she hurled it into a wing chair. So much for fantasies! she wanted to shriek.

She jerked on a bra and snatched a deep mulberry-colored blouse from her closet. It was severely tailored and buttoned up the front. Then she stepped into an off-white skirt of sleek sharkskin and tossed its demurely cut jacket to the foot of the bed. Three minutes of furious brushing brought her hair under control, and she viciously twisted it into a chignon. All the while she heaped long and loathing curses upon her weakness.

When Leigh breezed through the kitchen, Elizabeth had changed into a robe and was quietly brewing herself a cup of tea. The expression that swept across her face when she saw Leigh's suit was one of such utter disappointment that Leigh had difficulty in guessing who was the more miserable. But Elizabeth prudently refrained from uttering a single criticism. She pulled a sad smile across her face and murmured, "Be careful."

Leigh stepped from the kitchen entrance into the darkness of a star-studded spring night.

Be careful, she thought as she slid across the seat of the Buick. She should have been careful ten years ago at an American Legion dance. That's when she should have been careful.

Driving to the marina gave Leigh the time to whip herself emotionally back up onto the safe, detached perch where she felt comfortable looking down at life. By the time the launch transported her and a dozen television people she barely recognized out into the bay where the cruising yacht was anchored, she had come to view her evening as a perfunctory necessity. Out of need, she stripped the event of all excitement. She would meet new, possibly important people who would make her money to meet the expenses of a large house. She would do her ethical duty by Peter and return home to make up as much lost sleep as she could. Finis. End of evening.

The moment she walked into the smoke-filled stateroom, Peter spotted her. With a typically loose-jointed saunter, he wove his way through roving waiters carrying trays burdened with drinks and delectable finger-sized canapés. Laughing guests and stereo speakers blurred together in a dense cacophony of senseless phrases and a pulsing beat.

As Peter neared, a waiter placed a glass of dry California Chablis in front of Leigh, which she took. Sipping, she lifted teasing eyebrows at her client's designer jeans and his studiously casual shirt with racing stripes circling the sleeves. He playacted the doting boy and bent to kiss the smooth flush of her cheek.

"You disappoint me, lovely lady," he murmured out of the corner of his mouth, at the same time surveying the room for a possible high sign from someone who could push him a rung higher on the success ladder. "I thought you were going to let your hair down tonight."

Leigh laughed. "You handsome devil! Then I'd be as pretty as you are. You'd kill for that, and you know it. The only reason you insisted I come is because I make you look so good."

"Can you believe Padgett Williams?" he continued blithely. He was accustomed to her dismissals of his compliments by now. "Throwing a party for *tel-e-vision* riffraff? I thought it would be below his dignity, since my name isn't O'Toole or Chamberlain. We should celebrate my new clout."

Leigh stuck out her lower lip in a fetching pout. "We *are* celebrating, aren't we?"

"Oh." He tilted his head, letting a lock of golden hair flutter to his forehead, deliberately creating a wholesome lifeguard image. "But I meant *really* celebrate. Let's have an affair."

She narrowed her green eyes until they glinted through her lashes like threatening liquid emeralds. "I've already had one of those, Peter. Try another approach."

Peter was about to come back with one of his famous flatteries when the hostess for the evening, a Swedish-looking blonde flaunting diamonds on both hands and wrists, poured into one of the tightest black sheaths that Leigh had ever seen, attached herself adoringly to Peter's arm. After introducing herself as Helga and asking Leigh's name, she steered them toward one of the doors which opened out onto the deck.

The cluster of people parted like glittering schools of fish into walls of the sea. The world spun a full circle, and Leigh immediately discovered herself facing the dominating personality in the room: Padgett Williams.

If he were surprised, he didn't show it. But then, she guessed Padgett didn't show most of his emotions. He moved among these people as if bored with their adoration, as if he had tasted of everything which life had to offer and hadn't found it up to his exacting standards. Even dressing as casually as he did, though the cost was undoubtedly unspeakable, seemed to be a statement of his disillusionment.

Yet when he flicked his gaze over her own appearance, instantly appraising her conservative choice of dress in a room full of people who were trying to impress each other, a spark flared to life. Leigh found it flattering and, at the same time, infuriating. It was as if he were singling her out, putting some vague mark upon her.

She began to turn away. As she did Helga, who took her job as hostess very seriously, besides secretly planning to make Padgett her third husband, looped her other arm through his.

Flanked by the producer and the star, she said: "Padgett, darling, this is Miss Vinwick, Peter's agent. Miss Vinwick, this is our executive producer, Padgett Williams. He is just finishing a superb epic for MCA. A gem of a picture."

An affirmative ripple swept through the guests. As if he didn't hear, Padgett detached himself from Helga's grasp and took two intentional steps toward Leigh. His gray eyes drilled into her, pinning her as helplessly as a butterfly to a board. The smile which turned up the corners of his lips was nothing less than possessive.

"Miss Vinwick?" he repeated, his laughter suppressed. "How nice to see you again."

"Vin*cent*, Helga," hissed Peter, watching Padgett, as they all did, with acute suspicion.

So rarely did Padgett make an aggressive move where women were concerned that hands came promptly up to mouths. Whispers began weaving their unending tapestry about the stateroom.

"I think they've met," Peter added lamely to no one in particular.

Before she realized what was happening to her, Leigh felt Padgett's fingers closing upon her elbow, demanding, having no intention of being denied. The faint feminine stir beside them barely registered upon Leigh's swirling senses. He had been talking with another woman and had rudely left her standing. To cover her surprise, the woman made a quick move to speak with someone at her side with a laugh and a repetition of Padgett's name, as if she had known all along that he had been wanting to speak with Peter's agent on some important matter.

Leigh found Padgett's interest in her embarrassing. She pulled away, meaning to leave him standing as rudely as he had left the woman standing. They were probably having an affair anyway, she told herself.

Padgett's fingers tightened upon her arm—not a request but a demand. He guided her toward the main doors with such swiftness that the noise lulled. "Would you care to see the boat, Miss Vincent?" he asked with mocking charm.

With all those eyes watching and all those ears waiting to hear her slightest reply and report it, Leigh knew she had no choice. Lifting her head with the resignation of a duchess, she flashed him a glittering smile.

"That would be lovely," she answered with syrupy shrewdness.

As she left she cast a private glance at Peter, begging him to rescue her. Padgett, interpreting the look, inclined his silvering head as Helga dragged the film star into her own net of friends.

"I believe your Lancelot's being lured away," he observed, chuckling pleasantly. "There's no one to save you from the evil demon king."

"Do you think I need saving?" she replied lightly without considering the danger of flirting with him.

Beyond them the doors to the deck filled with laughing guests returning from a stroll. Cleverly placing himself between Leigh and half a dozen couples, he effectively trapped her against the wall adjoining the door. He braced an arm beside her head, almost touching but not quite. She found herself shattering inside and swallowed hard.

"I imagine you do," he agreed and drew infinitesimally nearer, so near she could feel his warmth. It matched her own warmth. Apparently content to just stand there and look at her, he let a smile tease his lips. "Do you know what a classy lady you are, Leigh? Every woman here is intent upon showing as much bosom and leg as possible, and you wear . . . this."

"My clothes offend you?"

"You know they don't. You have the instincts of a merciless gambler, girl."

"I don't. When I gamble I lose."

"Always?"

She had difficulty in believing his nerve. When he moved, he moved fast. He languidly contemplated the neck of her blouse and, hesitating for only a moment, touched the tiny pearl button with a slow, alarming fingertip.

"Always," she breathed and swore the entire center of her body was located below the feather-light touch.

As he pondered her answer, his tongue moved idly across the curve of his upper lip.

"I wasn't aware that an agent's attire was so crucial," she said with an exaggerated enunciation. She couldn't bear the silence.

Padgett frowned darkly then. "Do you have a comeback for every compliment a man pays you, or is it just my compliments?"

"I apologize, Mr. Williams. I didn't mean to bruise your ego."

Immediately, scornfully, the imprisoning arm released her. She heard him swear under his breath. Aware that she had insulted him, she expected him to walk away, to leave her. When he began propelling her through the door and onto the seclusion of the deck, she was surprised. At his firm touch, reality began a strange paralyzing spiral. He mustn't touch her! She drew herself beyond his reach.

The boat was a large one, so that the rise and fall was seductively smooth. Far beyond them the warm glow of Los Angeles burned into the sky. They walked in silence and let the cool breeze soothe the heat of their tempers.

"I was rude," Leigh said presently. His nearness and the lithe gait of his movement blurred her resolutions to despise him.

His reply was tight, still irritated. "You weren't rude. You were mistaken."

Turning, placing one hand on the rail, Leigh paused as an entwined couple passed them. They both watched as the folds of the night took them away. She wished she could blend into the darkness; then he couldn't see how exposed she was, how threatened he made her feel. Swirling the wine in her glass, she studied it so she wouldn't have to face the accusation on his face.

"You aren't used to a woman saying no, are you, Padgett?"

His laugh was short and harsh. "I don't ask women."

"I don't believe that."

"Why not? There's no future in it, my little firebrand. And don't tell me you don't understand, because your hostility toward men is written all over you, even in the way you walk."

Of all the egotists! She wanted to call him one to his face but did not dare.

"Tell me about yourself, Padgett," she said instead. "Were you in the army? Have you been married? How did you come to be the bitter chauvinist that you are?"

Heaving a frustrated sigh, Padgett clapped a hand

to the back of his neck. Without answering, he began walking again, as if he were searching behind her words for the motive which bothered him. Leigh sipped quickly and followed the pace of his steps. His trousers were tightly cut, and the power of his legs was evident as she furtively watched.

"Yes, I was in Vietnam for a couple of years," he said with no trace of emotion. "I found it devastatingly scarring. Some of the men adapted, some broke completely. I was one of those who got scarred inside and didn't really show it. I've never married—once, almost. And chauvinist? I don't consider myself to be one."

He was controlling himself with a great deal of effort, she guessed. She wanted, suddenly, to stop angering him, to touch the tautness of his neck, to thread her fingers into the crisp hair on the back of his head. She wanted to place his hand upon her breast and ask him how he could have forgotten what they had done together that night.

"I know you have a reputation for possessing a high standard of excellence that no one can satisfy," she said. "I wonder if you always please yourself."

He raked her with all-seeing eyes. "You mean please myself personally, as a man? No, I don't please myself as a man."

"I thought differently."

"Well, you thought wrong. I *satisfy* myself when the need arises, but I don't please myself. And I doubt seriously that you do, either, Leigh."

Leigh's natural reserve tempted her to retreat far inside herself. She had never allowed anyone to touch her on that level before.

"You're pulling away again," he accused before she could gather herself.

She blurted the lie without thinking. "No! Well, yes, I am, and I don't please myself very often."

His personality overwhelmed her. For a moment, in an attempt to escape him, she leaned over the rail and squinted to make out the dark, murky patterns of water sloshing against the hull.

"It's all a bit of punishment," she admitted softly. He braced his arms on the rail beside hers and listened. "I've made a lot of mistakes in my life. I think I must subconsciously flog myself, as they do in some cultures, you know, with ropes and chains. Anyway, pleasing oneself is relative. It isn't necessary for life."

"You think not?"

"There are many things which please, Mr. Williams, besides physical caresses and passionate lies which disappear with the dawn."

"Like what? Sacrificing oneself for a nine-year-old daughter?"

"How dare you say that?"

"You tell yourself, 'If I never allow another man to touch the inside of my soul, it will compensate for having borne this child without a father.'"

She turned furiously, spilling the wine, feeling it upon her fingers like the tears of another lifetime.

"You don't know what it was like for me. I don't have to take this kind of talk from you!"

"You don't have to take anything from anyone, Leigh. But those who are afraid to love invariably die. You're one of the most intriguing women I've ever known. You're aware that I think that, and you would like to respond."

Scalding tears banked threateningly behind her eyes. "Go to hell, Padgett Williams!" she choked. "Go straight to bloody hell!"

His lips curled in mockery. "Would that make you happy?"

"I would be happy if I never saw you again!"

Before she spun away from him to literally run from him, Padgett's hand came down hard upon her wrist. With a blaze of quick insanity, she drew back her remaining hand, fully intending to throw the glass of wine at him, like some vindictive heroine in one of his movies.

"Don't even think it, sweetheart," he drawled and twisted the glass from her fingers. With a catlike movement he flung the glass far out into the darkness, so far there was no splash when it broke through the surface of its watery grave.

Dark glittering eyes bent over her own, which were confused and prideful. One bruising hand found the small of her back and drew her hard against him until she felt every rigid contour of his body. His arousal, if it existed, was one of offended masculinity, not passion, and she bent as far back from him as she could. She should have listened to her first instincts; he *was* a dangerous man.

"Don't kiss me," she commanded hatefully. "Don't take your frustrated male ego out on me, Padgett."

"Be quiet," he growled as his mouth ground down upon hers.

He scorned the exposure of his heart she had made. For a moment he took the kiss without caring if she wanted it or not. Then she felt the abrupt gentling and the dissolving anger which washed outward like a tide as he groaned against her mouth. With the tenderness of his moving lips he apologized, and Leigh's eyes fluttered closed. When his hand slipped beneath her jacket, beneath her blouse to mold about her breast, she slumped against him.

But she stiffened immediately, knowing that if she let herself stop fighting him she was damned.

"Why are you so afraid?" he murmured against the warm moistness of her parted mouth.

She whimpered. "Don't hurt me."

His kiss moved to her ear and his tongue drew loving patterns on the side of her neck. "Has someone hurt you, Leigh? I won't hurt you."

She battled herself up from the depths of submission like a drowning person crazed for air. Don't hurt her? *Don't hurt her?* He had nearly killed her, and she was playing into his hands, letting him do it again. Wildly, blindly, her fists thrashed against him. She pulled herself from him, half stumbling, half running, to escape the folly of her own frail desires.

His protest was guttural, a primitive surprise. For a moment he was convinced she was mad.

"Leigh?" He caught her jacket, bringing her to a shuddering halt.

Her eyes flared wide and locked with his, begging like some wounded creature that knows the end has come.

"Leave me alone, Padgett Williams!" she whispered savagely. "Don't try to understand me. Don't try to save me from myself. Just leave me alone."

Leigh didn't pause to see if he followed her back into the stateroom. She didn't slow her steps until she was once again in the safe protection of dozens of people. If they stared at her, thinking she was oddly flushed and gave all the symptoms of just having suffered a lovers' quarrel, she didn't see it.

She searched the room for Peter. She wanted to get off the yacht at the first possible moment. All these years she had been working under a delusion, she thought as she faced the truth now. Padgett

Williams was not the enemy; he was not the factor which should send her spinning into panic. *She* was the enemy! In some bizarre concoction of hatred and love she would, if she did not find some inner strength to rid herself of this man, end up destroying herself.

## Chapter Four

The regal elegance of Leigh's back stayed in Padgett's mind even after she had disappeared through the rectangle of golden light into the celebration. For a frowning moment he stood, absently rubbing his jaw, his weight shifting to one foot as he tried to digest the impact of what had just happened between them.

Even though he knew his tardiness would raise a few tattling eyebrows, he didn't follow her immediately. He needed some time alone. He ambled about the deserted deck, his thumbs hooked loosely at the back of his belt. He pondered why he craved to smash something, to do some violent act.

A deluge of long-forgotten emotions had washed over him when he had kissed Leigh. Kissing and being kissed was a perfunctory ritual in his profession; it meant nothing.

But from the instant he had taken her in his arms he had known this would be different. The feel of her had been unbearably exciting. The taste of her lingered in his mouth even now and plunged him into the hazy memories of his youth, into the years of impulse and vigor when he feared nothing and tried everything.

He had often thought he had left all ability to feel in the jungles of Vietnam. Now he was a frightening mass of feeling, and he doubted himself. He was left with a disturbing need to explain his feelings to Leigh, and that made him angry—angry at her and angry at himself for allowing such a need to even exist.

Slowly Padgett let out his breath. Dreading to climb back on the human merry-go-round revolving inside, he toyed with a copper penny. He turned it over and over and finally closed a strong fist about it. Giving a throaty, derisive laugh at his male vulnerability, he flung the coin across the span of water to seek the path of Leigh's wineglass.

"Make a wish over the Pacific Ocean, you fool," he told himself and acquiesced to his own demand. "I wish the puzzle of that woman would get out of my head."

He straightened from the rail and let the night breeze fall on his face. Having shaped his resolve so precisely, so logically, he walked briskly across the deck. Calm, his broad shoulders squared, he stepped into the crowded room. The first person he saw was Leigh, just as Peter Joshua slipped a protective arm about her waist and steered her to the banquet table to select a dessert.

Quite naturally Leigh turned, as if she weren't

part of the room at all. Padgett's stare fixed, in spite
of himself, upon her aloof separation. It was amazing; she was dressed in a modestly cut suit that
revealed little that was sexual, only the willowy taper
of her legs and ankles. Yet there wasn't a woman in
the room who could equal her for sexual appeal. She
was soft and fluid and promised exquisite pleasures
beneath a dignified and proper attire.

He would not forget this picture easily, he knew.
It would persist in pinching him like a tight shoe. It
would keep him awake nights.

Oh, hell! In a darting reflex action the muscle in
his jaw tightened into a savage knot. Padgett went
directly to the bar and, without hesistating, asked for
a double Scotch, neat.


Leigh knew—with fascinating, alarming certainty
—when Padgett had returned to the cast party. It
wasn't the noisy stir or the obvious migration of the
guests toward him. It was an unnerving spiritual
intuition. They were like two people who had lived
together for a long time, sensing what the other was
about to say.

He had to know how splendid he was standing
there: his taut, trim waist, his muscular athlete's
chest, his majesty of height that most men would
never know. Yet he seemed oblivious of everything
except meeting her stare across the room. He wasn't
apologizing now; he was arrogantly reminding her
that she *had* responded. Before she had flown from
him she had let her body melt yieldingly into his.

Leigh thought that if he measured his kiss by how
devastating it was, he had triumphed. His mouth had
wielded the urgent poignancy of a lover's. For those
seconds it had aroused not only her lips but the tips
of her breasts and had begun a warm, throbbing

ache deep inside her. She had hoped he didn't know, but the steely glitter in his gaze told her he knew everything she had felt.

She turned away and struggled to give Peter all her attention. Her client was gently positioning her before a tempting table, complete with heavy starched linen and a vast array of sweets. Though Leigh's pleasant manner was an automatic skill no matter how distressed she was, she looked at but didn't really see garnished strawberries and sugared grapes, cherries iced in frosting and spilling from sterling compotes. Fruit salad swam in thick cream; silver platters were laden with melons and cold hors d'oeuvres and fruit pies. None of it appealed to her.

"Peter," she said, knowing she couldn't possibly choke down a single bite, "when could I get a launch back to the marina?"

Grasping her shoulders in both hands, rotating her, he peered down at her like a beautiful, indulgent parent. "Aren't you well, poor baby?"

Leigh grimaced an unhappy smile. Her emerald eyes were liquid, and she prayed he couldn't guess the truth of her distraction.

"Do I look well?" she teased.

"You look like—"

He chuckled and caught a chance glimpse of Padgett Williams in the far corner of his vision. The man's radiant force dominated the room as usual. People about him burst into delighted laughter at one of his dry quips. Even so, his features bore the same vague anxiety as Leigh's; his mind was somewhere besides where he was or what he was doing.

For a suspended moment the producer's sharp gray eyes met those of the star he had just spent a fortune to acquire. The actor sobered at the unmistakable blaze of jealousy that ricocheted across the room. The pat which he gave to Leigh's shoulder wasn't altogether reassuring.

"Stay here," he ordered her. "I'll arrange to get you back home."

Much to Margie's disappointment and much to Elizabeth's consternation, Leigh practically lived in her office for the next weeks. She threw herself into the problems and feelings of other people with such vigorous passion that those who knew her would have said she was trying to crush, or at least disguise, her own feelings.

Becky did little besides breeze along at her usual brisk pace and toss out succinct, smiling remarks that she had other ambitions in life than dying from overwork. Patiently she placed telephone messages from Padgett Williams on Leigh's desk, eight of them, underlining the words: He says he will call back again.

One month after the cast party Becky returned from the post office to find her usually indefatigable executive drooped over her desk like a wilting rose. Leigh's arms were folded, her head resting upon them face down. Several pins were stealthily slipping from their moorings to free the heavy cascade of black hair.

Leigh had not expected her secretary to return so soon. Her frenzied pretense, her smiles, and her self-discipline were wearing her out.

From a radio in the corner soft melodies had brought back haunting memories of the hours she had sat in her room, heavy with Padgett's child, grieving over her mistake. Now, when the door clicked shut, she lifted her face. She was unaware that her tears had not dried, that smudges of mascara had painted dusky hollows beneath her eyes. She smiled wanly at Becky.

When Becky didn't return the smile but stepped resolutely toward her, her concern stiffening her like a woman who has reached the final shreds of patience, Leigh tensed. Her smile disappeared.

"Leigh, am I your friend?" came the direct question.

Sighing, Leigh reached into her desk and snatched a tissue from a box. She blew her nose and began blotting at the streaked mascara.

"Of course you're my friend," she answered. "You're many things to me, Becky. Friend is at the top of the list."

"Then, for God's sake, Leigh, be honest with me."

Leigh's pause didn't break the tension as she had hoped. "Curious is second on the list," she added with a grim chuckle.

Becky's fists came up to rest on her hips, the mail still in one hand. "I've sat across from you all these years, especially these last weeks, and tried to ignore that something has chewed you to absolute slivers inside. I really can't stand this anymore."

"If you care about me," Leigh prompted, "you'll be patient."

"I do care about you! That's why I can't stand it anymore. *What's wrong, honey?*"

As if the slender fingers could prevent her distress from being a fact, Leigh buried her face in her hands. Becky waited. Neither said a word. After a long space of sympathy, Becky moved to repair Leigh's heavy chignon. With absent affection she smoothed back the rebellious wisps.

"For the next hour, Leigh Vincent, *I* am the boss

of this company. Now, pull yourself together. Fix your makeup and find your purse. You and I are going to the deli down the street for lunch. No arguments."

Leigh's expression, when she glanced upward, was part relief and part dread. After five years, she sensed that the truth about Padgett was about to come out. How she had kept it a secret this long was miraculous.

Keeping up with the progress of Padgett's career the last years had been a serious mistake, she now decided. The wise thing to do would have been to leave Los Angeles before Margie was born. She should have tried to start a new life in a new place. Now she was like a confused puppy chasing his own tail—delightful to see, perhaps, but spinning in a circle, accomplishing nothing.

Heaving a resigned sigh, she responded to her secretary's good sense. As Becky returned several urgent calls, postponing appointments and canceling one dinner engagement until later, Leigh made herself presentable.

David's Deli down the block was jammed between a laundry with a drive-in window and a bargain shoe store. It was the only eating place in a six-block strip, and the frantic bustle of the streets invariably flowed through David's establishment. He stood, smoothing a bibbed apron, behind his overstocked counter of cheeses, pickles, meats, and boiled chickpeas, and smiled through his curly beard.

Imprisoned behind an aisle which comprised the gift shop and the fresh produce huddled five round tables. Simple checkered tablecloths were centered with the usual clutter of napkins, salt and pepper shakers, and a hand-painted invitation to visit the craft shop across the street.

The two women dropped into cane-backed chairs and ordered Reuben sandwiches and coffee with chicory.

"I think I would like to answer your question here in the deli, Becky," Leigh said as they waited for their lunch to arrive. "That way, I can't let myself get out of control."

"It's Padgett Williams, isn't it?"

Flicking at her fingernail, chipping the rose-tinted polish, Leigh nodded. Against the level hum of chatter in the deli she wasn't overheard.

"I knew Padgett before I ever went into business with you. I've wanted to tell you many times. But you know, once the truth is postponed, then one is faced not only with the truth, but explaining why it took so long to come out with it. It all grew much too complicated."

"I can understand that. What did you two do, Leigh, have an affair?"

Leigh's smile was the hopeless expression of a forlorn child who looks at a wound and is certain that death, or worse, is imminent.

"I wish that an affair were all it was, my friend. Padgett is Margie's father."

Before Becky could gasp a reply, Leigh went on. "I was just a stupid kid when it happened, Becky. I didn't know enough to come in out of the rain. I don't think I'd dated a dozen guys, and all I'd ever done was let a few of them steal a quick kiss. I swear Padgett was the first and only one."

"I don't doubt that for a minute, honey. But *why?* Why didn't you tell the man? That's what I don't get. At least you could have made him shoulder some of the financial burden. Why didn't your parents go to him?"

Becky's thick fingers closed fondly over Leigh's as

the waitress placed their sandwiches before them. Between bites and blots of napkins, Leigh got out the rest of her story.

"They never knew who he was. Mother still doesn't know." The cup made a gentle clink in the saucer as she replaced it. "I tried to find him after I found out. I really did. But he had simply disappeared. It wasn't until several years later that I discovered he had only been home from 'Nam on furlough when it happened."

"You mean he went back overseas?"

"Yes. It was all such a freakish thing. He had come to a dance looking for one of the teachers, a friend of his. And we just kind of stumbled into it. After Margie was born I was so scarred I wouldn't have let him come anywhere near her."

Becky watched as Leigh placed her sandwich on its plate. Her stare was glazed and lost in the unheard laughter and sounds of energy which floated all about them, unconcerned with the unhappiness of a beautiful woman.

Leigh knew the temptation of a plain woman working with a pretty one. Never once, to her knowledge, had Becky reverted to being resentful. At this moment she probably thought that beauty was a curse. She was certain that Becky would have shot Padgett Williams had he walked into the room.

"You can't imagine how bitter I was after that," Leigh said with almost no emotion in her voice. "How much I wanted to hurt him."

Becky chuckled. "I've worked with you five years, sweetie. I've seen your bitterness, remember? You've gotten in your licks, believe me. That man doesn't know just how much he *has* paid for his sins. But what now? Will you tell him now?"

Leigh's green eyes widened and grew as brilliantly

hard as agates. "Are you mad, Becky? How could I do that? For one thing, he would deny it. And even if he didn't, he would be so angry he would only make things worse than they are. He doesn't even remember it, Becky. He has looked at my face. He's even kissed—"

Leigh hadn't meant to tell so much. Unable to swallow, she pushed the rest of her sandwich away. She rubbed at her temple and fixed a lying smile on her lips, hiding the disgust she felt at herself.

"Oh, Leigh," Becky crooned. "Try to remember what the war was doing to that man. He was as mixed up as you were, I imagine. You have to consider that factor."

"I've considered that. But look at him, damn it! He dates all those glamorous women. Every time I turn around I see a picture of him with some starlet on his arm. How can I fight that?" Leigh imitated a soldier at attention, saluting briskly. "Look, sir. I have this problem I'd like to talk to you about, sir."

Becky laughed so delightedly that heads turned to smile at them. Twisting her mouth out of shape then, she paused to finish her coffee. "If it's a fight you'd like to wage, m'dear, you have the ultimate weapon. Or have you forgotten your daughter?"

Thoughtfully Leigh narrowed her eyes, as if she were seeing visions and staging battles. She shook her head.

"I don't want to stake any claims. I only want to find some way to go on living with what I've done. I don't want to hurt my mother anymore. And I certainly don't want Margie getting shredded up more than she already has been. It frightens me, Becky, the pressure that girl is under because of what I've done. If I had it to do all over again, I think I would assume a name and lie to her about it.

I would tell her that her father had been killed or even that we had divorced. Anything is better than the truth."

Becky waved away the words with a wild gesture. "Bull! Single women deliberately have children nowadays. Margie has two women who are totally devoted to her. I say she's a very lucky girl. And she would tell you the same thing, I'll bet."

Balancing her chin on her fist, Leigh thought a moment. "What do I tell her ten years from now? What do I say to her when she comes to me as a mature woman?"

"That's a difficult question. I've always believed personally speaking, that a child has a right to know who her parents are. But I can't tell you what to do."

"If she were your daughter, would you tell her?"

Becky considered. "Yes, I probably would."

"Well, I can't. At least, not now. I can't live with it myself. I certainly can't ask her to."

Sniffing, Becky disagreed. "You're not giving her much credit. You're a strong woman. You've done a pretty good job of living with it by yourself. But you ought to think—what if the roles were reversed and you were Padgett Williams. Would *you* want to know the truth?"

Rising, Leigh fished in her bag for some bills. She picked up the check, indicating she couldn't talk about it much longer.

"Yes," she said, "I would want to know. But then, I wouldn't have taken so many lovers in my life that I couldn't remember who I'd seduced, either."

Laughing, scooping up her purse, Becky looped her arm through that of her friend and walked her to the counter. She placed her own money together with Leigh's.

"I get your point, Leigh," she agreed. "But then,

if a person were in my shoes, any relationship would be unforgettable. Believe me!"

The girl at the register pressed buttons and the cash drawer shot open with a fleeting ding. Her glance at the plain secretary, though she knew nothing of the conversation, did not disagree. Becky's habit of laughing at herself broke down her disadvantage of being less attractive. Leigh, however, thought the woman was lovely and enormously dear. As the clerk smiled, counting their change in a sleepy voice, it occurred to Leigh to wonder if she would always be doing this—eating lunch alone with another woman and letting the years slip by without a man in her life.

When Leigh parked her Buick neatly in the driveway, unable to get into the garage because of the Lincoln Continental blocking the door, she hardly thought it was unusual. She was accustomed to seeing cars parked in the drive of the old house. She couldn't remember a time when students hadn't wandered in and out the halls and parents hadn't sipped tea in the waiting room, reading magazines or consulting their wristwatches, waiting for piano lessons to finish.

Tonight, the first warning she had was that no music drifted from behind the heavy oak doors of her mother's teaching studio. Rather, the soft murmur of voices came from the living room.

As she walked smoothly down the hall, her soles hardly making a sound, the voices grew more distinct. Margie's girlish laughter rippled like crystal, and Leigh smiled, then frowned at the masculine richness of the next voice. One of Elizabeth's associates in the PTA, undoubtedly, she guessed. Elizabeth hadn't missed participating in a school function since her granddaughter started school.

Opening the door a crack before she proceeded on to the kitchen, Leigh froze—one of those death-craving moments when the heart almost stops beating and one wishes that it would so there would be an escape.

Lounging on the floor beside Margie, his tall height stretched full length as he watched his daughter draw figures with a protractor, was Padgett Williams.

Leigh pushed the door closed with only a hesitant whisper of sound. *Don't panic!* she frantically warned herself. *Deal with this!*

But the horror of a situation so out of hand sent her stepping back, pressing tightly against the wall like a shrinking, terrified criminal. The reactions spinning through her defied control—hysterical fury, consuming guilt, the violent need to retch.

What could she do? Running away wouldn't change the fact that Padgett lay sprawled on the carpet with his own daughter. Could she enter the room? Could she continue functioning like a rational human being?

Her hands trembled as she blotted away the fine line of moisture beading across her upper lip. She smoothed her hair back into its knot. It was as if her entire life had been forced into a giant pencil sharpener, tapering down to one point so sharp, so murderously dangerous, that everything consummated at the tip, at this precise moment in time.

She collected herself with a strength she hadn't dreamed she possessed. Hastily arranging her clothes, praying she wouldn't cry, she opened the door with a misleading energy and stepped into the very room where her father had leaned upon the mantel ten years before.

"Mom!" Margie beamed, not getting up but bouncing up to sit, her legs crossed like an Indian princess's.

Leigh's gaze flicked over the top of Padgett's dazzling head as he folded himself to stand. Waving him down with a dismissing motion, she stooped to place a perfunctory kiss on the top of Margie's head.

"Don't get up, Mr. Williams. Mother, I'm sorry I missed dinner."

Leigh perilously played for time with social amenities. Her lips said the right words—charming words, deceptive words. But as she sought her mother's eye, like some wild thing sniffing the wind for a threat it feels but cannot see, she cringed inside.

Elizabeth wore the blank, disoriented wonder of one who has suffered a serious shock. She smiled and acknowledged her daughter's arrival, but her vacant stare immediately returned to the pair sitting on the carpet.

Rising, Padgett let his tapered slacks settle gracefully over his long, athletic legs. By now Leigh's senses were so acutely honed that she noticed the darkness of the hair ruffling on his arms, his wrists, his knuckles flexing as he tucked in his shirt, the silver sideburns feathering back over his ears to frame his face.

"I finally came to the conclusion"— his deep voice seemed to fill the room—"that the only way to catch you was to enlist the assistance of your mother."

Moving with innocent, childlike sympathy, Margie stood beside the towering man. "Mr. Williams has been teaching me plane . . . ah—"

"Geometry," supplied Padgett with a quick, pleased smile.

Leigh heard all their words; she smiled as if she heartily approved. But her mind was racing, interpreting the same shocking truth Elizabeth undoubtedly saw. They stood side by side—father and daughter—and a fool could have seen it. Everyone could have seen it, except the two of them. Padgett was much too close, a participant who would logically be the last to see such a thing. And Margie was too young to realize that she was the exact image of her father, a perfect miniature copy, except for the liquid green eyes of her mother.

For a moment Leigh's strength completely dissolved. Blinking, coming to herself, Elizabeth gave her attention to her daughter.

"You look exhausted, Leigh," she insisted. She rose and stepped near, wanting to help. "Did you have dinner somewhere?"

"No." Leigh sought the friendly security of a chair and slowly lowered herself, as if she were in grievous pain. She ignored Padgett's low sound of instant concern. "I'm all right. Honestly. I'll eat something later."

Padgett's composure was so infuriating! she thought wildly. He stood beside her chair, frowning, his weight shifted to one foot, and watched her nerves unravel. She crossed her legs and smoothed her skirt. Then she thought the gesture made her look rattled, so she uncrossed her legs and folded her hands, forcing them still.

"I'm the solution to your problem, Leigh," he said smoothly. "I've come to take you to dinner."

"No!" came the explosive answer. She knew she was making herself look irrational. Her eyes fluttered closed. "I couldn't dream of putting you to so much trouble," she said more calmly.

"No trouble," he replied. "Consider it a business

dinner." He tossed out a sun-browned hand toward the room. "You're all invited, of course."

"Margie and I eat promptly at five," Elizabeth swiftly added, as if she felt Padgett deserved to know. "Leigh keeps such horrendous hours, you know. I try to keep Margie on a more sane schedule."

The room fell silent, a crawling, tedious silence. Leigh's head ached, as if someone were cruelly battering it.

"I think I'll get some wine," Elizabeth suddenly suggested.

"I'll help you!" Leigh popped out of her chair like a shot.

Padgett's eyebrows came together darkly over his narrow nose, and the gray eyes beneath them drew Leigh's gaze like a magnet which defied resistance.

"I would enjoy a glass of wine," he said carefully. He and Leigh could have been the only two in the room. Then he smiled at Margie. "While they're gone, Margie, perhaps you can be the hostess and show me this rock collection."

A delighted smile wreathed the girl's face. Leigh found herself breaking up inside. How quickly Margie adored him! Of all the things she had imagined about Padgett, this had never been one. Elizabeth seemed to understand her daughter's distress. She sedately drew her toward the door.

"These were my grandpa's rocks," Margie was proudly explaining as the two women left.

As Leigh trailed behind her tall, stately mother she couldn't remember ever feeling so repentant. Neither of them seemed to have the courage to say the obvious, and they moved silently about the large kitchen, fetching a tray, glasses, napkins, cheese, and wine. When everything was as orderly as they could arrange it, Elizabeth finally placed the tray on a long Romanesque table which monopolized the dining area just off the kitchen.

"Oh, Leigh," she breathed. "How can you do this?"

"Do what?" Leigh stalled. She stared at the herb cheese on a silver dish in her hands. She pinched off a sliver and nibbled distractedly.

"Keep such a terrible secret from a man. You must tell him. You have to tell him. How have you borne it all these years?" She sorrowfully turned her back. "When I think of the years you've suffered, the years . . ."

"You wouldn't understand, Mother. Sometimes I don't understand it myself."

Elizabeth Vincent was an artist by nature, and she had always been a demonstrative woman. Her family had been an artistic clan, with lots of boisterous hugging and kissing and loving banter. She had lavished years of cuddling and affection on Leigh in her childhood. Part of Leigh's wholesome attitude toward Marjorie's upbringing stemmed from a long background of loyalty and demonstrativeness.

Now Elizabeth lifted her strong pianist's hands to smooth back Leigh's hair. "I've always wondered about it, though I never asked."

"Asked what?"

"If you loved the father of your child. Now I think I have the courage to ask you."

*The* question! Leigh's eyes darted past her mother's shoulder to see nothing. In a more romantic age Margie would have been called a love child, wouldn't she? And would it have been true? Did she really love Padgett Williams?

One hand shaped itself distractedly about the older woman's forearm. "Oh, Mother, I've told myself for years that my attitude toward Padgett was a love-hate one. But when I look at it sanely, I wonder if it was love at all. We only knew each other for a few hours. A person sees all those touching love stories coming out of the war when women gave themselves to the men they loved and the men never came back. That's what happened to us, in a haphazard way. But love develops over a lifetime of living through good times and bad. You know that. How can I say I loved him then or that I still love him now? The one redeeming thing I take credit for is my honesty in all this, to you, to Margie, and to myself."

Elizabeth shook her head at Leigh's integrity. "My dear, dear girl. I've watched generations of marriages come and go, as I have watched you stand alone with such courage. It is my opinion—and I say this from my heart—that in an age when divorce and infidelity are a matter of routine, you have been more faithful to Padgett Williams than most women who own a ring and a certificate of marriage. It's not as if you haven't had offers from men to marry you. There have been a number of men you turned away."

"I couldn't have married another man. I've told you that over and over."

"I know you have. At the time, I didn't understand why you wouldn't marry, if for no other reason than to have some kind man as Margie's father. Marriage is, simply, the honoring of a commitment, darling. And you have honored your commitment to that man in there, in the broadest sense of the word."

Leigh detached herself, still holding the dish of cheese. She felt like weeping because another person agreed that she had done her best to act with honor in an unfortunate situation. She realized she actually had been faithful to Padgett. To behave any other way had been unthinkable. But a moral commitment and a legal one were two different things in the eyes of society. She wasn't certain how she stood—half right or half wrong.

Leigh's shoulders slumped. "It's all quite complex, isn't it?"

Elizabeth smiled, but Leigh didn't see it. "When one is dealing with human beings, my dear, it's always complex. I only want you to know that I understand now. Many times I have thought to myself, I don't understand why she doesn't make a new life for herself. But I promise you I won't think that again."

As Leigh paused in the doorway, watching her mother carry the tray with such a dignified carriage, a rush of love welled up inside her. How blessed she was to have someone who loved her completely.

By surprise, as it had come so often the past weeks, the memory of Padgett's kiss swept over her anew, like the burning of a fever. She didn't know if she could put the label *love* on the thrill she felt. Even now the intensity of his strength as he had smothered her sent shivers cascading through her. She remembered his chest molding her breasts to its hardness, the sweetness of his eager, demanding tongue.

It occurred to her, as she leaned weakly against the doorjamb and tried to breathe properly, that perhaps she actually did love Padgett Williams. But love wasn't just a swelling physical passion. She wouldn't fall into that trap.

Whatever, she was positive she didn't understand the magnitude of it. There were two absolutes in her life: Marjorie was Padgett's daughter, and there would never be another man except him. Ever. If that combination of principle and response and bitter resentment was love, she didn't know where the movies and novels got their inspiration. Love was a very painful process!

The living room, when Leigh returned to it, seemed changed. The snow-white walls were no different. The Chippendale bookcase and ribbon-back chairs were unmoved. The familiar crimson tapestry was still mounted over the fireplace, and the rich burgundy draperies were drawn, as before.

Yet life had changed. It had detoured and was seeking a new channel. Now Elizabeth knew her private, painful secret. And Padgett was in the room, filling it with an unaccustomed masculine vitality they were unused to. He dwarfed it with the subtle power of his voice and his moves, his hands which were capable of building such a room. Or destroying it.

Elizabeth placed the glasses and a decanter of wine on a low table. Margie's girlish chatter provided the moment of distraction Padgett had been waiting for. Carefully Margie filled the fragile glasses and drizzled a soft drink over the ice in her glass. Padgett easily removed the dish of cheese from Leigh's hand. He captured her eyes with a bold intensity.

She couldn't look away. Her pulse beat a persistent staccato in her ears.

"I want to talk to you," he murmured softly.

"I can't talk now. This is my home—"

She spun about, meaning to step away, but his palm clasped about the slender curve of her waist. His fingers tightened into the firm flesh. Hastily Leigh lowered her arm, afraid Elizabeth might glimpse the familiar caress.

"Come with me," he cajoled. "We'll drive some-where. Get something to eat."

"No."

"Yes, Leigh. I mean it."

"Don't threaten me."

The ensuing tension filtered through the room like the menace of fog, when the slightest movement is dangerous. Padgett broke it by walking leisurely to the table and drawing the attention to himself.

Leigh was positive he loved doing it. He held out a long-stemmed glass to her. She had no choice but to accept it, but she deliberately kept her head averted.

Margie appeared unaware of the volatile currents sparkling through the room. Her cherubic face was unquestioning as she tossed her head in a tease.

"Will we make a toast like they do in the television commercials?" she piped sweetly. She help up her glass of grape soda.

Leigh couldn't prevent the curling of her lips into a smile. She immediately became involved with her daughter, so she didn't see Padgett's sober perusal as she laughed and moved across the room with a classic, unstudied loveliness.

But Elizabeth's maternal expression grew solemn. Leigh's beauty was unusually heightened, enhanced by some inner sparkle; she had never seen her daughter so arrestingly alluring. She watched Pad-gett moisten his lips as he absorbed the charming portrait of mother and daughter. A vague hunger lurked about his eyes, an unsatisfied longing. That didn't surprise her. Leigh's underlying sensuality was never quite hidden, and her intelligence was obvious, laced as it was with a patience which the years had taught her. He admired Leigh, and Eliza-beth didn't know what to do. But she knew she wouldn't interfere in this relationship, no matter what it brought.

"You will notice my daughter is a modern thinker, Mr. Williams," Leigh said lightly. "She didn't say, make a toast like Spencer Tracy and Katherine Hepburn. Or Humphrey Bogart and Lauren Bacall. She said television commercial. Does that tell you anything?"

Padgett met her casual ploy. He blithely took up his role, like a skillful actor moving into the ongoing scene of a play.

"I may have to change my entire career." He chuckled. "In another generation we'll be a society of hairsprays and motor additives and detergents."

"And erotic designer jeans," added Elizabeth, smiling.

"And talking candy," Margie threw in.

"To commercialism, then," Padgett announced. He lifted his wineglass toward Margie's fizzing soda. "To the newly launched contract between producer and agent. May it prosper."

Though Leigh's smile remained beautifully intact, though the perfect oval of her face lifted and her glass clinked as it touched the other three, her eyes were a dark, moody green. Padgett's message over the glasses was unmistakable: he meant for the contract to prosper in other ways besides professional ones; he meant to see her alone tonight, and no excuse she could give him would suffice.

Arguing with Padgett, as much as she despised admitting it, would be as hopeless as reasoning with the caprices of the weather. Mellowed by her glass of wine, Leigh decided to meet Margie's father the same way she had faced her pregnancy—head on.

"I'll get a sweater, Mr. Williams," she said with

queenly finality. "Mother, I shouldn't be late. This little problem won't take long to iron out." She threw Padgett a serene smile. "Is it trouble with Peter Joshua, Mr. Williams? My client's usually very easy to work with."

Padgett's expression could have meant a dozen things. "Peter Joshua's the least of my concerns," he said and gave Margie a majestic bow. "Anytime you wish to spend a day on the set, young lady, arrange it with your mother and give me a call. I'll have someone pick you up."

Margie looked as elated as if she had just inherited Disneyland. Leigh could have slapped him. How dare he offer Margie something she could not possibly hope to match? She had been mother and father for all these years. It wasn't fair that Padgett could just stroll onto the scene and become an instant idol to a nine-year-old girl!

Leigh jerked a sweater from the hall closet without even looking at it. It was time, she decided, that Padgett learned he couldn't snap his fingers and change people's lives the way he could remodel a set or rewrite a script. And if *this* was love, it was all highly romanticized and grossly overrated!

# *Chapter Five*

*B*efore Padgett's Lincoln smoothly made its way out the tree-lined driveway, Leigh's compulsion to declare the rules of the charade bubbled out of her. She didn't want to say anything; she wished to be so perfectly blasé that her very presence overwhelmed him. But since she wasn't, she gripped the armrest with such tenacity that her knuckles were rigid and white.

"Mr. Williams," she blurted hastily, "considering what happened the last time we met, I think we should get something clear."

She prayed he wouldn't make a battle of it. And when he didn't but slammed on the brakes instead, she lurched forward. She caught herself with her palms upon the dash. Beneath the hood the powerful engine idled, aloofly purring, as if it were only enduring until she made a consummate idiot of herself.

In that first seductive darkness of dusk, Padgett's features were gently shadowed. His profile complemented the man he was. Caught in the glow of the dash, he had the aspect of a veteran hunter—not moving, not demanding, only waiting.

"I'm not going to run away, Leigh," he said with soft persuasion. "Tell me what you feel."

She wrenched her face away. "Don't pretend to be nice. It makes everything so much more difficult."

She felt him shifting his position on the seat, and she knew without looking that his knee was only inches from her thigh. With one arm casually outstretched on the back of the luxurious velour seat, he settled himself to talk. Beyond them the road was deserted. The beam of the headlights outlined the rolling hills skirting the San Gabriel Mountains.

Clearing her throat, moistening her dry lips until they were rosy pink, Leigh laced her hands together and sighed. She pointed outside her window.

"My great-great-grandfather built that stone fence. Over a hundred years ago. Can you imagine how much labor went into a stone fence surrounding eighty acres?"

He smiled. "I can imagine almost anything, darling, except what makes you tick."

Twisting around, her lips compressed with a tension she knew she could never explain, she glared at him. "Why did you call me that?"

He took a breath. "Darling? Oh, I don't know. Habit, I guess. Why, does it offend you?"

"If I knew why you were doing any of this, I might know how to answer that question. Why are you here, Padgett? Why am I even in this car with you?"

His hand moved unexpectedly. A bent knuckle brushed the troubled set of her chin, a caress that was strangely out of context with the confrontation. Jerking herself beyond his reach, Leigh forced down her craving to understand him. She wanted to feel blazing, all-consuming fury at him.

He laughed sardonically as she pulled into her pretended indifference. "Ah, the lady says my name. You don't do that very often, Leigh. Why now?"

"I asked you the first question," she snapped.

"What? Oh, so you did. Why am I doing this? Let's see." His head bent forward, and he lifted two fingers to touch it, as if he were pondering gravely. "I presume you mean, why have I called your office nearly a dozen times and why did I finally look up where you live."

"That'll do for a start, yes," she replied, stiffly fortifying herself to hear an evasive battery of half-truths.

Padgett shot her a questioning look. "Are you sure you don't want something to eat first?"

"I'm fine, Padgett. Would you just tell me?"

She wanted to scream, *Please don't lie to me, please don't hurt me again.* But she only huddled against the door, feeling, quite suddenly, chilled to the bone.

"When you pull away like that"—he shook his head as she hugged herself—"I want to just take you in my arms and hold you. Don't ask me to explain why I feel that. I don't know why, any more than I know why I kissed you or why I keep beating my head against this brick wall you've erected about yourself."

She sniffed in derision. "The same reason that

men climb mountains, I expect. It's there, and it's inaccessible. You know, the challenge of it."

Padgett's oath rumbled deep in his throat, angry and offended. For a moment Leigh thought he would throw the car into gear and spin out in a temper. But he lazily reached to close a hand upon her shoulder. It lay heavily upon her, not so much in passion as in sincerity.

"Look," he explained tightly. "I'm not launching a campaign against you, Leigh, or doing a number on you. I merely want to get to know you. What's so wrong in that?"

Outside, the darkness grew thick, isolating them. She could scarcely make out the stone fence now except for where the car lights caught it in relief. Weeds straggled along its edges, stark and ragged, and the mortar crumbled, in need of repair. It wasn't romantic now. It was only a man-made structure in need of attention at the hands of a strong caretaker. It was too poignantly symbolic of her own life.

She made a dismal sound against her teeth. "I'm not ordinarily a hostile person. I hope you believe that. Please, could you take me back to the house now?"

"Why?" he asked when he had finished studying her.

"Because!" she lashed out at him. Then, in an attempt to gentle her manner, her voice cracked. Her hands came up about her face, her fingers splayed in a gesture of futility. "Because," she repeated, "you've come into my life at a bad time, Padgett. Maybe any time would be a bad time, I don't know. But I do know what my instincts tell me."

He leaned so near that she drew back in alarm.

"What do your instincts tell you?" he probed softly. "What do they tell you, Leigh?"

"That you're an extremely dangerous person," she whispered. She pulled as far back as the door would allow her to escape from him. "That I'm a fool to be here with you."

Padgett's face was frighteningly near. The warmth of his breath caressed her face. His fingers dared to roam, hesitantly at first, then with a tantalizing pressure upon the bones of her shoulder, higher until they traced a soft, hypnotic trail up the side of her neck.

"Well, my instincts tell me that some part of me feels comfortable with you," he murmured. "I wish I could explain it, but I can't. All I know is, I haven't had a good day since that night I kissed you out in the bay. I've worked my head off, and all I've ended up doing is coming down hard on the people I care about and alienating the ones I should be cautious with."

If she turned her face the slightest amount, her lips would brush his jaw. If she did that, he would kiss her. Even though she wanted his kiss more than air to breathe, she dared not move.

"I don't know what to say," she said.

"Tell me that it's been like that for you, Leigh."

Even though the words would have been the truth, she couldn't get them out. Disappointed, Padgett let out his breath.

"Women think it's so easy for a man," he said, mocking his own vulnerability. "They think we're born with some insensitivity so that we don't feel like fools when we get rebuffed."

"I didn't rebuff you!" she denied hotly.

"Oh, really?"

His lack of retaliation made her wish she'd been

more tactful. "Well," she admitted, "I *have* thought about it some. I would be some kind of monster to not have thought about it."

When his hands moved unexpectedly to the back of her head, she froze into a breathless, trancelike immobility. He was enchanted with the perfection of her profile and solemnly touched the twisted coil of her hair. She wondered if he had imagined himself doing this before.

Thoughtfully Padgett searched out the hairpins, one by one, without a trace of awkwardness. As he removed them he dropped them into her lap, each one an unvoiced challenge to make him stop. But she was spellbound; she could scarcely draw a breath. In seconds the heavy locks tumbled over her shoulders and shrouded the curves of her bosom like an old-fashioned shawl.

"Ahh," he breathed, satisfied. He inhaled the delicate fragrance deep into his lungs. "I've wanted to do that since I saw you standing in your office with your mouth full of hairpins. I wanted to say then, please don't pin it up."

Much too warm, Leigh reached for the button to her window and pressed it hard. What was he *doing?*

Her jaw slackened as his fingertip traced one thick tress, following its wave down the column of her neck, past the hollow of her throat to the impish curl which lay with coy impertinence over the swell of her breast. She gasped at his audaciousness as he painted a lazy circle there, and at the ultimate betrayal when her own flesh surged to life beneath the tip of his finger. Now he knows, she thought. Now he knows.

"I'm going to kiss you, Leigh." His words came thickly. "Just once. That's all."

Her wisp of a protest was quite without conviction. Padgett felt the steady rising heat of her body and grasped her shoulders, turning her, wanting to be gentle in his urgency.

"Please don't fight me," he begged.

She moaned. "You're stronger than I am. You know you can force me."

"I don't want to force you." He gazed down at the conflict warring inside her, tensing her features. "You once called me a taker. Sometimes I am. I admit that. But I'm not always a taker." His lips traversed the line of her jaw. "Kiss me, Leigh."

She shivered. His caress would suffuse a passionate response all through her body. She was off balance and incapable of protecting herself. "I should never have gone to that party," she whispered.

He mumbled against the silkiness of her throat. "I would have come here anyway."

"I want to be strong, Padgett."

His face was buried in her hair, and the muscles in his back flexed. "I want you weak, like me."

He was hardly aware of what he was saying. The fragile remnants of her perfume intoxicated him like a heady liquor. Leigh reached to caress his neck, but she stopped, her hands outstretched, like one afraid to be burned.

"It's all right," he groaned and placed her trembling hands upon the sinews spanning the breadth of his back. She clung to him, and to the wonder of the moment, dreading when it would stop and knowing it must.

Padgett drew her downward on the seat until she conformed to the shape of his own lean body. The rise and fall of her breathing inflamed him, and his own breaths tore from his chest. His fingers slipped between them until they discovered her waist, the tiny buttons of her blouse.

"No." She drew out the word until it was a dying lament of one already conquered.

In a suspension of incredible torment, his face hovered close above hers.

"Kiss me," he said.

One kiss melted into another. Her eyes, before they closed, were smoky sapphires. Her drugged lips parted, warm and moist. Leigh opened herself to him completely and let him show her how hungrily he desired to taste, to feel, to fill his hands with her. One hand sought the curve of her hips, bringing her unbelievably near to the ache he suffered. They drifted deeper and deeper until, summoning the last vestiges of a waning strength, she broke away from him.

"That was more than once!" she gasped and hid her face in the wildness of her hair. She couldn't bear for him to see the naked desire, for never again would he believe her when she said she didn't care.

Padgett Williams had never tackled anything except in one way, the only way a strong-willed English background allowed him—full force, with every ounce of energy he possessed. Invariably he gave that extra bit and dared the task to outlast him. His remarkable achievements in his field were recognized by the numerous Oscars and other awards he had won. But these accomplishments weren't due to some secret supertalent; they were the result of relentless workdays lasting twelve hours or more. Most men found that such dedication was unappealing. He thrived on it.

His social life was an ongoing source of material

for the tabloids. Not only did he not care, he manipulated it to work for him. Padgett possessed an uncanny charisma with his people. That charisma depended on a good sense of timing and an impenetrable armor against social criticism. Juicy gossip, he found, only enhanced his productivity.

One of Padgett's most valuable assets was the ability to sell himself to men. He used just the right combination of cleverness, sincerity, and gambling instinct to convince a man that he was indeed privileged to work under him. His actors and directors performed better than even they thought they could.

Endearing himself to women was even easier; their feminine attributes offset his domineering tendencies. Yet, in spite of what the scandal sheets blazed in their headlines, Padgett was rarely involved sexually with a woman. Twelve-hour days didn't allow him the luxury.

Now, to his consternation, everything was backward. The one woman who appealed to the very best in him seemed the farthest out of reach: Leigh Vincent. Leigh put him off. She had a way of looking at him that made him feel incompetent, and he didn't understand why he felt driven to keep coming back for more of the same. She was very definitely *in* his life, from the first day he had met her.

But it all seemed to him like some star-crossed fate. It was a mysterious curse which he was doomed to bear. He wasn't certain how it had begun, and he sure as hell didn't know where it would end.

"There have been times I wished I could forget you," he said now, dragging his rangy limbs beneath the steering wheel with the cautious grace typical of tall men. "There were a couple of weeks when, I swear, if turning to drink would have solved anything, I would have drowned myself in very expensive Scotch."

"We're obviously unsuited to each other," she tonelessly agreed with his pessimism. "We should forget this ever happened."

As Padgett slipped the gearshift into drive the big car eased forward. Its lights sliced through the opaque darkness.

"You're right," he said.

"We should start forgetting immediately," she suggested with a gloomy sigh. "We should go back to the house and say a polite good night."

Padgett's brows knitted as he calculated the swiftest route to the upper San Fernando Valley, some miles northwest. "That would be the sensible thing," he said.

When Leigh began twisting and repinning her hair, he flicked her several frowns of disapproval. "I like it down."

"I look like a little round-faced chipmunk with my hair down, Padgett," she declared flatly.

He gave a short laugh. "Chipmunks are my favorite thing."

Neither mentioned the fact that he wasn't taking her home but was actually streaking toward the access road to the freeway. He handled the car with absentminded effort. Leigh gathered her hairpins and slipped them into her handbag.

He studied her from time to time. "Would you like to see where I live?"

She wanted very much to see where he lived. "Do I have a choice?"

"No." He smiled, smugly contented.

"You'll have a long drive to bring me back home."

"A man's lot is a hard one," he said.

They became aware of the double-entendre at the same moment. At her glare he turned on the radio and left her to her own musings.

Los Angeles was the third largest city in the United States. Bisected by the Santa Monica Mountains, it was an oddly shaped city, famous for its smog, its network of freeways for four million cars and trucks, its exploding ghettos, and the fact that it was still growing.

Padgett's car skimmed from the edge of the San Gabriel mountain range where Winthrop Vincent had bought eighty acres back in 1876 when the Southern Pacific and Santa Fe railroads had arrived in California. Los Angeles was a far cry from the small San Gabriel Arcangel Mission of 1771. Now *El Pueblo de Nuestra Señora la Reina de los Angeles* was no longer the Town of Our Lady the Queen of the Angels. The Lincoln skirted a bursting metropolis of palm trees, oil derricks, television and movie studios, and aerospace factories.

Once Leigh and Padgett were on their way, hunger finally caught up with them. Propping an elbow on the armrest, she buried her chin in her palm. Unintentionally, just as a wife would, she suggested places to stop. Padgett, like a typical husband, vetoed all of them.

Finally she gave up and told him to make the darned decision himself. Much to her surprise, he selected a congested truck stop which looked as if it were a series of disorganized additions and would serve absolutely abominable food.

"I like these places," he said happily, smiling across at her. "A person can sit back and observe all kinds of human nature at work."

Leigh's look would have wilted a lesser man.

"Really," he insisted. "Some of my best work's resulted from watching men when they're tired and hungry and in need of a bath."

"Do you propose that we do as the Romans do while we're in Rome?" she asked dryly. "I could run outside and rub dirt on my arms or something."

He assumed his favorite expression of misunderstood artist. "Meeting one of the requirements is enough, I think."

In spite of her badinage Leigh felt marvelously carefree and full of anticipation of what would happen next. Being desired as a woman must have gone straight to her head, she thought. Being able to lower her habitual guard, even that small amount, had been exhilarating. She never allowed herself to do that. Now that she had, she felt herself changing inside. She grew ravenously greedy and wanted to become even more of a woman.

Padgett parked the car and leveled a stern look at her. She laughed. Then he laughed, only because she had.

"Come on," he said and touched her jaw with a mock fist.

The truck stop was infectiously down-to-earth, an unglamorous cross section of working Californians. As they sat on opposite sides of a booth and munched roast-beef sandwiches—good ones—bearded truck drivers exchanged loud, earthy flirtations with wise-eyed waitresses dressed in tight Levi's and knit shirts with Al's Place written across the fronts. The short-order cook had to shout his orders over the country western song blasting from the jukebox.

"This scene keeps the world going round," Leigh

observed thoughtfully, half to herself. She watched diesel trucks groan and pull their monstrous trailers into place at the gas pumps outside the plate-glass windows. The front door never stopped opening and shutting for an endless stream of men climbing down from their cabs. "If they ever quit driving those things, this country would just about stop moving."

"They don't do too badly for the music industry, either," he added.

Leigh lifted her eyebrows in a question.

He grinned. "All those truckin' songs."

Beneath the table he moved his leg until his foot nestled possessively beside her smaller one and his knee braced against hers. Contented, Leigh leaned back to enjoy his warm intimacy. For a moment she almost forgot where they were. When he pinched off a bit of her sandwich, she opened her mouth as obediently as a child, chewed it, then smiled at him.

But both their smiles gradually faded. The seriousness in Padgett's study of her mood burned deeply, too near the truth of what she really felt. She lowered her stare to her hand curled softly upon the tabletop.

It only required a tiny movement from Padgett until the tips of their fingers touched. Impossible, she told herself, that such a fragile scrap of contact could wreck her composure so. It was more volatile than his kiss. Shattering inside, she peered down at the nearness of his hand until she couldn't bear the silence any longer.

Her open wonder, when she lifted her head, collided with his. They sat immobile, rapt in the unmoving awareness, until she forced a breathless laugh.

"You're not observing all this fabulous human

nature around you, Padgett," she chided, arranging her blouse, nervously brushing at her skirt.

He moistened his lips. "Oh, yes, I am," he said solemnly.

Then, because she really wanted to know, and because she had to do something to relieve the intensity building between them, she said, "Tell me about yourself, Padgett."

"I'm not very exciting."

"Spare me the false modesty. I know you love to talk about yourself."

He brushed his knuckle against the tip of his nose, an unconsciously sensual gesture. "I can't fool you, can I?"

"No." She arched her brows high, for his perusal had refused to leave her face. It relayed silent messages to her which said, I'm glad you're here with me. I think you're beautiful.

Finally Padgett pulled a face, then sighed. "Well, I guess I'm not so different from most men who were in the service. I tend to put everything about my life into two catagories—before Vietnam and after Vietnam."

At the mention of the war something in Leigh shifted—a warning, an intuition which alerted the most treacherously vulnerable part of her. Her whole distance from him changed, and she felt, for a few seconds, as if she were a third person looking at this scene from the outside.

Learning about people was so risky, she thought. Once people began to understand other people, they began making excuses for their mistakes and overlooking their flaws. Keeping a list of grievances became so difficult when people understood each other.

Headlights shone through the window as trucks pulled back on the highway. She spoke. "Those of us who didn't go to Vietnam read the books and saw the movies. But I don't think that any of us imagined what it was like. I know some men gave up everything they loved in this country rather than live with what was going on over there."

Padgett suddenly looked extremely tired. "I once thought about taking off. Desertion, some called it, but a lot of guys saw it as doing the right thing."

"Why didn't you? Leave, I mean?"

His stare grew misty and vacant. When he began stroking the curves and crevices of her hand, Leigh thought he wasn't even aware that he was touching her.

"I felt I owed more to the men I would leave than what I wanted for myself, I guess. There're things about that period I don't understand, to this day."

Over the distance they touched each other—not physically—and she grew overwhelmed at the depths of his feelings. A little frightened, too, for this period in his life had completely changed her own life.

"I've never talked to anyone about this before," he explained, remote and hesitant, as if he didn't want to now.

Leigh closed her fingers about his. He looked up.

"You don't have to talk about it now, Padgett."

"No, I think I want to tell you. They kept killing us, and we couldn't even see 'em. I remember sending my men out on those damned body counts. They waited for us. They knew we'd come."

Leigh felt she had to make him stop telling her. "What rank were you, Padgett?"

For a moment he came back from his pain, but his

grin was melancholy. "A lieutenant, one of those ninety-day wonders who usually didn't stay alive long enough to get to know their men. But I got to know mine. Nearly every time I sent them out I'd lose one or two. I held up pretty well for a while. Someone had to do it. But later . . ."

She had crushed her napkin into a tight, helpless wad. She wanted to understand why he hurt, why his face had been filled with pain that night they had created the life of a little girl. Padgett glanced about them, unseeing. But no one seemed to be noticing. He rubbed his upper lip.

"I had six men knocked out at one time. I don't know, I just kind of came unglued."

She nodded in encouragement that she understood. Half hoping he wouldn't say any more, she waited for him to continue.

"My sergeant had just been killed by a mortar, and the men up ahead got separated. I was bringing up the rear, this South Vietnamese and myself. The problem was, when you were separated out in those jungles, you didn't dare make a sound or respond to one. Nine times out of ten, the sound wasn't your buddy."

"Padgett—"

"I only know this because they told me later. They said I managed to locate the men, one by one, and got them back across the river. It took nearly all afternoon, under artillery fire part of the time. I remember that three of them were still alive. But the next thing I really knew, I was in a hospital."

"Wounded?"

"Not a scratch on me. We'd been out there on the front for five months with hardly a break. They called me a hero and all that garbage. They gave me a medal, but all I could think of was that I had finally snapped. That's why I've never talked about it, I think. They said I bandaged them all up, then radioed our position. When the helicopter came, I was just sitting there with all my men."

Padgett grew strangely quiet, and the noise of the truck stop seemed deafening. An enormous compassion surged up in Leigh. She hated all of it, especially the unspeakable terror he must have suffered.

"I say I don't remember," he finished quietly. "But somehow, I realized that I had bandaged up the dead men, too. I don't know why I did it. I just did."

For long moments Leigh held his hand in hers and smoothed the strong, slender length of his fingers. She examined the symmetry of his wrists and understood the love he had felt for his men when he had bandaged them.

"They sent me home for a few weeks after that, but I hardly even remember coming back to the States. After I returned to 'Nam I finally got better. I finished my months and got my discharge, but it was a good year before I was myself again. I try not to think about it much."

"Perhaps that's part of the reason you excel at what you do, Padgett. Making films is such a positive thing. It's there. You can see it. It's . . . touchable."

That wasn't what she wanted to say. If she had had the courage, she would have said that she forgave him, for all of it. As she lifted her face to smile back at him, half a lifetime of memories slipped into an astonishingly simple perspective. She forgave him because she loved him. She was the mother of his daughter, and *she loved him*. The years of grief dissolved like mist under the warmth of the sun.

For a moment neither of them said anything.

"Are you all right?" she asked finally, a little dazed because she didn't know where to go from here.

Reversing their hands, Padgett placed hers between his two large ones. "Sure."

Leigh wanted to lift his fingers to her lips and kiss them. Discovering love in the middle of a noisy, impersonal truck stop—the jukebox blaring, the doors opening and closing—could never happen. It *never* happened in the movies he made. Yet she knew it had. And she had been wrong about one thing, too: love wasn't overrated. Definitely not overrated.

Her eyes closed, as if drawing a curtain on a certain part of her life. Then she stirred, coming abruptly to life and blinking up at him.

"If I'm going to see where you live, Mr. Williams," she said huskily, checking her wristwatch, "we'd better leave. Else, neither of us will get much sleep tonight."

She didn't say that she wouldn't sleep a wink that night, anyway. But she wouldn't; she had far too many things on her mind to sleep.

In less than an hour Padgett swung the car off the highway into the hill country. For miles the distance glowed, lighted by hundreds and hundreds of homes. Leigh studied their starry windows and thought that behind each of those windows was a human being like her; they all had problems which they didn't know how to solve.

Even in the darkness Leigh was astonished at her first sight of the sprawling ranch. It graced a small rise and was golden with its own lights, a beacon set on a hill. The acres surrounding it were fenced with a white board fence which stretched so far it disappeared from sight.

"We're horse people here, Leigh," Padgett said cautiously. "Dad's raised horses for forty years. If you tell me you hate horses, I swear I'll turn this car around."

She laughed. "Horses and I have always gotten along. I don't ride, though. I sort of just stay in the saddle. I think they know I'm easy to please. They go out of their way to be nice."

"We'll see," he said skeptically.

They swooped down a long drive fenced on both sides, leaving clouds of dust rising behind them. Outlying buildings dotted the grounds, interspersed between training areas and stables. All the buildings were neatly painted white and trimmed with black shutters.

Padgett pointed. "There's the clinic. And that's the bunkhouse where the hands live. The main stables are out back."

"Oh," she said, impressed.

The main house, as the headlights captured it, looked as if it had been enlarged several times. It, too, was white and trimmed in black. But one complete end was swathed in a rampant growth of ivy. A shaded porch occupied the opposite end, providing a cool retreat from the heat of California summers.

As Leigh stepped from the car the delicate fragrance of honeysuckle and wisteria blended with the more pungent smell of horses. Large trees covered the half-acre lawn, and a gravel walk wound from the garage which housed two pickups and one Land-Rover.

At the slam of the car door a shadow stirred on the

porch some yards away. Leigh squinted to see the shadow detach itself. A splendid collie with black, tan, and white markings bounded down the steps and streaked across the lawn. She barked her greeting excitedly, and Padgett dropped to one knee to ruffle her thick coat.

Laughing, he pulled his hands from the eagerness of her tongue. She was a lithe dog with a fine, tapered head and alert, almond-shaped eyes. Her ears were erect, but one tipped forward more than the other. Leigh leaned over Padgett's shoulder to smooth the intelligent head.

As she bent, in one of those time-trapped intervals, he unintentionally leaned back. Her breasts fit perfectly against the firm broadness of his back. Instantly, in a reflex, she started to draw away, but his hand moved with lightning quickness to her arm.

Her heart was hammering frantically against his shoulder. He had to have felt it. But his voice, when he spoke, was steady, as if it were nothing.

"One of her ears would never tip," he explained, as if the tiny flaw were commendable. "Almost every day for a year I chewed a wad of bubble gum and stuck it to its tip. All I accomplished was this." He gently thumped the delinquent ear. "Her name is Bonnie. Bonnie, meet Leigh, another extraordinary female like yourself."

When Bonnie promptly dropped back on her haunches, Leigh had to lean even more tightly against Padgett's back to accept the proffered paw. They seemed to touch everywhere.

"She's gorgeous, Padgett," she said, hardly able to breathe.

"Thank you." His voice went on, placid and unhurried. "It isn't often that you see such a lady, is it, Bonnie girl? Be careful, though, or you'll get used to the sight of her pretty face. Then you'll lie awake nights thinking about her."

He wasn't making idle conversation. He was touching her heart, and she didn't know if she could bear it just now. She strained against his grip, but he only tightened it and readjusted his body until she was almost a second flesh to him.

"Once you reach that point, Bonnie, it seems like everything in the world is haywire. So don't get any ideas, 'cause this lady is habit-forming."

She must have made a small desperate sound in her throat. After a few seconds of mindless drifting, he slowly released her. They didn't speak of it. They began walking toward the brightly lit house and pretended their composure wasn't shattered to bits.

"You'll be the only woman on the place," he said unevenly. "Let's see if Dad is asleep in front of the television again."

"When do you have time to take care of all this property and horses and dogs?" she asked in a cheerful voice which didn't sound like hers at all.

He glanced out at the buildings, which demanded the full-time labor of four men and one house-keeper.

"I don't. I only make the money to operate it. And, believe me, this place devours money like a starving whale. By the way, you wouldn't happen to have a lake on your property, would you?"

Leigh stopped in her tracks and gaped at him in awe, then laughed. "Your mind has more twists to it than an eel. Yes, as a matter of fact, there's a lovely lake at the back. About two miles from the house. I haven't been there in a while."

"Good," he said and lengthened his stride until she had to nearly run to keep up with him. Bonnie trailed after them in a well-disciplined heel.

"Why?"

"I need a lake for the filming of *The Last Champion*. It'll have to be in the dead of winter, though. We can talk about it later."

Before she could ask, Talk about what, Padgett grasped one shoulder and probed deeply into her eyes.

"What is it?" she whispered.

Padgett glanced at the lighted porch, then back to her waiting face. "There's something about my dad I'd like to explain before we go in."

"Of course."

"Dad . . . well, Dad is one of the finest men I've ever known. I was the only child, you see, and when Mother died he and I became closer than ever. In some ways I don't think he's ever quite gotten over Mother's death."

"When did she die?"

"It's been over ten years now. But he loved her terribly. For a while there, I thought he would die, too. Sometimes, not too often, he forgets that she's not alive anymore. I just let him talk, and he remembers how things are. He'll get real quiet for a minute or two. I just want you to know."

Leigh patted his hand like a mother consoling a worried child. "I live with a widowed parent myself. Remember? I'm sure everything will be fine. Shall we make an entrée, Padgett?"

He teased her with his brows. "Our only stairs are the two steps from the den down into the kitchen. Will that do?"

"Perfectly." Leigh swirled out the side of her skirt in a grand flourish. "I'll do my best Scarlett O'Hara."

As they climbed the steps Leigh was impressed with the shrubbery and flowers. Though they needed tending, wisteria trailed on a trellis with great masses of climbing roses—frilled white ones, streaked and solid ones. They lacked a firm hand, climbing in places where they should have been trimmed. Leigh guessed that the flowers had been the domain of Padgett's mother.

Raymond Williams wasn't dozing in front of the television at all. In fact, the large raftered living room, furnished with ranch-style furnishings in beige leather and warm yellow tweeds, was quiet and empty.

They found him in the masculine, modernly equipped kitchen, stirring cream into a mug of steaming coffee. At the sight of Padgett, the man stopped stirring, then lifted shaggy gray brows at the sight of Leigh.

"I heard Bonnie," he said. "I guessed it was you. I was beginning to worry. Would either of you like some coffee?"

He seemed delighted at her presence, but Leigh had to choke down the sudden compulsion to explain herself. It was a rather late hour to come barging into a strange house unannounced. Padgett relieved her mind at once. Over his lengthy introductions and explanations, Leigh studied the striking lack of resemblance between the two men, except for some of the less noticeable features.

Raymond didn't have the height of his son. And he had been born with the fair, lightly freckled skin of a man who doesn't take well to the outdoors. Yet the ruddy tint to his cheeks indicated that the older man spent a good deal of his time outdoors.

"Did Ace High run today?" Padgett took a moment to discuss horses with his father.

Raymond shook his head. "His leg is still too sore. I don't like the looks of it, Paddy. But, say, you can't talk horses in front of your guest. Have you two had dinner?"

"No. We had a snack. I'm ready to raid the refrigerator."

Raymond tossed a hand toward the appliance. "Be my guest. Slim pickings, though. I've already tried it."

Playing the perfect host, Raymond moved easily about the kitchen. He fetched plates and glasses and an odd assortment of things from the fridge.

"May I help?" offered Leigh, feeling very much in the way.

He beamed at her with an unexpected charm. "I'm sorry. Most of Paddy's friends don't think of offering."

Liking him immensely, Leigh moved to the refrigerator and peered inside, pondering. When she began selecting this and that, pausing to ask if they had a specific item, the two men telegraphed amused messages back and forth.

Padgett, apparently content to straddle the back of a chair at the large dining table, watched Leigh assemble one of the most scantily improvised and thoroughly delectable dinners he had ever tasted.

# Chapter Six

Shortly before ten o'clock, the kitchen of the Williams ranch was brimming with men. One by one they had wandered through the back door wearing various states of work dress—stained khakis and dusty jeans, boots, and the inevitable western hats which they tossed onto hooks mounted beside the door.

They had come, they said, to get a cup of coffee or work orders for the next day. But Padgett guessed the word was out that a woman guest had arrived up at the main house. It wasn't often that the ranch got women visitors, unless there was a horse for sale. Bored ranch hands were as curious as friendly pets, he decided, and many times more annoying.

From time to time Padgett shifted in his chair. He

studied his wristwatch with barely controlled fretful-
ness, but no one—not even his own father—
appeared to notice.

Doc Sanders rubbed his pale, heavily veined
hands together as he soaked up the banter like a
thirsty blotter. The man was a listener, not a talker,
never putting more than half a dozen words together
at a time if he could help it. What he didn't know
about horses, however, wasn't worth knowing. His
sunburned face creased in a perpetual smile as he
watched Leigh's expression at one of the foreman's
tall tales.

Mac, the lanky foreman who had been with Raymond Williams when he had first bought the ranch,
prefaced nearly every dry quip with "Well, heck,
ma'am." Though Padgett swore by the man and
sympathized with Mac's fascination with Leigh—he
was a present victim of it himself—he hooked his
thumbs into the edges of his front pockets and
scowled darkly.

The trainer, Butch, slumped low on his spine and
smoked. Raymond kept a steady stream of coffee
flowing into their cups.

Finally, deciding that enough was enough, that
Leigh was his guest, not theirs, Padgett noticeably
scraped his chair on the floor. Rising, yawning his
annoyance, he stretched. Then he cleared his throat
and leveled a meaningful gaze at Mac.

The talk dwindled, then stopped altogether. After
one perceptive look at him, Butch came forward in
his chair and prudently stubbed out his cigarette.

"Butch," Padgett called as the trainer wisely
moved to fetch his hat, "if I took Leigh for a ride,
which saddle horses are there?"

Thinking for a moment, Butch threaded his hand

through his hair. Though he was only in his twenties, his hairline had begun to recede; he was terribly self-conscious about it.

"Sal, I'd say," he replied slowly, "for the lady. Garnet's got a busted shoe. You'll have to take Chancey."

Without altering his expression a fraction, Padgett quietly murmured, "Damn." When a series of chuckles rippled through the room, Leigh searched the men's faces.

Butch explained, grinning broadly. "The boss here ain't Chancey's favorite person, ma'am," he said.

"I'll be," said Padgett, as if he didn't hear a word they said.

Mac rose to amble out the door after the trainer. "Better take a long stick with you, Paddy. Give that stallion what-for, I say." Laughing, he settled his hat low on his forehead.

Padgett growled an unintelligible retort. A puzzled smile turned up the corners of Leigh's lips, and she tilted her head.

"What are they talking about, Padgett?" she asked.

"I should have gelded that beast years ago" was all the explanation she got from the frowning man.

Raymond threw back his head. "Chancey just loves the way you taste, boy." He turned to Leigh, eyes twinkling. "Every time Padgett rides that horse, Chancey decides to take himself a little nibble."

"He's addicted to human flesh," Padgett growled. "Mine. And I've got the scars to prove it."

"You want me to muzzle 'im, Paddy?" Mac offered slyly as he paused with his hand on the doorknob.

"Tie a pink ribbon around his nose," Doc suggested.

"Get out of here, Mac!" Padgett warned. "I'll take care of Chancey." His brow cocked at Leigh. "Okay with you? You can call your mother and tell her you'll be late and not to worry. Then we'll ride the north forty, as they say."

Smiling, Leigh stood up. "I'd love to. But let me take a minute to put these things away."

"Oh, no, you don't," protested Raymond, on his feet immediately to trap her hands in the act of gathering up coffee cups. "You're the first real woman that's eaten in the kitchen since . . . Judith died. You go along, now, and enjoy your ride before the wolves come out."

"Wolves?" Leigh coughed, sobering instantly. In dismay her hand flew to her throat. Her eyes widened as she searched for Padgett.

Clucking to himself, Mac winked at Butch. He said, "Don't pay any attention to this old codger, miss. He gets a kick out of frightening women and small children. There's not a wolf within two hundred miles of here. The bears killed 'em all off back in the forties."

Pausing, her mouth twisting out of shape in a delightful pose, Leigh narrowed suspicious eyes until she realized they were teasing her.

"Now, Mac," she chided and shook her finger.

Raymond's face crinkled with satisfaction. "Get off your lazy rump, Doc, and help me with these dishes."

Doc warily eyed the cluttered table. As he rose he adjusted the belt about his waist. "Hey, Butch," he called as the screen door swept shut, "wait up. I'll go with you."

Before he completely disappeared, his graying head popped back inside. "I got an ailin' animal that needs tendin'," he lied shamelessly.

Leigh laughed. The kitchen emptied with amazing rapidity.

"Nothing like a little dishwashing to clarify the issue," Padgett observed with a chuckle as he gave Leigh's clothes a swift inspection. Raymond happily switched on the radio and began puttering. His tall son grasped Leigh's hand and possessively drew her toward the back door.

"We'd better see if we can't find you something to ride in besides those," he said, enormously pleased with himself.

"I look ridiculous," Leigh complained as she stepped from a tack room out into a substantial open area between two wings of stalls.

Padgett was saddling a gentle roan mare for her: Sal. At her voice, he lifted his silver head from tightening the cinch. As if he were unexpectedly transfixed half through the act of dropping the stirrup back into place, he gave her a thorough once-over.

Leigh wore a pair of Butch's jeans. They were tight-fitting pants, a bit too tight in her opinion. Her own blouse was tucked into a waistband so snug it didn't need a belt. Someone's faded sneakers had been rotting away beside a tin of saddle soap, so she had confiscated those, too.

"Mmm," he appraised, staring, nibbling at his lip. "Turn around."

Leigh bridled, then covered her lips with her fingertips. He was wearing slightly flared jeans, boots, and a short-sleeved knit shirt with a decal

116

peeling off its front. She had difficulty in tearing her eyes from his rangy grace.

"Unh-uh." She shook her head. "They're *tight.*"

"You think I don't know that, girl?"

Padgett dropped the stirrup without looking and stepped near enough to take her shoulders in his hands. Giving her a slow spin, he whistled softly. When his large hand shaped about the enticing curve of her backside and he uttered a low moan, she flinched and spun away before he could do more damage to her equilibrium.

A slow crimson inched up her neck. "I came out here to ride with you, Padgett, not play with you."

He clapped the offending hand to the back of his neck, thinking that he had never desired a woman as much as he wanted her now. Though his words were light and fanciful, Leigh guessed the impulsive caress had unnerved him as much as it had her.

"Sorry, ma'am," he drawled. "That's the way of the West—wild and untamed. We cowpokes ride hard and play hard."

Smirking, she backed a few inches farther away. But she was nearer to the boarded wall than she thought and stumbled against it with a disheartening thump.

"Oh!" she said, surprised.

"Careful there, lady." He chuckled to disguise how perfect he found her to be, how easily he pictured the lovely womanliness beneath her clothes. "Don't figure as how those pants'll take too much roughing up until they come apart at the seams."

She threw him a playfully hostile glare. "You tend to the horses, cowboy. I'll tend to the pants."

"Yes'm," he said and disappeared.

She followed him to the tack room, where Padgett selected a bridle and a saddle which was obviously an old favorite of his. It was well worn and much scarred.

Handing her the bridle, he hefted the weight of the saddle to his hip. Leigh walked behind him to where Sal stood patiently waiting. After the notorious Chancey was led from his stall, Leigh stood back to admire the gleaming black beast. The rippling of his lines reminded her of a drawing in a picture book she had once had as a girl: Attila the Hun mounted on a magnificent wild steed whose hoofs struck sparks against the stones when he charged.

"Every year I threaten to sell this animal," Padgett interrupted her fancies. "He's the meanest devil ever born."

"Why d'you keep him, then?"

"Because he's sired some of the fastest horseflesh I've ever seen. *Stand still, you varmint!*" Padgett ordered tartly.

Padgett cautiously took up the bridle and inched beside Chancey's observant head. The dark eyes flared when the man closed a firm hand behind his ears. Despite his lack of time to work with his own animals, Padgett handled himself skillfully.

"Behave, now," he warned. "Don't throw a fit in front of the lady."

When he stepped beside the snorting nose, Chancey laid back his ears. His upper lip curled, and he jerked his head out of reach, skittering, crashing against the wall and kicking it with a cutting blow.

"Whoa!" Padgett lowered the bridle, letting the reins trail in the dirt floor. "You might as well settle this in your mind, killer. You're going to take this bridle if I have to bash in your head. Now, open that mouth."

He slipped the strap of leather over Chancey's ears, but Chancey gave another violent twist of his head. Prancing, snorting wildly, he eyed the man with a look that was almost human, daring him to try it again.

Padgett wasn't about to be bested by a stallion who had, in his opinion, been out to get him since day one. He scooped up the trailing reins and squared his shoulders with resolve.

"Padgett—" began Leigh.

In that slight second when Padgett turned to the sound of her voice, Chancey cleverly took his best opportunity. With a wicked curl of his lips he caught Padgett's forearm in the tender swell of muscle halfway between wrist and elbow.

No horseman alive would tolerate such a thing. Giving a low grunt of pain, Padgett spun, boxing the stallion with a glittering blow across the nose.

Leigh yelped with amazement, and poor Chancey plunged backward against the wall, snorting, shrilly voicing his complaint, and throwing his head back in a magnificently wild temper. Man and beast stood glaring at each other, nostrils flared, chests heaving.

"Shame on both of you," declared Leigh. She stepped toward the dancing horse with a fearlessness which quite staggered Padgett.

"Watch out," he grumbled, nursing his arm in wonder that the prints of Chancey's teeth hadn't brought blood.

"Poor darling," she crooned to the horse and lovingly smoothed the offended nose.

Chancey didn't seem certain if he minded being stroked by a female or not. He held suspiciously still, his flesh quivering when she cautiously handled his shoulder, then the arch of his powerful neck.

Before Padgett actually realized what she was

about, Leigh had retrieved the bridle from the floor and stepped beside the horse's head. Taking a firm grasp of his mane, she slipped the straps up over his nose. She moved the steel bit up against the teeth which had just taken a not so friendly nibble of his owner and easily moved it into place. Over the ears went the bridle, under the chin buckled the strap. Then she tied the reins together and touched them to Padgett's shoulder.

He turned his head.

After one look at the docile horse, Padgett's mouth twisted in a comically wry grimace. He glanced from her suppressed mirth back to the horse. His mouth puckered. Then he sighed with defeat and slumped.

"I don't believe this," he said. "You're a witch, aren't you?"

She smothered a laugh. "I told you, Padgett, horses and I get along. They know I'm not a horsewoman, so they humor me."

"Bull," he retorted with finality and moved to throw the saddle over an already tamed beast.

"Never mind him, Chancey. He's a sore loser."

"Just sore," protested Padgett. "And don't go putting any ideas in that nag's head."

Meaning to have the last word, Leigh tiptoed to the twitching ears. "He doesn't mean it," she whispered audibly.

Whereupon Padgett placed a sound slap upon her own little rump. "If you don't mind," he said wickedly and bent to tighten the cinch.

Their moonlit ride was wisely paced at a slow walk. Not that Leigh couldn't ride well enough, Padgett guessed, after watching her swing herself up into the saddle. But he wanted to prolong it as much as he dared.

The two horses stopped often and lowered their heads to nibble at the luxuriant growth of spring cover crop. Padgett guided them across a section of pasture which had been fenced off until now, and the grazing was over ankle high.

Leigh covertly observed his lighthearted posture. In spite of Chancey's dislike of his rider, once Padgett was mounted his firm rein demanded perfect obedience. He slouched in the saddle, seemingly an extension of the horse. His thighs, as they lay against Chancey's swelling sides, strained in the tight jeans. The moonlight teasingly ruffled the silver-streaked locks.

It was a mistake to become so fascinated with a man, she warned herself and squinted to penetrate the fuzzy darkness beyond. It was seldom that she allowed herself such freedom—out at night, carefree, with the wind whipping her hair, not worried about fretful clients or Margie or Elizabeth.

The sky was a polka-dotted mass of stars now. She breathed deeply and carefully wound her fingers about the saddle horn.

"Sometimes I forget how peaceful it is out here," he said quietly. "I get so caught up in the pressures of big money and risks, working from crisis to crisis. I wonder why I do it."

"Because you can't bear moments of being totally alone with yourself," she answered honestly before she weighed the possible offense of her words.

Her profile seemed to him like a piece of fine classic sculpture from the hand of a gifted Roman. Long strands of hair billowed out around her like the froth of some dark, mysterious waterfall. Her breasts swelled high and temptingly, and he suspected that they were not often touched. The image of their supple comfort drove a spear into the deep regions of his body. He wanted to touch her himself, but he was afraid to mar the serenity of the moment.

"I'm sure you're right," he said thickly. "Why do *you* get caught up in the gristmill of it?"

She shrugged without looking at him. "For the same reason you do, I expect."

The horses, contentedly chewing, bumped against each other. She loved the way everything smelled—the leather, the sweat of the horses, the tender grass as they clipped it off in their teeth. Occasionally her knee thrust into the back of Padgett's leg, and she didn't attempt to prevent it. His body was larger and stronger than hers, and the permanency of that fact comforted her like the eternity of the dawn, of the springtime, or of the rain.

His fingers suddenly imprisoned a floating lock of her hair, and she started. Logic flashed into her mind like an exposing flare: she was the mother of this man's child; he wasn't just another man; she must be careful.

When he leaned over the space separating them and cupped her face in his hand, she started guiltily. "Do you know what I'm feeling?" he asked hoarsely.

Far in the distance an owl hooted its lonely warning. The horses continued their munching, as if she were not snared in a conflict with no easy solution.

"Yes, I think so."

He leaned so near she could feel his breath fondling her cheeks. She thought he would touch her lips with his, but he didn't.

"There're so many things I would like to do to you," he murmured, "that it would take a lifetime."

Because his nearness made her mind whirl, she had no reply for such words. "Please don't tell me that," she begged him. "I can't think straight when you say things like that."

"Don't think, then. Just feel. Let it happen."

Her lashes drooped darkly. "It's not as simple as that."

"It can be as simple as you want it to be."

The truth loomed between them like a pile of heavy stones which would take great strength to remove, one at a time. The cruel starkness of her secret made her suddenly despise it. It wasn't fair to be trapped so.

"I want you," he said simply. "I want you a lot."

He didn't wait for a reply but straightened and drew the reins until Chancey moved forward a few inches.

How she wished she could be sensible and liberated, like women in magazines. How she wished she could place her secret in a separate part of her mind and take what she could of him. If she were wise he would probably fall in love with her. Perhaps he would ask her to marry him. He didn't *have* to be told the truth, did he?

She wondered, as she stared at the muscled elegance of his back, what his desires truly consisted of: lust or love. She wasn't a fool. She could make his desire grow into love if she didn't do something stupid. She had realized that when she sat listening to him tell about Vietnam. Perhaps she was a fool; she didn't know what to do.

Softly she clucked to Sal and inched up beside him. "We'd better ride to the fence and back. It's getting late, and I'll have to go home soon."

He kept his profile moodily etched against the sky. "You wouldn't have to go home," he said.

The wind whipped her hair across her face and disguised her astonishment. She hadn't expected this to come so quickly. After a moment, when she didn't reply, he took her silence to be refusal.

"Let's ride to the fence," he agreed without a thread of emotion in his voice.

Reflecting that this whole affair had grown amazingly complex, she followed hesitantly.

The fence line was marked by a dark row of shadowy clumps of trees—some small, one a grand old oak thrusting high into the sky. When they were less than fifty yards from it, Padgett swept out his hand in a lavish gesture.

"I'll bet there're wild blackberries along the fence. Let's walk."

Quite unable to resist his enthusiasm, she waited for him to drop lightly to the ground. He stood beside her foot in the stirrup. As she swung her leg over the saddle his arms lifted to catch her. Her hand closed tightly about his.

"Don't you drop me," she squeaked breathlessly and let her weight shift to his steady support.

"Never!" He laughed and pinned her very high against the span of his chest, her knees pressing into his waist.

Feeling herself weaving, Leigh grabbed his neck and gave a small cry of surprise when he buried his face between the softness of her breasts. Ever so slowly he let her slide downward in his arms, the smooth planes of her caught securely against his stomach, then his waist, then the hard shelf of his pelvis, his thighs.

His desire strained urgently against her; she couldn't ignore it. The barest moment before her toes touched the ground, he whispered, "I wouldn't drop you, little one."

Her lips were already parted in a trace of a laugh.

He groped hungrily, capturing them, fastening to them with the low groan of a starving man.

She murmured against his mouth, but he only eased her to the ground and framed her head between the wide span of both hands. Everything about him pleaded with her to relent—his tongue which tasted her burning sweetness, his breath which coaxed and spoke to her in a myriad of ways, his limbs which strained against her, driving with need.

The seductive trap opened its jaws wide, beckoning her into its exquisite depths, promising her she would have no regrets. His fingers were at her throat, then the buttons of her blouse. Leigh felt herself slipping into the warm abyss, felt her knees going.

"Oh, Padgett," she breathed as the tiny hook at the front of her bra yielded to him.

"Shh. Trust me, sweetheart," he said and brushed his wet, burning lips over the satiny curve to take the yearning tip into his mouth.

Her head dropped back and her eyes closed. She felt a dozen things at once and couldn't control any of them—her hair swinging free, her fingers threading about the back of his neck, his hands burying into the cushion of her hips, the two of them lowering in slow motion into a velvety cloud of green grass.

Far back in her mind—in a hidden corner of herself which was insanely logical—she thought, This is right. Margie is mine. Padgett is mine. I love them both, and this is right.

The first time that he took her was his—a blaze of unquenchable fire. But the second time was hers—a slow, languid intensity that built to such a torturing peak that she ended up begging him to help her end it. And he did, with a care which made her want to cry.

As the tension seeped gradually from her body, leaving her drifting in a languorous, peaceful contentment, she snuggled to Padgett's naked length. Sighing, she lay still upon the bed of their clothes and dreamily watched him prop himself on an elbow.

Their legs were still tangled together, and Padgett grew lazily absorbed in arranging the wisps of hair back from her face. It was the perfect time for one of life's cruel little twists of the blade. As Leigh gazed tenderly at the handsome set of his face she saw not him but the sweetness of their daughter. Real life bore down upon her with a crushing force.

"Padgett?" she said raggedly.

"What, darling?"

"Do you like me?"

Smiling, he kissed the tip of her nose. "I adore you."

She pushed against his chest, her forehead puckering. "No. I mean *like* me. Like, as in respect."

He drew back, wondering at her sudden earnestness. That inscrutable thing about her which had haunted him from the beginning was there again, painted across her face. He shook his head.

"Of course I like you."

"Well . . ." She paused, guessing she didn't have the right to invade every part of him. "Do you feel that way about many women? I mean, there *is* talk, you know."

Grinning, he shaped her cheekbones with a wandering finger. "Ah, we're getting possessive, aren't we?"

Leigh struggled to sit up, but he pushed her back down.

"I'm sorry," she muttered.

"There you go again, throwing up those defenses about yourself. Why can't you just admit you're jealous and have it done with?"

"I'm not jealous, Padgett!" She wrenched her head away, wishing that she were dressed. But his body lay half over hers, and she didn't have the strength to wrestle with him. "Oh, maybe I am, a little," she admitted.

"Well, since you're so magnanimous"—he chuckled—"I'll admit that I'm jealous, too. That night on the yacht when Pete hung on to you like a courtier I could have belted him."

"That was pride, not jealousy," she argued.

"Maybe."

He slid his palm up the slender calf of her leg, and she twitched, pushing at his hand. He moved it higher to her thigh and bent for her lips.

"You're beautiful," he murmured.

"No, I'm not. Padgett, I—"

"What?"

Heaving a sigh, he threw his leg across her waist and shaped his hand about her jaw, preventing her from jerking her face from him. "Don't *do* that! Don't pull away like that. We've shared something wonderful, Leigh. Whatever that thing is that gnaws at you, for God's sake tell me. I'm exasperated with trying to fight it."

She wasn't ready to tell him about Margie; she didn't know how. She lifted her hands to her face and hid behind them, wondering what to do. In the silence the steady munching of the horses seemed the only tangible thing about them.

"I can't," she whimpered.

He stiffened in disappointment, and she clutched

at his muscled arms which formed a protective haven about her.

"Don't be angry," she pleaded hurriedly. "Please, just try to understand that I . . ."

"But there is something, isn't there? I'm not just imagining it, am I?"

Her moan was low and weary of carrying the ten-year-old burden all by herself. She nodded her head.

"You're not imagining it. But it's kind of like you and the war, you know? Some things just have to have the right time to be said. Please don't be angry."

Padgett didn't understand at all, but he tenderly fastened his lips to hers and tasted of her one last time before they had to return. Deep in his heart he wondered if he shouldn't risk the exposure of himself. Perhaps he should tell her what he honestly believed—that he was falling in love with her.

If she had things she was afraid to say, however, he guessed he did, too. Telling a woman he loved her was a thing he'd done only once before in his life. And that had been a mistake.

So he helped her get dressed. They stood in the middle of the vast meadow and debated about whether he should drive her back home that night or not. She fretted about what his father would miscon-strue if she stayed over. She could sleep in the guest room, he argued; it wasn't a big deal.

Leigh's private conviction was that it was an enormous deal. Already they had reached the point where parting was painful. Now she was weary and sated with physical fulfillment. Perhaps she should trust him one more time. Later—tomorrow, next week—she could tell him the truth.

Later, lying between cool, crisp sheets, her eyes

wide with worry, she considered if she should even tell him the truth. At one point in her life she would have given anything to be able to fling it in Padgett's face. But now, in retrospect, she wasn't so sure.

If she let things take their natural course, Padgett would probably ask her to marry him. He would accept Margie without questioning her paternity and would be a good father to her. No law said he had to know Margie was his.

She had done her part, for goodness' sake! She'd been faithful to him without the benefits of marriage —the ultimate honor. Marrying him now would be fitting; she deserved the Cinderella ending to a bizarre wartime romance!

But if she told him the truth she would risk losing everything. After all, she had known where Padgett was for the past five years and had made no move to set things right. What would he do when he discovered that? He might believe her, he might even forgive her, but he would probably never trust her again. Could she take that chance?

It wasn't fair, she thought as she viciously pounded her pillow. She hadn't caused the war and thrown Padgett into a grotesque killing situation no human being should have to bear. Yet now it was *she* who had to risk—with a half dozen words—changing the future of a number of lives. What a price to pay for a few stolen moments of passion on a beach!

Most women would say she was crazy for even considering telling Padgett anything.

# Chapter Seven

*P*urple shadows shifted through Leigh's consciousness with the first dawn. Gray ghosts of daylight chased her in and out of slumber, and wakefulness presently won. Jerking up to a sitting position, she blinked and dragged herself into the reality of a new day.

Where was she? A strange bedroom with stark, masculine walls. *What had she done?* Then it all came back: she was in Padgett's home, she was vaguely sore, she had willingly, sublimely, given herself to him again.

Except now, in the honesty of daylight, making love didn't seem as right as it had beneath the moon. In fact, it seemed unbelievably foolish, even stupid, even wrong, even unforgivable. Though she was alone, she slumped, blistering with chagrin; She had made a fool of herself over him for the second time. As a result, there were the inevitable prices she must pay. Everything had a price, even love, *especially* love.

With her thoughts in a hopeless shambles, Leigh hastily improvised a toilette. After a few moments her appearance was almost as immaculate as when she had arrived, complete with her hair neatly brushed into its chignon and her soft swirling skirt and wedgies. She left the bedroom with a flagging enthusiasm.

Following her nose to the kitchen was an easy task. Raymond was beginning the weekend without the benefit of a cook. The rich aroma of perking coffee filled the whole house, and when her footsteps sounded he turned with a polite smile.

"How was the guest room?" he inquired hospitably and fetched down another ironstone cup.

Pretending to be composed, cuddling her cup, Leigh leaned back against the edge of the sink and sipped. With invented energy she described Padgett's duel with Chancey. As she talked she guessed Raymond was calculating how deeply the relationship between Padgett and herself actually went.

Not knowing Padgett's personal life was a disturbing disadvantage now. He didn't often bring women to the ranch, she knew, but she wasn't so naive as to believe she was the first one. What did Raymond think of his son's publicized love life? What did he think of *her*?

Raymond asked politely from beside the stove, "Would you enjoy walking out to the front porch? This is my favorite time of day. Judith and I always walked out when the roses were blooming. We'd sit on the steps and drink coffee and plan what we would do that day."

Pouring a bit more brew into her cup, she nodded. "I'd like that very much, Mr. Williams."

His head shook in a mild reproof. "You must call me Ray."

She observed the friendly warmth in his eyes, and it was not mere politeness; it was that irresistible charm of wanting to be liked in return. She found it quite wonderful. As they made their way through the stillness of the slumbering house she fell naturally into step beside him.

The early sun was bursting through the wide window—an impressionistic painting in brilliant orange and red. Raymond gestured at various things she had not noticed the night before. Pausing, he indicated a small portrait of a stunningly beautiful woman.

Leigh, as she studied the photograph, found herself quite unable to put one foot ahead of another.

Genetic material was so unexplainably treacherous at times. Considering that Padgett barely resembled his father and that Margie hardly resembled her own mother, Leigh now understood where the family traits lay. Judith's facial features were unerringly recorded upon Padgett, who in turn had passed them down to his daughter. If Elizabeth had been shocked at the likeness shared between Margie and Padgett, she would have been flabbergasted at this.

Feeling stranded and alone, knowing nothing else to do except remain silent, Leigh trailed behind Margie's grandfather to the porch. She pretended to be fascinated with Judith's roses as their verdant disorder upset him. Bending over the white railing, Ray scrutinized the undisciplined rampage of their thorny branches. For a few moments he attempted to fasten a few stems into some semblance of order, but the riot had gone untended too long. Nothing but a vigorous pruning would help matters.

Frowning, he muttered half to himself. "Judith hates to see them this way. I'll have to tend these things Monday morning." Then, as if consoled that he had come to a decision, he smiled and explained. "She's as strict with these flowers as some . . ."

His words dwindled into silence. Leigh returned his embarrassed smile and watched the lines of his face deepen, as if life seeped through some secret passageway and left him numb. His color drained away as he realized that, for those moments, Judith had been alive again. He didn't apologize for drifting into the past. He simply descended the steps to greet Bonnie, who waited patiently on the landing.

Leigh's face felt stiff from having observed such a private loneliness. Through the blood of her daughter she was connected to this man, she told herself. She owed him something. That obligation didn't surprise her too much; responsibility to Raymond was one of the prices she must pay.

The secret wasn't just between Padgett and herself. Its effects spread outward like ripples in a pond to touch other lives. If it were possible, the knowledge of Padgett's daughter would touch Raymond more deeply than it touched the rest of them. Elizabeth had had all those years to get used to Margie. It wouldn't be so easy for Raymond.

Feeling enormously weary, Leigh wished she were back home. Padgett's deep voice at the top of the steps made her stumble. She instinctively glanced upward, half expecting him to be standing astride like some demanding buccaneer in tight crimson pants, his fists planted brazenly on his hips.

But the tall man only slouched against the post

beside him and let his sleepy gaze wander as he rubbed the stubble of a beard.

"I hope you can cook, darling," he drawled with maddening good nature. "I'm going to shower and shave. Call me when breakfast's ready."

Jauntily he pulled himself away from the post and disappeared into the house. Leigh glanced back to find Raymond measuring her reaction with whetted interest. His expression was a mixture of amusement and intuition. He knew, she thought, and if he didn't know exactly, he guessed how deeply she was in love with Padgett.

He said quickly, "Paddy's damnably possessive when he wants something bad enough. I'm the culprit, I guess. He inherited it. We've always moved fast, Paddy and I—too fast. There were times I nearly drove Judith crazy with my arrogance. And Padgett's scared me to death with some of his assumptions. Don't let him run over you, girl."

The silence was too knowing and awkward. Leigh answered swiftly in order to end it. "You think it's me he wants?" she asked lightly.

"Undoubtedly. I can't say that I blame him."

Her eyes lowered. "Thank you, sir. I'm afraid that what Padgett wants, if you're right, isn't cut and dried. It's not like adding one and one and coming up with two."

For one mad, insane second she wanted to blurt that, in this case, one and one were three.

Raymond chuckled. "Cut and dried is dull, my dear. And dull is the one thing I suspect you're not. Shall we go scramble some eggs and make toast before the great movie mogul has our heads?"

Leigh made a small production out of looping her

arm through his. "Mercy, if he's that thirsty for blood"—she giggled—"I suggest we hurry."

"So this is where you work," Leigh remarked inanely as Padgett shoved open a heavy door to a room on the south side of the house.

The lines on either side of his mouth deepened into an indulgent smile. Nudging her forward, he introduced her to the spaciousness of his home office. "Come into my lair."

It was utter chaos. Below wide, sheerly draped windows ran a cushioned bench stacked with piles of bound scripts, tin canisters of film, and hardback books. To say nothing of a fifteen-foot semicircular desk in the center of the room with only inches of its surface visible. The furnishings were a mismatched collection of chairs and overflowing bookcases. A screen and projector crouched in one corner. It was a scholar's clutter and quite suited to him.

"Ahh"—she hesitated, laughing, spinning slowly to take it all in—"what kind of decor do you call this?"

"Late-century bachelorhood, and don't tell me you don't see how I can find a thing. I know where everything is. Perfectly."

She twisted her mouth comically out of shape. "Well, it takes all kinds."

The door slammed shut from an intent kick of Padgett's heel. Sighing, as if he had gone the ultimate limits of his endurance, he folded her into his arms.

"I've been wanting to kiss you since I woke up," he breathed into the small rebellious curls behind her ear. "It wasn't right waking up in an empty bed.

Couldn't you hear me thinking, Come to me so I can hold you, so I can touch you everywhere?"

"I—I needed to wake up and think . . . about us," she mumbled uncertainly against the soft, sweet-smelling terry of his shirt.

She would rest against him for just a moment. For a few seconds she would pretend everything was simple. She would memorize the rise and fall of his chest and gather strength to tell him. There were no doubts, now, about what she must do. In a way, Padgett loved her. He had the right to know about Margie.

Padgett balanced his jaw lightly on the silky crown of her head. "You're not sorry, are you, sweetheart?"

"About last night?"

"Yes. That I made love to you, that I learned everything"—his pleasure laughed deep in his chest —*"almost* everything about you."

"Yes," she said. "I mean, no. I'm not sorry. Not in the way you think."

Puzzled, growing still, Padgett forced her face upward with one hand. His gray eyes grew brooding and wondering. "In what way are you sorry, then?"

When Leigh hesitated, he gradually discarded his worry and bent to kiss the tip of her nose. As his lips moved persuasively lower Leigh pushed against his chest. His embrace tightened, and something in her blazed to life, rebelling. She shoved hard. Gasping to breathe, she whirled away and shook her head in protest.

"No!" she said and hurriedly began catching up stray strands of hair. "Please, don't. I mean, it's not you, Padgett. But you take me too fast when you do that. And I can't . . . think." She drooped wearily. "I need to think."

Padgett grimly watched her hands tremble as she tucked the tresses into place. She tried to avoid his eyes, and he wondered if he could believe what she said.

In a halfhearted attempt to postpone the unavoidable confrontation, she pretended to study the titles of the books covering the entire side of one wall.

"I saw this movie," she remarked and ran the tips of her fingers up and down the spine of one book.

He muttered, "I directed it myself." He wasn't the least interested in the movies she had seen.

"Oh." She smiled. "No wonder it was good."

Padgett didn't smile back. With troubled steps he drew behind her until she would be forced to touch him if she moved. Leigh remained perfectly still—a frightened doe now, being stalked by an experienced hunter. One of Padgett's arms came around her and braced itself upon the bookcase. Then the other, blocking any escape. His mouth, when it slowly lowered to the nape of her neck, sent a tremor shooting through her. Her forehead dropped in surrender to the sleek dust jackets in front of her.

"We'll move very slowly," he promised as he fitted his larger body to her back. "You don't need to be afraid of me, sweetheart."

"I'm not afraid of you," she answered in a small, thin voice. It was only half a lie.

"I won't even touch you if you don't want me to."

Leigh forced the words past her lips, fumbling with each one. "You—you know . . . I love it when you . . . touch me."

His head lifted, and the frustration in his breathing made her hate what she was doing to him.

"Then, damn it, Leigh," he said quietly. "I don't understand. Do you enjoy this Ferris wheel we keep spinning around on?"

Miserable, she shook her head. "I hate it."

As if he could transfuse some of his confident strength into her body, his strong arms crossed over her bosom. His hands closed over her shoulders until she was pulled back against his chest.

"You're not a child," he said. "I'm not a child. Whatever bothers you, we can work it out. Whatever it is."

She let out her breath. "I wish I were sure of that."

After a long moment, giving her room to compose herself, Padgett slowly withdrew. Leigh abruptly felt the sharp sting of resentment. Why hadn't he been overbearing about it and tried to force something? Why hadn't he thrown some sarcastic remark at her so her temper could seethe and she could strike out at him? So that she could have flung the entire blame in his face and gotten it over with?

She glared at the vague bewilderment in his eyes and doubted her ability to go through with it. The merciful thing would be to say it quickly. She caught a deep breath.

"You're always so in control," she threw at him, as if it were a grievous flaw. "I'm weaker than you. I've always been weaker."

His brows knitted. "I'm what I am, Leigh. I'm sorry if that offends you."

"But you're not, don't you see? You're only what you think you are. *I* know what you are." Her voice dropped to a hoarse pleading. "Believe me, I know what both of us are."

Leigh's fingers began to lace and unlace. She lifted her head and looked away, then back to measure his face with its fine, intelligent eyes and handsome mouth. She sensed his sarcasm before it came.

"Well, if I've missed something, babe," he drawled, "I'm sure you're about to tell me."

"Ohh." He was making it so difficult.

Wearying, Padgett caught her roughly in his arms. Her head tipped backward. "You want to make your confessions? You want to clear your conscience? Very well, do your trifling little penance. Tell me everything. But the past doesn't matter to me. *Now* is what matters to me."

His embrace, though gentle, was demanding. She could not escape.

"I've tried to tell you," she exclaimed. "A hundred times I've tried. At first I was so angry, and then you turned out to be nice. I didn't expect you to be nice and understanding. It was all so crazy, Padgett. I was so young back then, so . . ." She sighed. "So young."

Her green eyes were liquid pools which brimmed and threatened to spill. Realizing that her distraction was genuine, Padgett took her arm, prepared to lead her to a chair so she could recover herself. But somehow they were lowering to the softness of the carpet. He took her into his arms with great care. Making soft, comforting sounds, he cradled her in the nest of his own body. For a time he soothed her with a reassuring rocking motion, as if she were a hurt child.

"Back then, what?" he urged her.

With her head buried into his shoulder, her eyes closed, she began explaining in toneless words. "A long time ago. I was just a child myself. I didn't know then how it would all turn out. I never dreamed."

"We're all children at one time or another."

"I was only a child when I had a child." She could have been a robot repeating programmed words.

"You've done a magnificent job with Margie," he complimented her, not understanding. "I mean that. You can be proud of her, Leigh. Marjorie's a beautiful girl."

She twisted away from him as if he were poison. Inching as far away as possible, she leaned against the rows of books and struggled to search past the shell of the outer man into the inner one.

"Do you mean that?" she choked.

"Of course."

"Then how can you not remember? When you came into my office that day with Hugh Radnor I looked at you and thought, How can he not remember?"

Padgett's shift of body weight was gradual, a reflex of serious changes taking place inside him. Leigh felt him still, felt him balancing equations in his mind. The look that came down over his face was the most bleakly confused she had ever seen on any man. She must say it quickly now.

Her eyes fluttered shut. She continued. "When you told me about the war, then I understood why you didn't remember. I didn't know what to do after you told me that. So many years had gone by. There didn't seem to be a place to begin telling you."

Padgett thought that the apprehension crawling over him was not very different from the sweating horror he had suffered in the jungles of 'Nam. "What are you saying?" he demanded in a voice he hardly recognized.

She shook her head. "I don't know. Everything."

"Back then, you just said. Back *when?* Before the war?"

"No. In the middle of it."

A minute slipped by—the hacking of a dull blade, a mutilation. Neither of them spoke. When Padgett finally did speak, Leigh guessed he was recalling part of it, at least. She sat in a boneless huddle and feared what the outcome would be. He was facing her, his head dropped forward.

"But—" he said, then silenced again. "I knew we'd met. I've always known it, somewhere back in my subconscious. But you kept denying it. And those days, even now, are a little hazy to me." His silver head snapped up, his eyes glittering as they slammed into hers. "I shouldn't have listened to you when you laughed so coyly and said, '*Déjà vu,* Mr. Williams.' *Why,* Leigh. What did I say to you then that was so bad?"

A warning pulsed through Leigh at the sound of her own words. She saw herself, watched herself burn her own bridges. Already his bitter pride was simmering, choking out the embers of confused anger.

"I was eighteen, Padgett. We had a graduation party out at the American Legion Hall. You were in uniform and you—"

His hand cut off her words. She hushed instantly.

"There's no need to go any further. I remember now." He raked over the despair on her face, the cringing position of her body, everything. "I even remember your name now. I apologize. I don't have any excuse except that I was a little out of it then. But I've told you that, haven't I?"

Leigh's confidence melted away under the flame of his suspicion. "Believe me, Padgett, I really do understand."

"Do you, now?" His smile was mirthless. Between them stretched an infinite gulf. The room was no longer friendly; it was a strange enemy, dangerous.

Leigh drew herself tightly against the wall. "I

understand why you never called me as you promised you would. You disappeared, and I blamed you
then for breaking my heart. You were the first man
to ever love me, Padgett. Surely you knew that.''

He was in pain now, not only at what he had done
but that he had not known. He hadn't meant to hurt
anyone.

"My God!" he blurted out in misery, hardly
knowing what was happening to him. He was
amazed at the mystery of his own mind that could
trip him up so badly.

He unbent his long body and walked to the desk.
Opening a wooden box on the desk, he took out a
cigarette. He lit it, realized what he was doing, and
viciously ground it out in an empty ashtray. He
slammed the lid down on the box, and the fragile
wood splintered.

Moving near the windows, he stood staring out at
the well-clipped lawn. He took the stance of a man
when he ponders—his feet spread, his hands slipped
into his back pockets, palms out, watching as the
ranch came awake.

"At least," he said tightly, "I didn't wreck your
entire life, did I? Don't lay that guilt trip on me, too,
'cause I won't buy that."

Far in the distance Leigh heard the whine of the
Land-Rover as it ground into gear. She wanted the
advantage of standing up, but she didn't think she
could maneuver her legs. Drawing her knees securely beneath her chin, she wrapped her arms about
them and bowed her head. Dear God, she prayed,
please let him realize how difficult it had been for
her!

Padgett's voice spent its accusation like an arrow.
"I'll take the blame for my part of it, Leigh. If I was

insensitive and used you when you were innocent, I'm sorry. But don't pretend you . . . what shall we say . . . *wasted* your young life pining away over a mixed-up lieutenant."

Leigh felt like a wilted, condemned leaf, clinging by one thread to a tree. A fragile breath of wind would snatch her loose and hurtle her down to her death.

"Oh, Padgett," she said, her voice muffled against her knees, "there was never anyone but you. Never."

Her relief in saying it, after so many years of pretending, of protecting herself and Margie, could not compensate for her certainty she had lost him.

The silence wasn't merely an absence of sound; it was physical and glitteringly painful. After a moment her head slowly lifted.

In that first white-hot grip of disbelief Padgett's jaw slackened. He spun hard about. Leigh wished she could lose consciousness so she wouldn't have to see it. As if his arm had lifted to strike her from across the room, she flinched and threw up her hand. His eyes, uncaring if he hurt her, were granite-hard, cold.

Leigh was hardly lucid when he strode across the room. His fingers bit into her arms as he jerked her to her feet, and she found it impossible to look away. Deep lines cut into his features from nostrils to mouth. His lips, as the rage spurted through him, were bitterly compressed.

"You're not lying, are you?" He spat it out, satisfied, obviously, that her lifelessness was proof.

Leigh shook her head in agreement.

"My God!" he breathed and abruptly released her so that she stumbled back against the books.

He jerked away, then turned to stare at her fingers pressed cruelly against her mouth. "Oh, my God!" he repeated. He moistened his lips, his mind racing madly.

They stood on opposite sides of a misunderstanding so abysmal she dared not even approach it. She felt him reliving the last years in a vast panorama, battling to shift scenes into some sane, meaningful order. When his finger pointed at her, it cut her to raw bone.

"How could you do this to me?" he thundered.

She choked out the explanation and shrank, as she was doing it, into a tiny knot. "I couldn't find you, Padgett. I swear it. I tried for weeks. I didn't know where you lived or anything. I called every Williams in the Los Angeles phone book. I thought of going to the police. And then the nausea hit me, and I had to tell my parents."

"But you've known where I was for the last five years. Why didn't you come to me? I would have believed you! I would have done the right thing!"

Some of the years-old determination seeped back into Leigh's spirit. She drew herself up—queenlike, defensive—and faced him. After all, hadn't she had ten years of practice in forcing up her head? She didn't have to grovel before this man, even if he were Margie's father.

"I didn't want the *right thing* from you, Padgett Williams. I wanted someone who would love me. I did the best I could do. You have no idea what it was like, going through something like that, having to take all of those silent accusations, the funny looks, the humiliation."

She stepped toward him, her eyes glistening. "You have no idea of the thousands of ways that society has of embarrassing an unmarried mother. Don't you dare talk to me about the right thing! You wouldn't know the first thing about it. You only sired her, Padgett. *I bore her!*"

He paced the carpet of his office like some caged animal, muttering to himself, trying to make sense out of something which could turn his life upside down in the space of seconds.

"It's unforgivable," he lashed out blindly, eager to destroy something. "Five years. Five years! All this time I've been the father of a daughter, and you could have told me five years ago!"

She followed stupidly in his wake, wincing when he whirled, thrusting glare for glare, bitterness for bitterness.

"I was nothing but a girl," she said. "You were a man. You knew what you were doing."

He threw out an arm, his brows working. "Oh, don't give me that garbage about it being the man's fault, honey. You didn't exactly fight me off, if I remember."

She wanted to slap him. "Ohh."

She started for the door, stomping, declaring that she was going home, that she wasn't going to demean herself any longer by listening to his raving.

He grabbed her arm.

"Keep your miserable hands off me!" she shrieked at him.

"She's my daughter, too! I have rights!"

"You have no rights, not like this. Stay out of her life, Padgett! I'll take my share of the blame, but you're not charging into Margie's little world and making it a shambles, too. Do you hear what I say?"

Padgett forced her back against the door, his teeth grinding. "If you think I'm going to let another day go by without claiming a daughter I've had for nine years, my darling, you're a bigger fool than I take you for."

The miracle of maternal instinct transformed Leigh into a dangerous adversary. "I'm warning you," she said in a calm, deadly voice. "I won't let you hurt her."

He towered over her, his shoulders heaving. An oath rumbled deep in his throat. "I'm not a monster, Leigh. I don't want to hurt you, and I don't want to hurt her. But I mean to have what's mine."

"Then pay your dues," she countered savagely. "Pay your damn dues like I did!"

She reached for the door, meaning to leave the room, meaning to take one of his cars if she had to in order to return home. She was sick to her bones, and she wasn't certain at this point if lying would not have been the better way.

Putting her hand on the knob, she was startled at the knock from the other side. Without hesitating, she flung the door open. Raymond Williams stood outside, agitation lining his face.

"Come in," she invited. "As it turns out, this quarrel is a family affair."

Raymond shook his head. "Forgive me. I don't mean to interfere, truly. But—"

"Come on in, Dad. You'll learn soon enough, anyway. But you'd better sit down. Leigh has just put a nice little bomb in my lap."

"Padgett!"

"Oh, hell, Leigh. What's the use of tiptoeing around. Dad's a big boy now."

Leigh drew herself up regally, poking a fingernail into the span of Padgett's chest. "For once you'll listen to someone," she ordered him. "Now, sit down and be quiet. If your father must be told, I'll do it. Decently."

Shock drained Padgett of the strength to fight with her anymore. Slumping down at his desk, he moaned a soft, private grief and buried his silvering head into spread hands. Leigh swallowed down such an enormous wave of compassion for him that it nearly blinded her to what must be done.

It hadn't been easy on the man everyone admired for his tough, glittering genius. Now he was a motionless, wounded human being. She loved him so badly she wanted to go to him and draw his head down to her breast and hold him.

Unfortunately, the time wasn't right for sympathies. With the remaining vestiges of her strength, she took Raymond Williams by the hand and meekly guided him to a chair.

"Sir," she said tenderly. "Padgett's right. What I'm going to tell you won't be easy. But I swear before heaven that I've done the best that I know. You will try to understand, won't you?"

Raymond gazed at her with such loving patience that she motioned for him to sit down. As if she were a young girl, she lowered herself beside his feet. The older man instinctively took her hand and spread it carefully upon his knee.

As Leigh explained her difficult story he kept his eyes fastened upon the small white hand. He thoughtfully smoothed the fingers, one by one. And when she had told it all—uninterrupted by the moody, withdrawn man on the other side of the room—he lifted the hand to his lips. The kiss he placed upon it was one of unmistakable caring, of trust and respect. She wanted badly to weep.

That was the only response Raymond made. He

didn't say that he was glad or that he was sorry. He rose and moved toward the desk where Padgett sat in some dark world of his own making. He studied the frustrated marks upon a paper which, if someone had analyzed them, would have been unbelievably tormented.

"I'm taking Leigh home, Paddy," he said quietly. "We'll talk when I get back."

The room threatened to shatter from the silence. Leigh wanted to scream. She wanted to rush to Padgett and shake him until he was limp. *Tell me that you understand!* her thoughts raged at him. *Say you love me! Say you hate me, but say something!*

The eyes of the grieved man remained riveted upon the paper he was covering with marks. Leigh knew then that this part of her life was over. She had taken the risk of telling because she thought it was the fair thing to do. Well, she'd lost. It wasn't the first time she had lost. She would survive.

Her feet, when they carried her from the room, were heavy, like those of a tired old woman.

As Raymond drove down the long, dusty driveway Leigh did not look back. Standing before the window, Padgett watched with unblinking eyes as the pickup glided along the lane toward the county road beyond.

The pencil in his hand snapped into two pieces. He closed a tight fist about them.

The house, without her, grew deathly still.

Padgett made no move to brush away the tears as they glistened and spilled. They slid with symbolic slowness over the strong planes of his cheeks to drizzle into his mouth. He had found her and lost her, both at the same time. He didn't know if he wanted to go on.

# Chapter Eight

Leigh didn't consider herself to be faking when she stayed in her bed for the rest of the weekend. She was sick—sick in a way she hadn't been for years, sick with an illness of the soul.

Oh, she wouldn't huddle under the covers and try to hide for the rest of her life. Life wasn't some dainty little game that one could elect to take or leave. There were phones to be answered and clients to be consoled. There was a mother to be cherished and a daughter to be adored.

But—and the guilt of admitting it made her want to die—everything seemed like an infinity of meaningless ritual now. It seemed an exercise of the body just to keep moving and smiling when tears gushed out of her eyes at nothing and her throat was so knotted with disappointment she could hardly talk.

Only a passionately loved man could hurt a woman as badly as this. And she did love Padgett, damn him! She realized now that the private vendetta she had waged for five years against Everest Productions had kept her alive. It had kept them together, too, as he always lurked in her mind. Vengeance was a compelling motive. Telling Padgett the truth had robbed her of even that.

Moping about the house was so unusual for Leigh —she absolutely would not *tolerate* being sick—that Elizabeth ignored the glum orders to stay out of the bedroom. She bent over the pale, inert form of her daughter beneath a crumpled sheet and frowned down into her swollen red eyes.

"Should I call a doctor?"

"No, I don't want any doctor." Leigh pretended a stuffy nose to match her eyes and strategically went through the ruse of searching for a tissue. "I've caught a virus or something. I'll be better in a day or so. Don't worry."

Elizabeth rolled her eyes to the ceiling. "Don't worry," she mimicked and left the room with an armful of clothes for the laundry.

Elizabeth did worry. She had watched as Leigh, burning with fever, refused to be ill, dragging herself about the house as if putting on at least one garment would confuse her body into thinking it was well again. So, after Leigh's first day home from work, she stood at the kitchen sink and pondered the untouched bowl of tomato soup, the last of a half dozen which had been snubbed. Then she pictured Leigh's blazing resentment if she should interfere in this private matter without being asked. Deciding her offspring's health was more important than a temper, Elizabeth called information, then briskly dialed Padgett Williams's home.

Raymond answered and identified himself.

"Ah . . . yes, Mr. Williams," she said, not really knowing how to begin. "You don't know me. I'm Leigh Vincent's mother."

Silence hovered on the other end of the line.

The sympathy in Raymond's voice when it drifted across the miles of telephone cable was wonderful. "Yes," he said agreeably. "Well, Mrs. Vincent, you don't know me, either. But I think it's time we ended that. How about you?"

For the first time since Gentry Vincent had died, Elizabeth felt the consolation of an ally.

"I completely agree," she said with relief. "Would you like to meet for lunch, Mr. Williams?"

He chuckled. "Anywhere you say."

Leigh's inbred practicality finally defeated her depression. After three days of solitary mourning over the death of something she had cherished for ten years, she forced herself out of bed and showered and shampooed her hair. She changed the bed linens and made the bed. When the room was once again put to rights, she dropped to a chair and stared dejectedly at the stark whiteness of the telephone.

The one thing she refused to admit was that skulking behind her rivalry with Everest Productions had existed the hope that she would one day be married to Padgett Williams. In spite of her certainty now that it would never, never be, she starved for the sound of his voice. She was tempted to indulge in the teenage tactic of dialing to hear him say hello, then hanging up. That would be impossible, though; only through a front-line battalion of underlings could a person reach Padgett when he was working.

She sighed wearily and dialed her office. She told

Becky she would be in to work the next day and to keep putting everyone off a little longer.

Becky hesitated. "What'll I tell them? I've run out of excuses."

"A lie, naturally," Leigh replied. A fragile smile barely teased the edges of her lips, the first in many days. "Tell them I have a wisdom tooth acting up. That's not even a lie. When I get there tomorrow, I'll give you the day off and do everything myself."

Becky snorted. "You couldn't, even if you wanted to. This place is a disaster."

Refusing to be wheedled, Leigh hung up and dressed herself.

Not once had Leigh ever taken the time to analyze why she persisted in bouncing back after every blow life gave her. If she had, perhaps she would have said that she might as well, she got what she deserved. Somewhere in her childhood she had learned that whining never got her the things she wanted. That philosophy had served her well through an unfortunate love affair and the setbacks of a cutthroat business. The more difficult circumstances had grown, the more angry she had become. Giving up was something she never considered.

Now she took her checkbook and drove into Los Angeles and did something completely extravagant. She spent six months' salary on two additions to her wardrobe and one carefully selected piece of jewelry.

Leigh had always possessed a careful sense of style, and she rarely spent money foolishly. Today, after painstaking contemplation, she bought a beige pants and blazer suit by Saint-Laurent with a claret-colored silk blouse which fit as if it were tailored precisely for her. For nearly an hour she debated before choosing a Chanel classic, a two-piece suit in a soft muted tangerine. Both ensembles were perfect for what she wanted, subdued, yet chic and fashionable.

Lunch was marvelous after nearly four days of starvation. After eating a spinach salad so large she amazed her waitress, she spent the remainder of the afternoon in a beauty salon having her hair styled. It took two tiresome hours, but the image which the mirror reflected of gleaming, shoulder-length hair, caught at the crown on both sides to form a softly layered frame, was worth it.

"What do you think?" asked the anxious stylist. She lifted the sides and let them drop with a silky bounce. "It's perfect for those cheekbones, don't you think?"

"I think you're very talented," observed Leigh, negotiating an extra tip in her head. "How long have you been in this business"—she glanced at the name tag—"Claire?"

With a professional flourish Claire removed the protective cape and began putting away her accouterments. She couldn't have been any older than herself, Leigh thought as she noticed the fine lines about the girl's face and the dry roughness of her hands.

"I didn't plan to be a cosmetologist, believe me. But after my husband and I got divorced I had two little girls to raise. I went to school nights." She threw Leigh a knowing look. "It was hard."

Leigh smiled. "Tell me about it." Pausing, she searched for her checkbook. "Couldn't you and your husband work things out? I mean, I've always told myself that there is nothing that can't be worked out somehow."

The hairdresser shrugged, as if it were an old wives' tale she had heard often. "Both people have to want to work it out. He wanted it, but I had had all I could take. I thought I could do *anything* on my own. It got to where we couldn't talk anymore. When you can't talk, where do you go?"

"I don't know, Claire. I wish I did."

The other woman looked up from putting away her blow dryer. "You getting a divorce?"

Leigh shook her head. "Not exactly. But I think it hurts as much."

"Yeah. I guess it could. You know the song, 'Breaking Up Is Hard to Do.' But you'll make it, all right. You're so pretty."

Leigh wanted to clasp one of those rough hands in hers. For one impulsive moment she wanted to hold it and tell Claire that being pretty had nothing to do with anything. But, of course, to do that was unthinkable. She placed the folded tip beneath a bottle of hairspray. "Thank you, Claire."

When Leigh walked into the office the next day, Becky stopped short on her way to the file cabinet, her hands filled. She gave a low whistle. "You should get sick more often."

"Bite your tongue," Leigh retorted and immediately began rifling through the stack of mail and telephone messages. "What's this?"

As she waved a message Becky moved to peer over her shoulder. "Hugh Radnor called. He said something about Mr. Williams making a trust. He wants your signature."

The knowledgeable stare her secretary gave her was not comforting. Becky knew too much about too much.

"Damn!" breathed Leigh.

"Shall I tell him you're unavailable right now and to check back in a week?"

Leigh would have liked to tell Hugh Radnor to go to hell. She tugged on a gold chain and envisioned Padgett telling his attorney everything about their weekend, about the past, and about his daughter. She could see Radnor's smirk, as if he had always known there was something suspicious about "that Vincent woman."

"No," she said with forced energy. "Just wait until the papers arrive. I'll deal with them then. I want you to get four people on the phone and set up individual lunch engagements at Ma Maison's."

On a scrap of paper was judiciously scribbled the names of four clients. The top one was Peter Joshua.

"What're you planning to do," asked Becky as she skeptically inspected the list, "gain weight? You need to, by the way. You've lost at least another five pounds."

Leigh glared at her. "I'm doing what is commonly called taking a new lease on life. I'm going to . . ." She shrugged, momentarily at a loss.

"You're going to put a fancy frosting over a bitter piece of life and pretend you enjoy eating it. Right?"

Leigh pinched the telephone between her ear and her shoulder. "Hang out your shingle, Dr. Freud," she said with a smirk. "And don't look so smug. Padgett Williams won't be the end of me." She thought of Claire at the beauty salon. "I'm not the only one starting over, my dear. Everyone's doing it."

As Becky placed a cup of black coffee on the desk she grew absorbed with the pale oval of Leigh's face. "You told him, didn't you?"

"How'd you guess?"

Becky tilted her head with a comforting familiarity. Leigh was struck by the memories she shared with this woman: good ones, bad ones, and the times when neither wanted to talk but knew that the other would, if the need arose, be a compassionate listener.

Now Becky answered. "By the battle wounds underneath all those expensive clothes, honey."

Settling at her desk, Leigh placed her palms together as if she were praying and balanced her chin upon them. Becky turned her back to pour herself a cup of coffee, which made it easier for Leigh to pour out the truth.

"Ten years is a long time out of a woman's life," she said. "Do you realize that?"

"Yes, I do," the secretary replied.

"If I had known, soon after, that Padgett were dead or even that he had married, I wouldn't have . . ."

Becky faced her. "Kept yourself for him?"

Laughing, Leigh said, "Yes, as weird as that sounds, yes. I have been so certain that I hated him, yet when I looked into his eyes and told him the truth I realized that I've never really hated him. The circumstances of it, perhaps, but not the man."

"And now what, Leigh? After ten years and it's all out, now what?"

Opening her hands, Leigh formed a curved mask of them and hid her face. Her words were muffled. "He wants to be a father to his daughter."

Becky took a long sip of her coffee and then mused, as if to herself, "A father to his daughter. Everything you have ever wanted."

"Everything I've ever wanted," Leigh echoed pensively.

"Well, then, what's keeping you from taking it?"

For a moment Leigh pinched the bridge of her nose. Then she smiled, more at herself than the subject of the conversation. "Now I'm greedy," she admitted. "You know how it goes. Offer a man a hundred dollars for something, and he gets visions of asking for two hundred."

Becky laughed her rich, broad-minded laugh. In spite of the complexity of the situation, Leigh smiled.

"Now you're not satisfied with Padgett Williams, the father." Becky lifted her cup in a salute. "Now you want Padgett Williams, the husband."

Leigh shook her head. "Not only Padgett Williams, the husband. That would not be impossible, all things considered. I want Padgett Williams, the husband who is madly in love with his wife."

"Oh-ho," crowed Becky, arising to resume her work. "You *are* greedy, Leigh."

Rummaging in her desk, Leigh did not reply. Only when the office had resumed its normal buzz of activity did she pause and stare down at her hands. "Ravenously greedy," she murmured and felt as if something monumental had just been decided.

For the next weeks Leigh planned and executed a strategy to promote the LEV Agency from the ranks of comfortable mediocrity up into the vague ionosphere of the big time. Why she launched this campaign was only partially clear. Was she trying to prove that her excellence could make her *equal* with Padgett? Was she trying to earn his professional respect since she couldn't have his love? Or was she simply trying to show him? Perhaps she was filling in a void of her dream. Or she could have been pretending to herself that her heart wasn't breaking with loneliness. She wasn't certain, only that she was driven to be the best she could be.

After two weeks of calling in past favors which were owed her she landed Peter Joshua a spread, with pictures, in *Celebrity Magazine.* At Ma Maison's she and Pete were seen lunching with the co-star of *The Investigator* series.

Since Teresa Jessell's second movie with Robert Atly was a week away from release, Leigh captured her a spot on an afternoon talk show. Neil Cord's cutting of a new album made a featured spot on *Solid Gold* and a taping for England an easy enough matter to arrange.

Leigh kept a just low enough profile to prevent her from being accused of random socializing, but in each case she made certain enough credit went to the star's agent that her presence was felt.

On the week she was to fly to New York to see a literary agent who often showed her manuscripts suitable for movie rights, Hugh Radnor phoned to request that she drop by his office. It was late Thursday afternoon. With his most syrupy diplomacy he hinted at an invitation for dinner.

Automatically Leigh refused him. "We'll see how it goes, Mr. Radnor."

"Call me Hugh," he said sweetly.

By the time Leigh finally stepped into the elevator of the newly erected high rise in the heart of the city, she was in a volatile mood. Parking had been abominably difficult.

With brisk, irritated steps she left the elevator on the twelfth floor and walked into a luxuriously decorated office—an apology for the bad parking, she told herself. A secretary, with customary efficiency and surprising friendliness, ushered her into an empty office of Hugh Radnor and Associates.

Hugh Radnor was thirty-nine years old. Leigh doubted that everyone disliked him as much as she did; she was biased because of his connections with her old aversary, Everest Productions. She glanced about at the genuine antiques and their artful settings. An original painting was framed impressively on a walnut wall.

To her way of thinking, Hugh's only redeeming quality was his clever grasp of corporate law. He was a walking genius, which was undoubtedly the reason Padgett employed him. She wondered if Hugh had ever had a real love affair in his life. Probably not. She pictured him living with his mother.

He strolled into the office with such studied propriety she wouldn't have been shocked to see him click his heels and offer to kiss her hand. However, he reached out a thoroughly Americanized handshake, which she took.

"You're looking better than I've ever seen you, Miss Vincent."

"I'm looking terrible. It's the new suit."

"Ah, yes, very becoming. Very becoming."

Leigh bristled. "Did Padgett really want some business with me? For your sake, I sincerely hope so. The parking on this block would drive a person to madness."

Hooking a hip on his desk, he picked up a file and spread it open. He bent over it. "I'm sorry about that."

Leigh crossed her legs, then felt so ill at ease she rose to stare at the still-life painting of a violin, an ancient manuscript, and a bowl of fruit. The man did have good taste, she thought.

"Look, Mr. Radnor," she said, turning.

He didn't look up. "Hugh."

Before she could telegraph him a glance which she reserved for men she liked the least, he began rattling a rehearsed speech about trust funds. These forms, he explained, were perfectly routine: Marjorie Vincent was, upon her twenty-first birthday, to receive a semiannual amount of money payable from dividends of Everest stock owned by Padgett. When Hugh lifted his perfectly combed head from the sheaf of papers, his look said, I had no idea you and Padgett Williams were so close.

"I'll need Marjorie's correct birth date and place of birth, Leigh," he said softly.

Leigh numbly watched him remove a pen from the inside pocket of his suit. His eyes, when they lowered, swept over her legs and the open-toed slings she wore. Women's legs were obviously his weakness, and he couldn't have been more obvious if he had made a pass.

When she hesitated, he said, "Maybe you'd like to do this in a more pleasant place. Dinner, perhaps. I know of this delightful little place—"

Without warning he rose and moved across the ten or so feet which separated them. He was so proper in his Oxford clothes that she didn't actually believe he would be stupid enough to touch her. He stood beside her and smoothed her head with the same indulgence with which one pets a favorite puppy. When she tried to pull away, his fingers trailed up the long curve of her neck.

She spun away from him, flushed with high outrage, her breasts heaving indignantly.

Hugh didn't often touch a woman. All of his insecurities seemed to lie in the area of interplay between the sexes. And when Leigh wrenched away from him, it addled him so badly that he reacted with the gut instincts of a hysterical man who is drowning or trapped.

He grabbed her and forcibly crushed her against him so tightly he had to bury his chin into his chest just to talk down at the top of her head.

"Don't fight me," he begged hoarsely. "Please don't fight me."

Leigh could hardly breathe, much less argue with him. He frightened her badly with that brightness lurking in his eyes, that completely serious streak which was neither flirtation nor jest. She bluffed with every shred of resource she could muster.

"Let me go, Mr. Radnor," she demanded with amazing steadiness. "Leave me alone, and we'll forget about this."

He moaned, bending lower to search for her lips. His breath was raspy and harsh with unexpected arousal, and he trembled as if taken with a fever. "You let him; why not me? I would be good to you. I wouldn't treat you as he has. You don't deserve that."

Violence of any sort had never been Leigh's way. When she shoved hard at the attorney's chest, the glancing blow she struck him was quite by accident, the result of stumbling against a grasp she could hardly break. The toe of her shoe caught him a keen, deflecting kick on the sensitive bone of the ankle.

The man gasped with quick, excruciating pain and stepped from her.

"I didn't mean to!" she blurted before she realized the advantage of her position. He glared up at her from an inspection of the poor ankle. The unjust accusation glittering in his eyes stiffened her. "Who do you think you are?" she shouted at him.

"Who do you think *you* are?" he yelled back. "Miss Decorum of the year?"

"What I am and what is between Padgett and me is none of your concern. Padgett would . . . *kill* you if he knew what you'd just done."

Though he was embarrassed at his lapse of control, he arched one brow high in mockery at her impetuous verb.

"Well," he said and removed his handkerchief to mop up the moisture on his forehead, "let's not get melodramatic, dear. I don't think Mr. Williams would add murder to his list of crimes."

Truly angry now, Leigh snapped, "Could you please get him on the phone?"

A look of genuine dread chased across Radnor's face, and Leigh knew immediately how much he feared being caught in a dilemma with Everest Productions. Unprofessionalism, she guessed, was the one thing he would not tolerate in himself, in spite of this momentary weakness.

Hugh bowed his head in defeat and pressed the knuckle of an index finger to his lips. With a more entreating manner he looked at her. "There is another matter," he said coolly.

Her eyes glistened, brilliantly green. *"What* other matter?"

"Mr. Williams, uh . . . well, you see, he has set up a special allowance to be paid to you personally on a monthly basis. The principal of this fund is invested, and you will be drawing the interest, which is a formidable figure, Miss Vincent."

He ignored her choked protest. "The agreement stipulates," he went on, "that the principal of the allowance is retroactive for the past ten years." Without lifting his head he shot her a your-secret-is-out look.

*"What?"* She practically screamed the word.

The sting left her abruptly. With her jaw slackened she lowered onto a chair and struggled to figure what this all meant, where it would end. Obviously Padgett was doing the only thing his honor would let him do: he was making up for the years she had raised their daughter alone. But she didn't want money; she had never wanted money!

The depth of Padgett's concern amazed her. No, she corrected herself. Her memory flashed back to that evening in the truck stop when she had listened to his indescribable compassion for his men. She wasn't amazed at all. A gesture of this magnitude from the man she had come to love was perfectly predictable.

She studied the deflated counselor as he sat on the edge of his desk and worried with a misshapen paper clip. His mouth twisted, as if he marveled at her unconcern for such a large sum of money. "If you never work another day in your life, Miss Vincent, you will be an enormously wealthy woman."

Leigh gestured limply at the polished telephone beside his hand. "Will you, or shall I?"

It took precisely fifteen minutes for Hugh to locate Padgett. After he had explained to the producer that Leigh was waiting to speak with him, he handed her the phone and discreetly made his way from the room.

For several seconds Leigh could hardly lift the receiver to her ear. When her voice came it was hoarsely dry and brittle, a thin, desperate sound.

"If you think," she began without saying hello, "that I will accept a single penny of this, you're . . . mad."

The tense silence made her wonder if Padgett were even on the other end of the line.

His voice was deep and resolute. "Did I ask you?"

She started. "Padgett—"

"She's my daughter. Both of you are, and have been for years, my responsibility."

"Oh, don't be so correct, Padgett. I'm not going to fault you on a technicality. I don't want grudge money, or charity, or anything else that you want to call it."

"It isn't any of those, and it's done."

"It isn't done!" she cried. "I won't accept it."

His inflexibility was a king's decree, stamped with a signet into never-to-be-revoked law. "The money will remain where it is. You might as well use it."

"So you can appease your conscience?" she countered unfairly.

His oath echoed distinctly and meaningfully in her ear. Getting up from the chair, Leigh paced the length of the telephone cord. She absently turned and thought she must be in a dream, hopelessly fighting the distortion of images.

"I do it to atone for my sin of ignorance," he said dryly.

None of this was working out the way she wanted it to. He should have been saying how much he desired her, how he wanted to pick up where they had begun on the beach an infinity ago. But that was ridiculous! One could never pick up things or go back. One had to go forward; it was a fact of life.

"It wasn't your fault," she said brokenly, wishing now that she could hold his face between her palms. "A man can't help what he doesn't know. You have nothing to regret, Padgett. I promise you."

When he didn't speak, she guessed she had said the wrong thing. He caught a short breath, as if he had started to tell her something and changed his mind.

"I have much to regret," he said finally.

With her eyes closed she visualized what he looked like at this moment. She remembered his gentleness in the meadow, the protective tenderness of his hands, the softness of his words.

"Why do you say that?" she asked him, hardly

aware of what she said; she was in his arms once again, melting into him, loving him.

He answered simply. "Because I care too much."

The gentle click on the other end of the wire was as final as a sword piercing sharply through her heart. When she moved again, she realized, half paralyzed, that she had no idea of how long she had been sitting there. Padgett's words revolved about her head like the blurring cacophony of a merry-go-round. He cared. He didn't love her, he only *cared!* She was a confused little girl again; everything seemed too big for her. She hugged herself dejectedly.

By some means which she didn't understand, Padgett had brought her to a place where life divided into two distinct paths. Somehow, he was forcing her to make a decision she didn't want to make yet. Could they balance the equation: her everything equaling his *caring?* Many people built a relationship on that inequality and made it work, but could she and Padgett? She honestly didn't know. Far back in her dreams she had never pictured herself settling for so little.

Laughter rippled from the kitchen of the old Vincent house like waves at the caprice of a fanciful wind. Outside, about to enter, Leigh smiled and leaned against the door, thankful to be home again.

The cheerfulness was as it used to be, and she was happy that Margie and Elizabeth, at least, were carefree. The one thing she absolutely must not do was burden them with the weight of her problems.

It was the delicious yipping of a puppy that sobered Leigh, that froze her in her tracks. Astonishment passed over her face, then sternness, as she jerked open the door and strode rapidly into the house. There, on all fours, her impish face buried into the most adorable ball of fluff Leigh had ever seen, was Margie.

Hearing the swift determination of Leigh's steps, Elizabeth's head twisted toward her. The expression on the older woman's face said that she knew all the questions and had all the answers in one solemn pronouncement: Padgett Williams. She shrugged, amused at her daughter's predicament.

Bracing her fists on both hips, Leigh surveyed the rollicking scene on the floor. Margie scrambled up, eyes sparkling, and threw her arms about her mother's waist.

"Isn't he neat, Mom?" she bubbled. "He's exactly what I've wanted forever and forever. How did he know?"

"How did *who* know?" Leigh asked unnecessarily as the sinking feeling plummeted clear to her toes.

"Mr. Williams," assured the girl. She stooped and planted the wriggling, licking bundle of fuzzy exuberance into Leigh's arms.

Leigh refused to look at the squirming charmer.

"Here," she protested. "I don't want this thing. You can't possibly keep this puppy." When Margie twisted her mouth into a disappointed pucker, Leigh wailed, "How could Padgett do this to me?"

Giving her head a vigorous toss, Margie made certain that Leigh didn't miss the point this time. She drew her mother's hand near enough to receive a thorough washing by the eager pink tongue.

"He's got the prettiest face, Mom." She began pointing out the puppy's virtues. "Look, you can see how smart he is. I'll bet I can teach him to shake hands and speak and sit down. He knows everything I tell him. He won't be any trouble at all. I've already fixed him a place in the garage and everything. He won't cost much to feed, 'cause I'll do without my supper every day so we can afford his food. I'll keep him out of your way. And I'll teach him to keep the rabbits from chewing up the nasturtiums and—"

"*Stop!*" Holding up one hand like a distraught traffic policeman, trying to dodge the avid adoration of the animal she held, Leigh leaned her head back and frowned down into his eyes. She was positive the collie pup fully understood the delicate balance of his destiny. Tipping his head to one side, he adorably melted her resistance with two blinks of velvety brown eyes.

Elizabeth laughed, then caught sight of Leigh's glare and hurriedly busied herself with setting the table.

Margie wielded the final blow. "I've picked out a name for him," she announced with perfect innocence.

Leigh groaned. "And what is that, pray tell?"

The girl smiled angelically. "Gunther. Doesn't he look like a Gunther to you, Mom?"

Elizabeth's silent appraisal, which Leigh morosely felt she could have done without at that moment, said, He's breaking you down, daughter. You can't win against the man. He's too strong for you.

Having visions of strange and varied retributions upon Padgett for this underhanded trick, Leigh shook her head. "Gunther?" She deposited the puppy into Margie's eager arms. "Absolutely not. Not Gunther, no."

She didn't think anyone even heard her.

It wasn't until well after midnight, when the large old house rested in slumber, that Leigh made her way down the creaking stairs. She wore a long white straight-cut gown that made her look like a restless ghost on the prowl. Outside, the moon was bright, almost like daylight, and she furtively walked toward the garage.

From the empty section where Gentry Vincent had kept his tools came a lonely whine from a strategically placed box. Leigh peered down inside at a pile of clean shredded newspaper and an old blanket which formed a cozy bed for the canine waif. A jar of warm water was wrapped in a towel, supposedly to deceive him into thinking he wasn't alone. Margie had performed her mothering exactly as she had promised she would.

Kneeling, Leigh scratched the furry ears, one of which didn't tip as much as the other.

"Well, Gunther," she whispered, "I'll make an educated guess and say that you're one of Bonnie's grandsons."

Gunther agreed completely. Placing his two front paws on the rim of the box, he sniffed her hands and arms. Leigh, caught up in the memory of that night at Padgett's ranch, remained still for so long that Gunther finally grew bored. He dropped back into his box, rotated in a circle until he found the exact spot he wanted, then curled up into a warm ball and promptly went to sleep.

I've underestimated you, Padgett, Leigh thought. After all that talk about money, you finally get to me in a way I can't deny. How do you manage to turn me to jelly so easily?"

Leigh's outlook mellowed during the next weeks. Gradually her purpose clarified in her mind, primarily because Padgett made no attempt to see her or talk to her.

After a great deal of contemplation, Leigh knew .

she could never reconcile herself to some one-way relationship with Padgett. Besides, living without him, loving what she had of him, was an old habit by now. She was a woman capable of great love, and she couldn't expend it in polite exchanges, which was what she and Padgett would end up doing eventually. No, if she married him—and he would if she demanded it—he had to return as much love as she gave. She would hold out, she decided; she would go for broke.

The tranquility of routine came to an abrupt halt, however, when she recognized Raymond Williams's pickup in the driveway one summer Tuesday midafternoon.

Wasn't anything predictable anymore? she asked herself as she and Margie climbed out of the car and hurried into the house. Nothing ever came at a convenient time. She carried in her daughter's wet bathing suit and towel, goggles, fins, suntan lotion, and a cassette tape. In one hour she was due back at the office.

"Mother?" Leigh worriedly called as she walked through the strangely quiet house.

"We're in here, darling," answered the familiar voice.

"Who's we?" asked Margie, not waiting for an answer as she darted around her mother, grabbed a couple of cookies, and dashed outside to hunt for Gunther, who usually spent his afternoons chasing rabbits down by the lake.

Pausing, reflecting that coming home and opening doors was growing into a dangerous business these days, Leigh entered the living room. Padgett's father rose and stepped toward her, his hand fondly extended.

Ignoring the hand, Leigh hugged him warmly and

glanced beyond him. Spread upon the sofa was a collage of scrapbooks and photograph albums. Immediately she knew they had been looking at Margie's baby pictures.

Her face darkened with concern. "Well," she said tightly, "I wasn't aware that you two were friends."

"Oh, Leigh," Elizabeth chided before her daughter could say more, "this is entirely my doing. Raymond and I have been getting acquainted for weeks. I hope you're not upset that I didn't tell you."

Slumping down to a chair, Leigh studied Raymond's neatly polished boots. "That's sort of a pattern these days," she said. "I'm always the last to know." Straightening, as if she were ready to deal with anything, she said, "Well, Ray, how is Padgett these days? Flourishing, I guess."

Raymond chided her sarcasm with a jutting of his chin. He gathered up the albums and placed them neatly on a table.

"Padgett keeps pretty much to himself these days. Usually he's barricaded in his office and only comes out to eat or go to the bathroom. I hear him in there, late at night, studying film or pounding on a typewriter. None of the men will dare come around him anymore. I don't do it myself if I can find a way out of it."

Only too well Leigh remembered her own days of despair. "I shouldn't have asked," she apologized. "But you're looking well."

The older man's steady logic kept her on balance. He gestured toward the albums, and his eyes filled with such touching hunger that Leigh leaned far back in her chair. She felt powerless to cope with such an honest need.

"Can you imagine what it's done for me," he

asked, "seeing these photographs? Margie is Judith, all over again. You must have sensed that when you saw Judith's portrait that morning."

She nodded. "You're right. It's . . . unreal."

"Oh, I won't press you to let me get to know Marjorie, I promise. I know you've gone through a major upheaval during the last weeks. Only, I wish you would let me do things, little things. A birthday gift, a—"

"A puppy?" interrupted Leigh, a wry twist to her mouth.

Raymond chuckled. "I told Padgett you'd be livid about that. I warned you, didn't I, how aggressive he can be when he wants something?"

Not wishing to discuss Padgett's desire for his daughter—a fact about which there had never been any question—Leigh glanced down at her wrist-watch. "Look, I have an appointment that I can't miss. I really am forced to trust the discretion of you both." Her face grew bleak with entreaty. "Please," she begged, "be careful with Margie. She's just a little girl, and this Pandora's box I've opened is catching up with me. I don't know where it's going to end. I find myself fighting everything, sunup to sundown."

In a movement which completely disarmed her, Raymond stepped forward to fold Leigh into his arms. "Oh, sweet girl, give an old man credit for a few things. I wouldn't hurt that child if it cost me my life's breath. And neither would her grandmother. All I want of you is permission to just see her once in a while. I promise I won't become a meddlesome old grandpa."

Leaning against him, torn in the conflict of a need to trust and anger at Padgett for taking control of her life, Leigh rested for a moment. The two people she knew she could depend upon were Raymond and Elizabeth.

Ray's chin touched the crown of her head. "I know what I do," he said in quiet reflection. "I worry Paddy. Up until now I haven't cared to truly face it."

Pulling back in his arms, Leigh searched his face. It was drawn with lines of unselfish concern. "Face what?"

"That Judith's gone. I know she is. I just haven't completely arranged my life around it. But seeing this daughter of yours, knowing that part of Judith still goes on living, well . . ."

Leigh held him tightly. "I know. You don't have to explain it. For many years I have been loving Padgett through her, and I didn't even know it. That's selfish, isn't it?"

He shook his head. "Not selfish. Human, maybe. But loving someone through another person is part of what keeps two people bound together. When the stormy times come, that common denominator is a lifeline. Talk to your mother if you don't believe me."

Leigh inched up her fingertips to blot at the secret moistness which dampened her cheeks. "I really do have to go," she whispered, straightening, feeling as if her life were becoming a snowball which was growing out of control. "I do trust both of you. Honestly. Mother?"

Elizabeth smiled. "Everything will be all right, darling. Rest your mind."

The green in Leigh's eyes smoldered as she disagreed, but she said no more. They might think everything was all right, but the knotted panic in her throat warned her it wasn't.

She slammed the door to the Buick with a viciousness which was part confusion and part helplessness. She couldn't go on living like this, sitting on a time bomb which could go off anytime. This pattern—a few weeks of peace, a few days of despair—had to be broken somehow.

Her afternoon appointment could wait, even if it cost an account. She had to see Padgett now. Today the woman would confront the man. If she wound up with less than she had, at least it would be different. And at this period of her life, that much was worth something.

## *Chapter Nine*

*P*adgett's relationship to Everest Productions was anything but superficial. Not only did he control a vast amount of stock in the studio, he was on its payroll. To make the working bond even more intimate, he occasionally put up his own money as capital for a particular film.

As a producer Padgett benefited from observing the policies of his more colorful colleagues. He believed in his work and aimed for aesthetic excellence. Yet he never attempted a picture purely on aesthetic values. His gut instinct—often the crucial factor between success and failure—was a knack of consistently achieving the right balance between film quality and box-office triumph.

On the set of *The Last Champion* Padgett discreetly filtered into all aspects of the filming process. Though he maintained a low profile and gave the director his freedom, both the director and the screenwriter consulted him regularly. Any of the crew who had objections to his omnipresence voiced them in private. All of them knew that nothing except excellence would ever reach the theater screen with Padgett William's name in the credits. They had come to expect the best and relished the status it gave them; they tolerated whatever they had to and worked their hearts out.

Leigh was only an agent, but when she had told the man at the gate she was there to see Mr. Williams at the request of his attorney, he had admitted her without a hassle. Now she lurked in the shadows of the set, hating to place herself at an unnecessary disadvantage of dealing with Padgett where he reigned as king. After waiting for him to finish and leave, something she began to despair he would ever do, she finally scribbled a note and asked one of the stagehands to deliver it to him.

From a distance she could see Padgett accept the tiny missive, get sidetracked, and, after another fifteen minutes, read it. He jerked up his head, his brows blunting. His gaze scoured anxiously over the set in search of her.

Across the huge expanse she met his surprised expression at seeing her. She also interpreted the spontaneous guard he threw up. It rankled her. More than that, it slapped her brutally. She wished desperately that she had not come.

Spinning on her heel, she ducked behind cameras and set equipment which sprouted out of the floor like pitched tepees. Cables snaking across her path impeded her. She aroused the curiosity of at least a half dozen crew members with her unexplainable haste. "Hey, lady!" yelled a man loaded down with a roll of carpeting.

She almost accomplished her escape. The double doors at the entrance, painted in that nauseating dark green common to high-school gymnasiums and football stadiums, opened only a mere ten feet away. Skimming over the remaining distance, Leigh yelped as a fierce hand closed over the bones of her shoulder. The possessive grip yanked her to a humiliating standstill.

Neatly sidestepping her, Padgett towered between her and the doors. All around them flicked overalert sidelong glances, and Leigh shivered with hot-and-cold embarrassment. With the automatic reaction of a thief caught in his unlawful act, she smiled brightly and tilted up a face crinkling with sublime innocence.

"I'm sorry," she murmured between curved, laughing lips, wishing vehemently that the others would mind their own business. "I made a mistake. I shouldn't have come. I'll call you later."

"You'll talk to me right now, darling. Keep that sweet face intact and come along."

Inclining his head, he looked her over with an air of familiar interest, nothing more. He gave her slacks, her tailored silk blouse, and the flattering new cut of her hair his leisurely inspection.

"You're wearing your hair down," he lazily approved.

He circled an arm about her waist and drew her beside him to walk. Leigh's nerves coiled as taut as a spring. She attempted—only once—to pull away from the blatantly familiar embrace, but he only strengthened his hold. With each step their thighs brushed together.

She had forgotten how thoroughly his nearness dissolved her anger. "You're causing more attention than the star, Padgett," she remarked shakily.

Padgett caught a quick breath but didn't look at her. He nodded a signal to someone across the set. "Don't fight with me now, Leigh," he warned. "You'll lose. Are you in trouble?"

"How could I be in trouble?"

"Easily."

Her green eyes narrowed. "Except for a little bundle of puppy joy Margie has named Gunther, everything is fine. We . . ." She paused. "We did have an unexpected visit from your father."

Padgett's guise of subtle indifference crumbled. He took her shoulders, firmly, with both hands, and his concern engraved deep lines across his forehead. "Dad?"

"Smile, Padgett," she warned him.

"Be quiet."

His virility was even more impelling because of his unselfish concern. It filled her entire vision. The alluring scent of musk triggered her senses across the inches which separated them. It never failed, did it? That longing to be held?

"Your . . . macho is slipping," she accused brokenly.

Realizing that the director was conducting a conference with the screenwriter, Padgett drew Leigh near a half-constructed prop and partially blocked her from the business of the set with his back. The dappling of the shadows enriched the blackness of her hair, he noticed grimly. It enhanced the lustrous tint of her lips.

Indiscreetly, mercilessly, the stab of desire knifed through his body. The bitter misunderstanding when he had last seen her disappeared like a wind-chased cloud. He experienced difficulty even recalling why they had been so upset with each other.

"Gunther, hm?" he mused, then laughed deep in his chest. "That's an insanely abominable name for a thoroughbred collie."

"Your father wanted to see Margie." She ignored his roving eyes.

"Did Dad upset her?"

"Of course he didn't. But you promised me—"

"I know what I promised. What's the problem?"

Her head was beginning to throb. "You don't *understand*, Padgett!"

Leigh found it impossible to ignore Padgett's legs as he braced one foot on a crate of electrical apparatus. Settling his weight, he pulled her forward into the small space created between his knee and the wall.

Actually, Leigh meant to prevent Padgett from growing so intimate, but when she dropped one hand to shove against the imprisoning barrier of his thigh, he trapped her hand with his. To her regret, trying to recover her hand only increased his amused determination to keep it.

A blistering flush swept up her neck and burst into flame upon her cheeks.

"You're the problem, I think!" she choked.

"Me?" he teased. "I didn't give our daughter such ghastly taste in selecting a name for a pet."

"Let me go. People are beginning to stare."

"They can't see what's going on over here. Relax."

"What they're imagining is even worse, you idiot!"

Padgett's mouth curved in the white flash of an enormously pleased smile. "And she inherited her mother's sweet temper." He chuckled. "My daughter's mother—a lady who coddles temperamental horses and takes in orphan pups. A quality every man looks for in a woman."

It was unfair that he should be so big and so sexy, that even his shift of weight could arouse her. When he drew a fingertip along the line of her jaw, her mouth quivered.

She twisted her face away, trying to see past him, fearing everyone would see him undo her. Padgett traced a swift path to the corner of her mouth. She had never been subjected to male liberties in public before, none except clumsy passes which repulsed her to the point of rude brush-offs. Leigh was caught off guard. She must do something! she thought wildly as he caressed the swell of her mouth.

Leisurely, as some men would undress a lover, Padgett slipped the tip of his finger between her lips and touched the edge of a tooth. Their looks captured each other. She stupidly envisioned herself striking out at him, but she weakly groped to stand. Her lips parted with a wisp of unexpected yearning.

The seduction—and that was all she could call it—spun a cocoon about them. Daringly, his eyes burning, he drew a slow line across the edge of her lower teeth.

"Oh, damn," he whispered.

The vulnerability of his response inflamed her far past the point of discretion. Touching her tongue to his finger, she tasted him, she nibbled and closed her lips over him. Kissing him would have been much less devastating.

"Oh, damn," he groaned again and slumped heavily against the wall at his side.

Leigh's eyes glazed over, drugged with arousal.

The ability to remain standing fled. Stumbling slightly, she reached for him, the silent shape of his name moving her lips.

"I think the main attraction in this studio isn't being filmed," drawled the husky insolence of a female voice from somewhere behind Padgett's head.

Like a pair of child culprits caught stealing sugar, they both started.

Padgett's nerves fared better than Leigh's own. He casually straightened himself and turned toward the smile of Cynthia Trivitt, a familiar face in film circles.

With a television viewing audience which rivaled Rona Barrett's, everyone, especially producers, exercised caution regarding Cynthia. Most of her so-called Hollywood sensations began as innocent trivia. Since she was like a virus with no known cure, most people exposed themselves to her as little as possible.

"Don't you and I have something to talk about, Padgett, darling?" cooed Cynthia as she raked a glance over Leigh's willowy height.

Except where Padgett was concerned, Leigh was tough. Now, to all outward appearances, she collected herself with the confident grace of royalty. She threw the woman a cool emerald stare.

"If Padgett doesn't," she said, "perhaps I could scrape up something to discuss. I can always do with a little publicity. The more scandalous the better."

She smiled prettily at Padgett, who, with amused prudence, stepped back to watch. With a sparkle, she added, "A certain amount of scandal lends the necessary mystique to an agent, don't you think so, Padgett, *darling?*"

"My opinion isn't worth anything," Padgett countered, trying not to smile.

"That's unfortunate," sympathized Leigh. She stepped beside Cynthia Trivitt, who was puzzling whether Leigh were putting her on or not. "If it's a stage romance you're looking for, Miss Trivitt, let me give you a lead that'll blow your mind. Peter Joshua is infatuated with his leading lady, three weeks after arriving on location."

Cynthia shot Leigh a gimlet glance. *"Real-ly?"*

"Would I lie about a rumor?"

Though the reporter's own notoriety was a feature story in itself, Cynthia hesitated to push the agent too far. Leigh was beautiful and obviously involved with Padgett Williams in some way. Control by intimidation might work well with some people, but even a writer of a scandal sheet had the sixth sense to know when not to touch. Leigh Vincent was a hands-off woman.

The woman flitted diamond-studded fingers about her face, as if the conversation were simply delightful. "Oh, sweetie," she gushed, "I'm not in the business of dishing out free publicity to aspiring television actors. Or agents."

"Oh?" asked Leigh. "Just what business are you in, then, Cynthia?"

Even Padgett figured that Leigh's temper might set off a chain reaction she would regret. Playing the smooth diplomat, he flourished a bow and looped one arm through Cynthia's, the other through Leigh's. He muttered something about having some margaritas on ice in his office and if Cynthia really needed material he'd be happy to give her a behind-the-scenes account of the shooting of *The Last Champion*.

"I have some film clips we made in Brazil," he offered with calculated generosity. "We were intending to use them for our own publicity, but we're not selfish." His grin was as dazzling as the silver hair curling about his collar. "We'll share resources, Cynthia. Would you like to see them?"

Cynthia made no secret of it; she was of the opinion that watching a producer's publicity clips was as disgusting as viewing home movies of someone's grandchildren.

"I'll have to pass on this one, doll baby," she purred. "I really would *love* to, you *know* I would, but I'm supposed to be over at Columbia in half an hour. Would you *be-lieve* the schedule I try to keep?"

"I find it hard to believe myself." Leigh smiled.

Cynthia didn't take the time to throw Leigh a glare. She shook Padgett's hand with the utmost politeness and kissed the director, also the associate producer who was dictating some changes in the script and didn't see her coming, plus one of the electricians who stood gaping after her with fifty feet of wire looped over his shoulder.

Padgett plunged both hands in his pockets and absently followed several steps after the female reporter as she blazed a glittering trail to the doors. Distracted by such a show, Leigh ambled beside him.

"Remind me to never take you on," he whispered, leaning over the crown of her head. "Tangling with you is like cuddling a barracuda."

Bridling at his caustic wit, Leigh was struck at how easily it had happened: being thrown into a set of circumstances with Padgett, joining forces with him, agreeing, liking it, hating for it to end. She experienced a certain twinge of failure; in a space of minutes her resentments had all dissolved again.

The ease of slipping back into a friendship with him alarmed her. She didn't want him to think he could lead her anywhere he chose to take her. From years of habit, she squared her shoulders and lifted her chin to a determined angle, an accurate barometer for one who took time to read it.

"Ah." Padgett frowned, easily recognizing the banking storm. "You're back to the old I-refuse-to-admit-I'm-only-human game, eh? Well, all right, my darling." Turning, he began walking away. "I know a scam when I see one," he called without looking back.

He motioned to the assistant producer that he was finished for the day. Feeling like a negligent student being dismissed by a professor, Leigh dully walked in the opposite direction toward the double doors. Then the full impact of Padgett's irony registered on her. Whirling, she glared at the sight of him disappearing around a corner.

"Damn that man!" she swore under her breath.

Not about to allow such an aspersion to her integrity, she bolted after him. Once around the corner, she hurriedly contemplated the problem of four closed, unmarked doors.

She stepped into the path of a harried script girl. "Which one is the producer's office?" she asked, gesturing.

The young woman's arms were filled with sheafs of typed material; she nodded to the first door on Leigh's right, nearest her.

Without knocking, Leigh shoved the door open, entered, and slammed it shatteringly behind her. Padgett buried his head in the papers in front of him.

What a ham he was! she thought; he just adored playing this role.

Not caring how unreasonable she looked, she braced both fists upon her hips, positioned herself, and refused to speak for at least thirty ponderous seconds. She mutely called him several names; he was outlasting her. Finally she blurted: "Just what did you mean by that last remark, Padgett?"

He still refused to glance up and meticulously underlined several words with a ball-point pen. She knew he couldn't be reading. "I think the statement is self-explanatory," he calmly observed.

Leigh leaned across his desk like some heavy-handed television gangster. She slammed both her palms loudly on the top of it.

"You think so, huh?" she snapped.

He shrugged. "Yes."

"Well, for your information, Padgett Williams, my intentions in coming over here were to tell you that I don't mind your Dad's visits to Margie. I think she should get to know her grandfather, but if anyone tells her *anything,* I want it to be me. I don't want any 'accidents' happening."

Padgett finally met her gaze without a glimmer of humor in his cool gray eyes. He said, "If I were in your place, I guess I'd lie, too."

Leigh had had all the taunting she intended to take. He was baiting her now, and she knew it. Still, in the same breath she lashed out at him. Fiercely grabbing the pen from his hands, she bounced it off the wall, which did absolutely no damage whatsoever and made very little impression on the placable producer.

He cast a rather impassive eye toward his pen lying twenty feet away and clucked absurdly sorrowful sounds. "Perhaps I would do that, too," he admitted.

Making an insulting hiss through her teeth, Leigh spun about and stomped toward the door in the face of such mockery. Ordinarily, she would have laughed.

An arm suddenly crossed in front of her and effectively blocked the door. "I dare you to touch that doorknob," he warned.

Her mouth turned downward in an attractive sulk. "There's such a thing as self-confidence, Padgett. But don't you think you're taking it a bit too far?"

Padgett, following his arm with his body, drew up to his intimidating height. She stared hard at a button in the center of his chest and caught her lower lip between her teeth.

"I forgive you for throwing a childish tantrum," he said lightly, "because you do it so adorably."

"Your teasing reminds me of barbed wire," she retorted. "This is ridiculous."

"Of course it is. That's why we both enjoy standing here like duelists. It's the one chance we get to be kids again and bash our heads against the wall."

Her shoulders lowered, and she wanted to smile. "You're right, naturally. And I really do have to go now, Padgett. That's all I came to say—I didn't mind Ray coming. I just want him to be careful."

"Liar," he challenged huskily. "You're still throwing the tantrum."

"I am not," she protested. "Now, get out of the way."

"Is the truth so hard, darling?"

Padgett made a grave error when he placed a knuckle beneath her chin. Leigh promptly knocked it away, and her smile degenerated into something more closely resembling the brewing of a temper.

"What truth?" she demanded shrilly. "I've told you the truth. I'm tired of this hassle. I mean it."

Sighing, he let a grin flicker across his face. "My, my. The pride of a woman. Okay, I'll say it for you, then, my dear. Dad was only a handy excuse. You really wanted to see me, and your stubborn little head refused to admit it."

Angry now because he was more right than wrong, Leigh felt violated and stripped of her innocent feminine devices. Complete honesty was cruelly naked—openness to study, exposure to examination.

"I give up on you!" she cried, exasperated. "Get away from that door."

He laughed. "Make me." Like a prankster, he added the final insult by shaping his mouth into a maddeningly suggestive kiss.

If she had dared, she would have boxed one of his ears. Instead, she closed her fingers into the faded denim of his jacket and attempted to shove him aside. It served only to bring them closer together, which was, buried far back in her mind, what she had been wanting all afternoon.

Padgett gripped her forearm with explosive frustration. She knew in the last reeling seconds that he had no intention of letting her go without having his say. With his free hand he caught her just below the swell of her hips and lifted her completely off the floor. Leigh found herself lodged against an unleashed desire that was as urgent as it had been when he had taken her beneath the moon in the meadow.

"You're the most infuriating woman I ever saw," he said before he groped for her mouth.

The next movements defied rational reaction. They happened too quickly, too primitively. She meant to dodge him as she wrenched her head aside, but she only succeeded in getting herself pinned securely against the wall. The first time Padgett missed her mouth and his kiss landed on the edge of her jaw, then her nose. Determined now, he kept her trapped and forced her head still with his own.

"Stop!" he choked against her cheek.

"*You* stop!"

"It's an ego trip? You're satisfied that you've brought me to this point?"

Not giving her a chance to answer, his mouth ground hard over hers. He thrust his tongue relentlessly between her teeth, and his body melted painfully into hers.

Then it was over, and she was stumbling forward, unable to cope with it. The one thing she was certain of in the seconds which blazed between them was his embarrassment. Padgett's sensitivity—that singular quality which separated him from most men—was his finest asset. She knew she had pushed him further than he meant to go.

For an instant Leigh was outside herself, drawing back to watch the blood pulse in his temple. His irritation, because of that one act ten years before, became part of her own reaction. His new sense of guilt tore at her own breath. That he should be suffering now because of something she was capable of soothing hurt her unbearably.

"I'm taking you home," he muttered and opened the door.

Helpless, she stood in the opening, wringing her fingers. "But I have my car."

"I'll have someone drive it over. Give me the keys."

It didn't occur to her to refuse. She slipped her bag off her shoulder and searched for her keys while he patiently waited. Numb, wondering inanely where they would go from here, she handed over the keys. He didn't look at her when he took them, and she was glad. She followed him back onto the set, waited, then clumped along beside him across the darkening parking lot, wishing he would say something—anything, a silly remark about the heat.

Seized by a sudden irrational exhaustion, swallowing down a knot in her throat which threatened to choke her, she lifted pleading, brimming eyes. He had to open the door for her, because in her bleary regret that everything had gotten out of hand she couldn't press the button on the handle.

Padgett was turning off the ignition in her driveway before he said the first word. For the past three quarters of an hour they had listened to two dozen ballads about unrequited love, about love gone bad, about the hopelessness of a life without love. Most of the time Leigh had kept her eyes safely closed, with her head resting back on the seat. Her only real awareness had been the power of his physical presence maneuvering the car and the full sound of music about her.

The radio clicked off, and she opened her eyes to realize they were home. Except for a faint glow from Elizabeth's room, the house was dark. The clock on the dash read ten o'clock. Elizabeth and Margie must have gone to bed early, she thought. She should have called them.

"I'll marry you," he said tonelessly.

Stunned, she felt her jaw drop, her hands grow cold, a shiver begin at her feet and radiate through her whole body. She couldn't move, but if she could have she would have bent her head to her knees. How many years had she wanted to hear those words?

Padgett gave her a few seconds to realize the echoing implications of what he said. They sat motionless for a tedious lapse of time while she focused on the diamondlike dew which collected on the windshield.

She pressed a button beneath her fingers, and the window whispered open. With an acuteness she rarely paused long enough to indulge in, she listened: distant highway traffic, delirious katydids, the powerful drone of an airplane high enough overhead that she couldn't see its lights blinking.

"You have a way of bringing out my worst suspicions," she said quietly.

"Why are you so afraid to trust me?"

She laughed at the ironic question and wondered if she could give him an honest answer. "Life," she said. "And how things have a way of never working out the way a sane person would expect them to. Sometimes I think I have life all figured out. I give it a reasonable margin for error and don't expect miracles. It always surprises me."

He looked pitifully tired. "That's my fault."

The familiar flick of her own guilt twisted in her stomach. "It's no one person's fault. Margie happened a long time ago, Padgett. We were an unfortunate combination of impetuous youth and a crazy war."

Leigh thought, when he formed his next words, that she had never known a man to be so intensely serious. "If," he began slowly, "if you could undo everything—and I mean me, how it happened, Margie, everything—would you?"

He was so attuned to her response that she knew he sensed everything, even her pulse rate. Letting out her breath carefully, she said, "If I could separate you and Margie from the heartache, I suppose I would undo it."

A deep groove cut between the fine classic line of

his brows, distorting them. "But if you had to take it *all,* one way or another, which way would you go?"

"I've asked that question at least a thousand times," she told him, smiling. "I would do it all over again."

His head leaned to one side, his eyes as sharp as razors. "You're sure?"

"Of course I'm sure."

Padgett dropped his forehead upon the steering wheel the way a woman might do, with his hands loosely circling it. The gesture was so completely exposed that she guessed his hands trembled. She needed badly to touch him.

Impulsively she removed one of his hands and placed it in her lap, smoothing the long hard fingers, the palm which should be smooth but was callused from work he did at the ranch. He didn't lift his head.

"I don't think I can bear living with what I did to you," he confessed thickly.

For a moment Leigh said nothing.

"You don't have to atone for it," she finally assured him. "I can't cope with a proposal of marriage that only tries to set things right, either."

Both their words were earnest. He lifted his head to study her. His features were so strikingly handsome, so disturbed, that she was amazed all over again. She knew he thought she was being stupidly stubborn. Most women would have done almost anything to marry Padgett Williams.

She leaned forward. "Call it pride or whatever you want to. But no matter how I felt about a man, I would never accept him upon those terms. I would deny every physical need, every emotional craving I possessed, before I would do that."

Discomfited by such open honesty, doubting that

anyone knew his heart that completely, Padgett sighed. "Is *that* why you never told me I was a father?"

As if her hair were so many cobwebs cluttering her mind, she threaded her fingers through it and swept it out from her head. She dropped the strands, and the silky locks tumbled back into place.

"Would you believe it was all such a complex tangle of things, I don't even understand all I felt then?"

Padgett made no attempt to analyze her; he stepped from the car and opened her door. Closing her hand in his own larger one, he drew her beside him in a prolonged, inch-by-inch advance toward the silent house.

The massive treetops knitted above them, forming a green-black canopy. The few shimmering shreds of starlight which stole through it weren't enough to see clearly. Leigh wished she could read what he was thinking.

"You will take the money, won't you?" he asked with edginess. "You do understand that I want you to have it?"

Her head dropped forward. "I know you want to help Margie. I'll cooperate with anything you decide to do. But money for me?"

Her feet abruptly ceased moving, and her head lifted proudly. He quietly waited for her answer. "Can't you understand," she told him, "that taking your money would be . . . unequal?"

"My money would be *what?*"

Her voice cut like a whip. "Unequal. *Unequal!*"

"What in hell does equality have to do with anything?" His fingers bit, more painfully than he knew, into the tender flesh of her shoulders.

Wincing, she cried, "Why do you force me to say these things to you?"

"Say 'em!" Padgett ground his teeth. "Say 'em, and get it over with."

Leigh turned away, as if she would not tell him more, then spun back. "You hurt me so badly back then . . . I was blind with hurt. And then I hurt you back. We did terrible things to each other. But at least, the way things stand now, we're even, can't you see? Hurt for hurt. I don't have to feel ashamed every time I look at you."

She watched him squint through the darkness, trying to reconcile his man's logic with her woman's pride. "Garbage," he growled.

Twisting herself free, she began walking so quickly she was almost running. Then she did run. Padgett broke into a sprint to catch up with her. Her torrent bubbled over her shoulder as if it had been pent up so long that a bulwark the size of Boulder Dam wouldn't contain the force of it.

"You have money!" she lashed out. "The universal Band-Aid for any kind of wound. I don't even have a good reason for what I did except revenge." As she whirled, her hair swirling in a wild cascade, her shoulder bag struck him squarely in the chest. Instinctively he caught it, seeing only the passionate beauty twisting her face.

"Wait a minute," he said.

"I can't ease your pain, Padgett. I can only say I'm sorry, and that doesn't go very far."

Padgett, since he had never faced the responsibilities of supporting a child as a single parent, now suffered a swift disillusionment. Money had never been a problem for him, and he swiped a frustrated hand across his mouth.

Finally, beginning to see things more from her

point of view, he nodded, his big shoulders drooping. "Okay, okay. See that Margie's taken care of the way I want her to be, and that will settle that. We won't fight over that particular bone anymore. Agreed?"

Glumly she acquiesced with a gesture.

"We've created another human being between us, Leigh," he went on. "That means something to me." He hesitated. "It means everything to me. We can't let it go, walk away. We have to . . . do something."

Scanty fragments of pale moonlight captured her face. Tiny tears glinted in her eyes like scattered jewels. Their sparkling path over the curve of her cheek was incongruous with the corners of her mouth which tipped bravely upward.

She shook her head. "I won't marry you because of duty, Padgett. I'm old-fashioned in a number of ways. Maybe if we lived in the days of our grandparents you would be forced to marry me, no matter what your feelings were. But marriage is hard, Padgett, even at its best. Doing it because of a child doesn't work as well as it should."

"But our circumstances are special," he countered hotly.

"Everyone says their circumstances are special." Leigh's words grew dull and bleak as she stared out at the land her father had bought before she had ever been born. "Margie has gone through a lot. To take the chance of making her watch us fail would . . . well, it would be inhumane."

"I wouldn't marry you if I intended to divorce you."

She wanted badly, as she turned to look up at him, to hold his face between her hands. She wanted to say, *Why don't you tell me you love me, then?* But she didn't have the courage. All she could do was smile a sad, very old smile. She felt years older than the troubled man who loomed so disturbingly over her.

"Very few couples marry with the intention of divorcing," she said. "Times aren't like they used to be."

Padgett's face grew haggard with lines of frustration. His words were bitter, almost hostile. He rammed his fists deeply into the pockets of his jeans. "You've got things all figured out, haven't you?" He took several steps from her.

The sight of him, as surly as he was, sent admiration pulsing through her. His back was perfect and capable, his waist tapered and as elastic as that of a man half his age. His tight, lean hips and long, agile legs were proof of a man who took himself seriously. But she would love him if he had none of those physical beauties. But she wanted him to make a commitment to her.

"I believe," she said huskily, "that until two people reach the point where they absolutely *cannot* live without each other, they shouldn't marry."

His silent frown was a slow death for her. The angles of his face cut sharply in the darkness. "A very convenient ultimatum," he said stiffly. "Convenient for you," he added and turned his head.

When his hand dropped to swing loosely by his side, Leigh, in mad desperation, captured his wrist. She was shameless, she told herself, for he hadn't committed anything.

As if she had struck him in the back, Padgett froze in his tracks. She had no possible way of knowing that such a small isolated act had inflamed him to the point of a blistering, aching need to love her. She was groping for her own reassurance, and she guessed, mistakenly, that he resented her touching him.

Padgett stood mutely still, not resisting, not speaking. Hesitantly she lifted the hard masculine structure of bone and muscle in both her hands. Underneath his wrist the sinews spread up his arm. A man's arm, she marveled; one of the most powerful things in existence, capable of fighting wars or wreaking incomprehensible destruction, yet capable also of building a city or cradling a baby's head.

She loved him so utterly she wanted to shriek it to the heavens above them. She wanted to cry out to him that all she needed from him was to return that love and promise to try.

But the time wasn't right to say such words, and she couldn't beg him to say he loved her. His love, if it ever did come, must flow from his heart, not from any sense of duty, even if the duty was a good one.

She waited, and found herself praying, Say you love me. Please say you love me.

Padgett said nothing, and in that blinding misery she didn't know if life was worth living without his love.

Lowering her head slowly in a saddened, resigned gesture of defeat, she drew his wrist to her cheek as if she were bestowing a parting kiss on it. Its granite toughness against her soft, moist cheek was such a contrast that the words slipped from her lips before she thought—illogical words to him, a symbolic omen to her.

"So different," she murmured. "So different."

Padgett drew his wrist upward, tipping her head while her eyes fluttered closed. "Different?" he said quizzically, not understanding.

She pressed back the tears which threatened to

spill. She didn't want him to see her cry. "Oil and water," she choked. "They have never mixed. We're both fools."

She couldn't talk any longer. Spinning, hurrying across the long expanse of clipped grass to the front door, she fumbled for her key. In only seconds he caught up with her. But she gave him no time to say good night or to question her about the cryptic verdict of her words.

"It's all right," she said and opened the door only enough to pass the slender frame of her body through its portal. "I'll call you soon."

The door shut with solemn finality.

Brokenhearted, she slumped against the heavy oak barrier erected between them. In the unfriendly interior she moved and pressed her cheek against the long inlays of beveled glass. Listening to the knotted tearing of her own breathing, she barely distinguished the shadow of the tall man she loved so dearly.

Slowly, with something near despair the tall shadow moved. It drifted hesitantly away and gradually grew more indistinct until it blurred into the black jungle of shadows beneath the trees.

"Fool!" she cursed herself. The accusation scraped across her mind: a needle scarring an oft-played record. *"Fool, fool, fool!"*

The crash of the door, when it swept back on its hinges, cracked like the unexpected violation of gunfire when the peace treaty has already been signed.

The gaunt shadow halted, dead still and alert.

And she, skimming across the dew-soaked lawn, forgetting every sensible thing she had ever told herself, dashed to throw herself against him.

# *Chapter Ten*

*P*adgett didn't ask her what she wanted when she sped across the lawn to reach him. He didn't need to. He just caught her up in his arms, turning with her, holding her to himself as if he could never, under any circumstances, be persuaded to let her go.

Leigh clung to him tenaciously. Her arms wound tightly about the secure pillar of his neck. Then their garbled words of need and apology and starving hunger jumbled together as they tried to say everything at once.

Somehow their lips came together and for a second they touched, pausing for that glittering, wondering moment when the universe holds its breath. Then their mouths twisted and clung with a fierce craving for reassurance. Trails of moistly passionate kisses wandered everywhere, and breathy fragments of love talk made no sense at all.

Leigh, uncertain for a time whether she was laughing or crying, threaded her fingers through the familiar crispness of his hair and leaned back across the powerful support of his arm, her throat arched, her mouth parted and moaning. His tongue tasted her again, as sweetly satisfying as a baby's gentle croon.

Padgett's hands didn't tease or torment her. They clasped her with a mastery which she never once doubted. For those dizzy, infinite moments they were not two but one, before heaven, before the world, before themselves. She knew, in that timeless space, that even if he never loved her, he would never leave her. Perhaps, she prayed fervently, she could make it be enough.

"I came because I—"

"It doesn't matter," he muttered thickly.

She feared she was weeping as his mouth opened to reach again and find her, as demanding as the fire of her own flesh.

"Marry me," he pleaded against her lips. "Say it. Say yes. Now. Tomorrow."

"It's not that I—" She wanted to explain that she really did want the ceremony; she believed in it with all her heart. It wasn't so simple.

Padgett's insatiable kisses assaulted her, and she could hardly breathe anymore. "You want me. You need me. We're good together."

"But, Padgett—"

"Margie needs us both." His mouth ravaged her throat. His bones ground against her bones. She was unbearably hot!

"Soon," she whispered into his hair. She kissed his ear and felt him shiver. "Soon," she promised.

"You vow it?"

"Yes, yes."

The sound he groaned combined relief and plea-sure and freedom from a heavy burden. Leigh had no idea that her legs were even carrying her toward the secluded discretion of the dark house until they stood on the broad, vine-shrouded stoop. Padgett moved against the soft, willing curves of her body, tenderly pressing her back with his greater weight.

As the swell of her breasts conformed naturally to his chest she knew the truth. She had never been a gambler, but did she honestly have a choice? Were kisses and the heat of passion enough? Had they ever been?

Already her body was betraying her, turning to liquid desire. Padgett's cleverness with buttons as-tonished her. She grabbed at the suddenly open blouse and pushed at his fingers. But they agilely invaded everything she tried to keep from him.

"No, sweetheart, don't do that," he softly coaxed into her ear when she tried to rebutton her blouse. Then, nibbling the tiny tip of her ear, he forced the clip of her bra to surrender.

A violent shudder rippled through Leigh's legs before they traitorously humiliated her by buckling against his. Padgett smiled and moved her against the security of the balustrade.

She breathed his name like some misguided prayer for mercy.

"Everyone's asleep," he pleaded hoarsely into the hollow below her chin, then lower against her throat. "Let me love you. It's all right if I love you."

Leigh's head was tipped backward, and one of his hands filled itself with masses of her hair. "Stop, Padgett. You're making me drunk."

"I can't stop. Not now."

She couldn't fight the treacherous blouse any longer, nor the agility of his fingers and his mouth that closed over her naked breast and drove needles of paralysis through her. She didn't care that she whimpered again and again as he swept her up into his arms and stepped through the open door and carried her up the stairs.

"Is this your room?" he murmured when he reached the top. She lifted her hand limply.

He lowered himself to the edge of her bed easily, like a husband of many years, bracing an arm possessively on each side of her. Leigh's thoughts sharpened into focus. This room—a room she had known all her life—was about to change. Never again would it be the same, for now it was overpowered with the masculinity of Margie's father, the man who wanted to marry her.

"I don't know how you've managed this," she said quietly from the pillow. "There's a little sanity straggling around in my head."

Grinning, he touched the center of her lip and moved toward the open window, where a breeze flung the curtains against his waist. Unbuttoning his shirt without consciously thinking about it, he dropped it to the floor where he stood.

He was unconcerned about everything except his desire for her, and he forced himself to move slowly, to wait, to prolong the sweet torture. As she lay on her side, stretched full length before him, he studied her.

Leigh's gaze flicked over the naked expanse of his chest, the dark smattering of curls as they swept down his chest and tapered across his belly into a thin wisp which disappeared beneath the loose waist of his jeans.

"Nothing will happen that you don't want to, Leigh," he promised her. "I won't ever hurt you again. Tomorrow I will give you a ring, something as special as you are."

Involuntarily Leigh's hands covered her face. "I'm not special," she mumbled, shaking her head.

His knee bent to the bed as he leaned over her, and she, needing him terribly, lifted herself to be folded into his arms.

His lips crushed into the silky swirls of her hair, and his voice was broken and hesitant. "You're special to me."

Wasn't that the same as saying he loved her? she comforted herself. And even if it came a little short of the mark, many women never had that much.

Leigh turned to search for the shell of his ear. She thought, I'll whisper that I love him, and then he'll say it back. But the smell of him was clean and drugging; the hardness of him was quickly compelling, and her fingers fumbled with his pants. Her mind began to splinter in torn directions, and her lips moved wetly across his chest. As the last piece of clothing fluttered to the floor she told herself the lie: her love was enough for both of them.

She decided later that she didn't need to hear the words. He had shown her his love eloquently enough. The warm tides which had broken over her were their own unique type of love's confession. Again and again, he had taken her there and back. It had been enough, she thought drowsily. Enough. Enough.

Yet, when she lay thinking in his arms just before dawn and listened to the peaceful satisfaction of Padgett's slumber, her eyes peered unseeing into the darkness. This wasn't a new love affair. They were both adults, and they had a child. They were planning for the rest of their lives, and Margie's future, too. She couldn't tell herself lies, not about that.

A tiny sense of loss pressed hard against the back of her throat: a grief, a little death inside. Physical love and spiritual love were united—one, yet two, clearly distinct. To have one without the other was not enough; that would be tragic!

As the grayness of dawn crept into the fringes of the room her decision was already made. She had to be sure. She couldn't marry him until she was sure, for Margie's sake, for his sake, and for her own. Nothing would be lost by the wait. Love, like a delicate wine, only grew sweeter with the keeping. And in the waiting he would come to truly love her. He had to.

Blinking herself awake the next morning, Leigh realized two things at once: the brilliant blaze of the sun and the fact that Padgett was gone. Mystified, for she had gone to sleep worrying about the uncertain dilemmas of a tryst, she bolted upright. At once she suffered the throes of a simulated jet lag and the consequences of overindulgence in matters of love. She fervently wished she could snuggle beneath the cover and sleep until noon.

Being the dilettante that she was at deception, however, she quickly grew frantic that she had ruined herself. Her secret was probably no secret at all by now. She took a swift look in the mirror, groaned, and twisted on the water jet in the shower.

"Mother!" squeaked Margie as she dashed up the stairs in shorts and halter and ragged tennis shoes, her braids flying. She practically collided with her rushing, freshly showered mother.

"Shh!" Leigh cautioned.

Leigh wore a pink-and-white-checkered wrap-around dress—feminine and frothy like freshly spun cotton candy. Her toes peeped out from white strap sandals. "I think a truck has just run over me," she halfheartedly joked. "I should be in the hospital this very minute."

Margie giggled. "Guess who stayed overnight in the guest room?" Before Leigh could assemble the shattered fragments of herself, her daughter paused thoughtfully. "Oh," she reconsidered, her lower lip puckered adorably, "I guess you know about that."

Leigh was already prepared for the cataclysmic worst. She said, "Of course I know Mr. Williams spent the night. There're some extremely important things he wants me to help him with today. The drive over from his ranch is a long one, you know."

She was about to congratulate herself on her control, to say nothing of Padgett's ruse of the guest room—so clever of him—when Marjorie corrected her.

"He said I should call him Padgett," Margie informed her, very grown up, very official, not noticing Leigh's sudden surprise.

Margie could not know what that announcement triggered in her, Leigh thought: a whole new chain reaction of delicate responsibilities. She and Padgett must be careful when they told their daughter the truth. In some ways, however, she was beginning to suspect she could trust Padgett more than herself. Padgett's sensitivity was, in some respects, unsurpassed. All of them loved Margie without measure. She knew her daughter would come out intact, better than before. It was her own yearning heart she should worry about. Why didn't Padgett just say the words she needed to hear and put her mind at rest? *Why?*

In the marvelous way of children, Margie saved Leigh with bubbling, girlish chatter as they descended the stairs together.

"Padgett's going to take me to the bookstore at the mall," Margie informed her. "There's a book about training dogs he says I need to have." She paused to reflect. "Mom?"

"Hm?"

"Did you know Gunther has papers that are two hundred years old? Don't you think we should get him some new ones?"

Leigh's laughter rippled like fresh spring water. She stopped to lovingly repair her daughter's braid. "In this case, my precious, I think old is good."

Panic, however, nibbled at Leigh's heels as she and Margie entered the high-ceilinged kitchen. The aromas of freshly brewed coffee and cinnamon toast invited them in, but dread of her mother's disapproval made her cautious. Lifting her head, Elizabeth smiled when she heard their laughter.

Obviously, from the pleased expression written on her mother's face, Leigh's own night with Padgett wasn't written all over her. Leigh felt instant relief. Her glance darted apprehensively toward Padgett as he lazily lounged in his chair, his hands laced innocently behind his head while he watched them. What did he intend to do? Would he give her a cue?

In the unspoken way of lovers and spouses the message passed between them; he moistened his lips a certain way and smiled a certain slow smile. Intuitively Leigh knew he had covered for her with her family. She wouldn't be embarrassed in any way.

After her mind was satisfied that Padgett was behaving nicely, Leigh began fretting whether Elizabeth knew he had wrangled a promise from her to marry him—posthaste, as the saying went. But if Elizabeth knew about a forthcoming wedding, she was discretion itself. She moved graciously about the kitchen. One would have thought by her manner that Padgett always ate his breakfast at this table.

"Coffee, Leigh?" inquired the older woman, lifting the percolator.

"Marvelous." Leigh smiled cheerfully. After sipping, she said with pointed energy, "Well, Padgett, Margie tells me you've already planned an excursion to the mall."

Except for the knowing glint which he quickly masked, the man was so cool that Leigh slightly doubted her own senses. Perhaps she had missed something. Padgett moved skillfully from one subject to the next, anticipating, making everything seem natural and proper, answering questions before they were ever raised. Always he was careful to see that Margie was undisturbed by his presence and was included in everything.

With a confusing twinge of disappointment, not quite sure what she had expected, Leigh carefully took the chair beside her husband-to-be. He didn't have to be *that* perfect, she mused and felt the warm awareness of his lanky height resettle itself beside her. His first indication of his human frailty was when he reached to pour cream into her coffee. The hard swell of his thigh shifted meaningfully against hers beneath the table, as if he were telling her, *Trust me. Everything will be all right.* As he readjusted his weight, his hand grazed the gentle swell of her hip.

Leigh's lashes brushed against the flushed curve of her cheek, and her gaze, half hidden by the rim of her cup, flirted outrageously with him.

All through breakfast the strong sense that they were a family prevailed. Margie smiled more often than usual, Leigh noted. There was a certain zest about the girl, a self-assurance she had not exhibited so openly before. With those wide green eyes she followed Padgett's every move, hung on his every word, and her adoration was as honest and untarnished as Padgett's love was for her.

The deep sense of maternal satisfaction Leigh felt humbled her. He loved her. Already Margie was confident of it, though she didn't know it for what it was.

Why, then, didn't Leigh feel more confident of Padgett's love herself? The past. The indelible past. She warned herself to be patient. Above all, she mustn't fall into the vicious trap of being jealous that things were so easy for the father and the daughter and not so instantaneous for the father and the mother. Padgett would love her in time.

Gunther, in his typically eager manner, greeted the three of them as they strolled about the old estate in the cool of the morning. The day was alive with the eagerness of nature: birds busily feeding, honeybees carrying nectar to their hives miles away.

Kneeling, Padgett studied Gunther's ears and tapped his upper lip with a thoughtful finger as Margie waited patiently.

"I'm afraid, kitten," he said gravely upon arising, "that we're going to have to revert to the bubble-gum treatment in this case. A sad state of genetic affairs, I must say."

Her small hands braced on her hips, Margie understood about half of what he was talking about and shook her head at Gunther as woefully as Padgett did. Gunther, happily ignorant of his malady, wagged his tail at both of them.

"It should be droopier, shouldn't it?" Margie accepted without question Padgett's appraisal and heaved a disappointed sigh at poor Gunther.

With mock seriousness, Padgett agreed. "You wouldn't have any chewing gum about the place, would you?"

The smile she shot him was shrewdly triumphant. "I have to sneak it past Mother. She says I'll cost her a fortune in dental bills."

"You rascal!" exclaimed Leigh, tweaking a braid.

"Very clever," congratulated Padgett. "Scoot off and bring us a piece. Well chewed," he called after her as she gaily scampered toward the kitchen door.

Laughing, Leigh looped her arm through Padgett's. "Very clever yourself, you devil," she said softly.

Before she realized what Padgett was about—his decorum at the breakfast table had begun to border on the ridiculous—he grabbed her hand and whisked her around the corner of the garage. Beyond them stretched nothing but trees and grass and fencing.

"I love her to death, but I thought she'd never go," he mumbled and lustily swept Leigh into his arms.

He placed a series of breathy kisses all over her mouth, her nose, her eyelids, her ears, her hair. All the while his fingers grappled with the intricacies of her wraparound dress. Stepping back, glaring at the series of offending ties, he swore a hearty and pertinent oath.

"Did you have to wear such a complicated affair?" he growled.

"It keeps me in it as well as you out of it, my darling," she answered, trying to pretend she was unruffled.

His handsome mouth turned downward at the

corners. "Which is precisely my point," he argued and ravaged her mouth again. Some moments later he lifted his head, and Leigh leaned weakly back against his arm, attempting to keep her balance by hooking a finger into a belt loop of his jeans.

A dark, urgent color swept above the neck of his shirt, and one masculine hand stole inside the low neck of her dress. It stealthily trespassed beneath the fragile lace of underwear she wore.

"Let's go get married," he said, his voice deep and earnest. "We can fly to Vegas and be married before dark."

She grabbed at his fingers, which were nearly destroying her as they teased the tip of her breast. "You know I can't think when you do that."

"Exactly," he whispered as his lips dipped again.

When Padgett finally did release her, he tucked in his chin and stared down at her, considering her silence. "You aren't saying anything," he said and kissed her temple.

She toyed absently with a button on his shirt, and her laugh was breathy. "You haven't really given me time to say anything, Padgett."

"Yes doesn't take very long. It's settled? Today? We'll catch a noon flight, and for your wedding gift I'll teach you how to gamble."

It didn't take long to wage a battle in one's mind. Was the wait for a declaration of love worth it? Yes? No? But the thoughtful man had grown much too sensitive to miss the slight hesitation. He pushed her out at arm's length and studied her. Feeling like a child caught in the wrong, she kept her eyes lowered.

Lamely she said, "Margie will be back any second."

"Don't pretend, Leigh," he said soberly. He tried,

unsuccessfully, to tilt up her face. "What's the matter?"

"Nothing's the matter."

Knowing she wasn't being honest, he released her arms and strode a couple of steps beyond her. Leigh watched his hips flex as he shifted his weight. Shading his eyes against the sun, he gazed far into the distance where the small lake rippled within a circle of oaks and willows. When he turned back to her, his gaze was dull with concern.

"This isn't right," he said. "I don't believe I'm so big a fool that I concocted what happened between us last night—the promises you made, the truth of what you felt inside."

Leigh impulsively reached out her hand to touch him, then drew back. "Please, let's not let Margie find us like this. I said I would marry you, and I will. I want to marry you. Honestly."

Uncertainty defeated her posture, the slant of her head, making her touch her lips briefly with her fingertips. Padgett couldn't be blamed for misreading her, she knew. Before her eyes he assumed some vague, unnamed pain. She watched it tighten his mouth and deepen the fine web of lines about his eyes. Laughing it off would be disastrous. She slumped with relief at the happy noise of Margie and Gunther returning.

They both forced themselves to be enthusiastic as Padgett applied the chewing gum to Gunther's ear, explaining as he did so how to care for it. The charm of the moment waned. Then it disappeared altogether. Over Margie's head Padgett coolly met Leigh's eyes and accused her of leading him on, of making promises she had no intention of keeping.

During the welcome bluster of Padgett's leave-taking from his daughter, Leigh found her mother scrutinizing her sharply. Elizabeth's intuition—habitually sensitive—realized that something had changed.

"Everything going all right?" she inquired casually as she broke open a tray of ice and got out the brewed tea.

Leigh automatically began dropping ice cubes into the glasses. They clinked with ironic cheerfulness against the glass, and she paused with her hand on the rim. "Nothing that can't be fixed with a little time," she answered. "Padgett wants me to marry him. Immediately. He doesn't want to wait another day."

Presently, with deceptive calm, Elizabeth moved nearer. She removed Leigh's hand from the glass and smoothed it in her own, examining the length of her fingers. "For many years I thought I would make these hands into those of a musical artiste. Do you remember winding the clock ahead and trying to trick me into thinking you'd practiced your hour at the piano?"

The memory coaxed a small laugh from Leigh. Her hair shimmered as she shook her head. "It always amazed me how you knew."

The silence carried them back in years, through a tunnel of sweet memories.

"You never were very skilled at deception, my daughter. Then, or now."

Withdrawing her hand from Elizabeth's, Leigh averted her head in embarrassment. Keeping her head erect, she placed the open hand across her eyes. "I'm so stupid," she breathed.

"That's your father's line," Elizabeth said. "I usually agreed with him. Aren't you being too hard on yourself?"

"Padgett and I have been," Leigh replied, after swallowing and adjusting herself to the growing tension in the room, "well, intimate. Oh, don't ask me to spell it all out. It makes me feel ridiculous to even tell you why I'm—"

"Upset?"

"Yes, upset! You get a dream fixed in your mind, you know? Of the man declaring his passion and saying how much he loves you and that he can't *live* without you."

Lifting the glass to her lips, Leigh drank without realizing what she was doing.

"And Padgett hasn't done any of those things." Her mother's words were not a question but a statement of fact.

Leigh breathed a long, disillusioned sigh.

"I'm being unfair. Padgett has shown me in a dozen different ways that he can be a wonderful husband. Would you marry a man who didn't say those 'three little words'?"

Elizabeth shrugged and smoothed her demurely parted hair. "You can't ask me that question. Our circumstances were too different."

"You think I should do it, don't you? Just do it and hope that Padgett's affections will evolve into that mystical thing that makes the good marriage different from the ones that end up in the divorce courts or in separate bedrooms."

"That's a little strong, isn't it?" asked Elizabeth, frowning.

Pinching her nose, Leigh admitted, "Oh, yes, I'm going off the deep end like I always do."

"Have you said those three words to him, Leigh?"

Elizabeth rarely called her by her name; it was always some endearment or a teasing pet name. Leigh knew her mother considered this to be a crisis, though she would never say such a thing. Not urging the conversation forward, she waited patiently and only shook her head as an answer.

At last Elizabeth cleared her throat. "I thought about leaving your father once."

Leigh's green eyes flared. "I never knew that."

The smile teasing the older woman's mouth was wise and knowing. "There are several things about me that I've never told you, my darling. I never told you I once lost a baby."

"Mother!"

"There was no reason to. You were about three years old. Gentry and I were having some marital troubles." At Leigh's dropped jaw Elizabeth lifted her brows. "Yes, despite what you think, we did have our little troubles. Some of them not so little."

Leigh had never considered that her parents' marriage had ever been less than idyllic. "I'm sorry," she said helplessly.

"We were having a five-year crisis or something. I was certain he regretted being tied down to a wife and child. I even believed he was interested in another woman."

Taken completely by surprise at the direction the conversation was going, Leigh asked warily, "Was he?"

Elizabeth shook her head, smiling. "You know, I was never certain. Anyway, when I lost the baby I was devastated. Gentry's comfort was somewhat lacking, I thought, and as the weeks passed things grew very bad between us."

Leigh realized her mother's difficulty in telling this, and when Elizabeth paused she waited patiently.

"We did talk about it. And when he said some

things I didn't like, I lashed back by saying I was glad I had lost the baby. We hurt each other terribly. He threatened to move out of the house. I told him I wished he would."

Leigh watched the woman remember. Elizabeth distractedly ran the tip of her fingers around the rim of her glass.

"What happened?" Leigh asked.

"After that I was sure we could never have a good relationship again. But we had so much invested in it, Leigh. And what else would we have done? I didn't want anyone else. And even if I didn't really want your father at the time, we had nowhere to go. And there was you."

"I always thought you were so close."

Elizabeth nodded. "We were."

"But you said—"

"Some of the best years of our lives came after that, darling. I thought we could never be happy again, much less fall in love with each other. But with care and work those things are possible. We both swallowed a little pride, took a little blame for things we didn't altogether do."

Bracing her elbows on the table, Leigh leaned forward, unable to picture Elizabeth and Gentry Vincent as Elizabeth had described them. "Oh, Mother."

"The reason I'm telling you this, Leigh, is to beg you to not foolishly let something good slip through your fingers when it might turn out to be the most wonderful thing you could have done for yourself."

A pain passed across Leigh's face, drawing it tight. "If he would just say he loved me."

"Sometimes it's easier for a man to show it than say it. And I believe that Padgett does love you. He's a fine man. Give him a little time." Elizabeth, when she drew herself very straight, reminded Leigh of a queen. "In the meantime, you could tell *him*."

"I've done everything, Mother. I've been faithful to him. I've raised our daughter as well as I knew how. I shouldn't have to do everything."

Rising, walking to the sink, Elizabeth ended one of the most difficult conversations they had ever had. "Well, don't wait too long, sweetheart. Someone has to be the first, even in that."

Leigh moved to stare out at the long, tree-lined drive. She wished they would return from the mall. Unconsciously she plucked at her lower lip, pulling it out of shape.

"You would think," she mused softly, as if to herself, "that in a liberated age two people wouldn't get hung up on something as simple as communication."

Behind her, Elizabeth laughed gently. "There is nothing simple about communication."

# Chapter Eleven

*P*adgett was so damnably proud! Leigh cursed that quality in him which she vowed during the coming weeks was nothing but stubborn male vanity.

Then she turned the inner raging upon herself. Everything was her fault; Padgett had asked her to marry him, several times. But no, she had to have it all. She had to cling to a hopeless dream and marry for love, on *both* sides!

Who would have thought that a mere hesitation, no more than a hairsbreadth, would have triggered such a change in a man? Or have erected such a high, unscalable barrier between two people?

Months had passed. The oak trees by the little lake behind the Vincent house had turned brown, and the willows had lost their lacy green frill. The huge lawn surrounding the two-story house was banked deep with drifts of dying leaves now. The acres of grazing land at Padgett's ranch were bitten with frost.

But the grassland wasn't all that had died with the approach of winter; marriage was a subject she and Padgett had never discussed again. The season had changed, Leigh told herself glumly, in more ways than one.

During the passing season Padgett showered Leigh with the usual courtesies. With unerring faithfulness he took her out to dinner twice a week. He was charming, a pleasure to be with. Every day they spoke on the telephone. The weekends belonged to Margie and to them both: fun-filled days of horseback riding, picnicking, Disneyland, swimming. When the weather turned colder there were movies and skating and Leigh's comically disastrous attempt at bowling.

In some ways, it was as if she and Padgett had actually played by all the rules, as if they were an established married couple of ten years who had somehow lapsed into a comfortable, predictable routine where everything was taken for granted.

Leigh's instincts warned her, however, that things were far from routine with Padgett. Below the surface of her world, as the weeks slipped past, some giant fuse burned dangerously low to the point of explosion.

Padgett didn't try to wheedle her into bed again. Still, she was positive he ached to do it. She was aching. At times she caught him watching her with a barely concealed hunger that kept her awake nights.

When he kissed her she longed to let the shrouds of her forced detachment flutter to her feet. She wanted to shake him, to beg him to either do what he longed to do or not do anything. But she was afraid to lose what little she had left of him. Her whole life was bound up in him, and if she lost him now, she didn't know if she could pick up the pieces.

She often stood on the stoop of the big house and said good night to him. Their breaths sent wintry mist curling about their faces, and she remembered another time when he had nearly shattered with pent-up desire for her. His self-discipline tautened his tall man's body, and there was nothing she could do to stop it.

Her smile curved politely upon her lips and she pretended she was satisfied and happy. She told him she would talk to him tomorrow. After he had gone, she would sip a glass of wine and sit staring into the melancholy darkness of her bedroom and hate herself. After weeping a few wasted tears of self-pity, she would lie down upon her empty bed and drift into a troubled sleep.

Toward the close of the year the Neilsen ratings placed *The Investigator* within the top ten of the year's new series. It was a cause for celebration, Peter Joshua said as he phoned Leigh with an invitation for a cast party. The Christmas episode of the season had just been wrapped up, and Peter was thinking ahead to a contract renewal. He wanted, naturally, more money.

"We're in a recession, Peter," Leigh sweetly reminded him. "Don't get greedy."

"Greedy, schmeedy. Everest Productions has made plenty off me this year. They can afford it. Talk to someone." He chuckled with friendly suggestiveness. "Talk to your . . . friend, Mr. Williams."

Scowling prettily, Leigh pinched the telephone between her ear and shoulder and flourished her signature across the correspondence Becky kept slipping in front of her. *Leigh Vincent. Leigh Vincent.*

"All right, Pete. I'll see Padgett in a day or so." *Leigh Vincent.*

"I thought you two were going to get married," came Peter's laughing observation over the wire. "Everyone thought you'd do it this summer. I should be a member of the family by now, Leigh. What's going on?"

"Stay out of my love life, Pete," Leigh warned with a sniff. *Leigh Williams,* she wrote on the bottom of a letter to the Internal Revenue. Amazed, she stopped in midsentence to stare at what she had done. Becky bent over her shoulder. Neither woman said a word. The mistake flashed like some garish neon sign.

Straightening, Becky whisked the ruined letter away. "I'll type it over," she said to ease the sudden nervous edge in the room.

Leigh drooped tiredly and jammed her pen into its brass holder. Nearly every day for the past two months Becky had waged a discreetly silent war with her. With looks and gestures the secretary told her employer that she should swallow her foolish pride and go after Padgett. Telephone calls were impossible to not overhear in an open office, and careless remarks were too easy to catch. It would have taken a deaf and blind person to not guess that things were nearly to the flash point whenever Padgett came to the office.

Sensing an unwelcome confrontation in the making, Leigh frowned. "Look, Peter, I'll come to the party. Talk to you later."

"What're you wearing?" he asked.

"Don't get me flowers." Leigh shook her head, not wishing to think about parties or clothes just now. What did she have to party about? She was being tactless, and she gentled her tone. "I don't know yet. I'll do some shopping. And, Peter?"

"What?"

"Get a haircut."

He laughed. "Would I forget?"

"Yes."

Leigh smirked at his happy-go-lucky attitude and dropped the receiver back into its cradle. Becky sat hunched over her desk as her typewriter clattered over one hundred words a minute. Out ripped the new letter. The woman rose, slapped it on Leigh's desk like a summons, then folded her arms. "V-i-n-c-e-n-t," she spelled solemnly.

"What's the matter with you?" Leigh demanded as she signed her name correctly this time.

"Nothing."

"Don't give me that."

Becky's habit was to fold letters with no wasted motion. Now she carefully placed them in a row, their edges precisely even. But she was so agitated she became mixed up in her order and inserted half the afternoon's mail in wrong envelopes. Realizing what she had done, she muttered something hotly under her breath and swooped them up in one frightful disorderly mess.

"In all the years I've worked for you, Leigh," she practically shouted, "I've never considered you to be a total imbecile."

This was one time she could do without Becky's principled honesty, Leigh thought. She plopped her chin onto both fists and dourly waited for the lecture she knew was coming. "Until now?"

"Until now."

Leigh groaned. "I'm going to hate myself for this, but *why?*"

"Because Williams should be your name, damn it! Because you're throwing away one of the best chances you'll ever have to be happy. Only a demented person would throw away something she wanted more than anything else in the world. Right?"

Nodding, Leigh agreed. "Right."

It was the end of an infinitely long day. Leigh, figuring that Becky had had her say now and that was the end of it, gathered up some loose contracts to take home. She washed her hands before putting on gloves, hat, and raincoat and searching for her umbrella. The last thing she felt like doing was shopping for an evening gown, but not to go with Peter was, of course, unthinkable.

Pausing on her way out the office door, she turned to tell Becky she didn't mean to worry her. "Becky?"

Swiveling in her chair, Becky covered the mouthpiece of the telephone and looked up, waiting for Leigh to speak. When Leigh didn't but absentmindedly removed one glove and then the other, Becky spoke softly into the mouthpiece. "Just a minute."

Leigh arched perfectly curved brows, puzzled brows. "Go on. I can wait."

"Ah . . ." The secretary hedged, curiously refraining from looking Leigh straight in the eye. "It's just . . . Pete."

"Peter?" Leigh was astonished. The telephone hadn't rung; Becky had to have dialed the actor. What reason could Becky possibly have for telephoning Peter Joshua?

Becky beamed her bright, wonderful, homely smile as if it explained everything. "He wanted to do something for you," she said. "I was just telling him, uh, what perfume you like."

"Really?" Leigh drew out the word as if she thought they were conspirators.

Shifting uncomfortably, Becky finally removed her hand from the receiver again. "Can you hold a little longer, Pete?" Then she leaned back in her chair with a sheepish shrug.

Leigh received the distinct impression that she had walked into a chattering, gossipy room only to have it abruptly fall silent and everyone turn to look at her. The feeling annoyed her so badly that she clamped her jaw hard to keep from saying something she would regret. She even forgot what she had begun to say in the first place.

Realizing Becky wasn't about to disclose her purpose for talking to Peter, Leigh gave the brim of her rain hat a disapproving jerk and flung a suspicious grimace toward the telephone receiver still buried in Becky's palm.

"Well, if it's all *that* important," she said tartly, "I suggest you don't keep the imperial Mr. Joshua waiting on the line."


"I've been to Harrod's beach house once before," Peter told Leigh over the powerful roar of his TransAm as it swept them up the twisting coast road of Big Sur.

In the west, deep wooded knolls of redwoods and sycamores sprouted up to edge one of the most extraordinary coastlines in existence. Even the majesty of the Shostakovich symphony which poured from the car stereo was dwarfed by the primitive grandeur visible through the shadows of dusk.

"Back a couple of years ago," Peter continued over the music, "before I made it big." He flashed her a gorgeous, toothy smile. "It's one of those stark, modern affairs, a Bertram Helman home, you know?"

"Where the house is part of nature?"

"Yeah. Half the second floor juts out over the rocks." He gestured with a slicing motion. "A thousand feet below, the breakers roll in like you wouldn't believe."

Ben Harrod, the director of *The Investigator*, was throwing a lavishly expensive party, Leigh mused. His liquor bill alone would probably feed Elizabeth, Margie, and herself for a month. She snuggled down into her ankle-length cape of soft velour and crossed her legs, grateful for the warm stream of air bathing her feet.

"Still cold?" asked the fair-haired actor, slowing the big car down to a more reasonable speed as patches of fog drifted in over the highway.

"I'm fine." She smiled at him. "You're really doing a good job with the series, Peter. Padgett told me he was quite pleased. You've been easy to work with and have done your homework thoroughly. I'm proud of you."

Peter wasn't often serious, but at this moment his mood sobered. He didn't reply as he turned off into a rock-lined gravel drive which wound through wild grasses to a weathered redwood house far off the highway. Gently he nosed the car along a strip of drive which was filling on both sides with custom vans and long sedans.

"Looks like everyone is about here," he said.

"Except the star."

Between selecting a spot to park and bringing the tires to rest with crunchy spurts of gravel, he threw Leigh short appreciative glances. Close behind, the daggers of headlight beams stabbed into the darkening interior. Ducking his head, Peter peered out the rear window, then double-checked his side mirror.

Laughing guests spilled out of automobiles and called greetings to one another, hurrying toward the front door some hundred feet away. The house sat between two great gnarled cypress trees and was ablaze with Christmas lights. On this wintry evening, with the ocean wind whining bitterly at the edge of the car windows, the colored holiday decorations blinked a gracious welcome.

For a moment Pete left the engine idling. Leigh studied his familiar profile—familiar to almost everyone in the country now—as he reached across her with one of those muscled arms that teenage girls swooned over. A gold chain shifted about his neck, and he snapped open the glove compartment with long, tanned fingers.

"Hell, Leigh," he said as shadows of people continued to move past them and their conversations were swallowed up by the wind. "I'm no Dustin Hoffman or anything. I know what you've done for me. Frankly, you and Padgett Williams being what you are has helped more than anything. I have a feeling the reason the scripts were so decent is because the Old Man took a personal interest in the series. Some producers as big as him would say 'Hey, it's only television.' "

At the mention of Padgett's name Leigh's eyes deepened to a thoughtful, misty green. In her lap her hands curled inside each other, and she threaded them tightly in frustration. Then she flicked at some imaginary piece of lint but said nothing.

"Here," he said huskily, almost bashfully, and popped open a small box.

Leigh caught her breath in surprise. A gleaming

gold bracelet blinked at her from the light of the dashboard—not too expensive a gift for one's agent, and not too cheap, either. Stunning.

"Oh, Peter," she breathed and suddenly wanted to cry. It had been a long time since someone had given her a gift of simple gratitude.

"Here, put it on," he urged. "Will it go with what you're wearing?"

"Of course, silly. This would go with anything, anywhere. It's really lovely, Peter."

Chuckling, the actor pitched his voice into a high falsetto and teased her by saying, "Oh, my dear, dear boy, you really shouldn't have. It's too, too much."

"You ham! Someday you're going to walk off with a Grammy, I swear."

"I don't need a Grammy. Just get me more money, sugar. A new car is what I need."

As he joked Peter lifted her hand from her lap and clasped the piece of jewelry about the slender column of her wrist. Holding her arm extended, delighted, she watched the dash light sparkle off it. She giggled.

As the heater poured seductively into the car a fine haze painted the windows. They were enclosed in a fine sheen of mist, and in that one special moment Peter Joshua bent his dazzling blond head to Leigh's. Gently, for the first time, he touched her lips with his own. She didn't pull away; it was a kiss of friendship, not of passion. His mouth was firm and warmly affectionate. She cupped his jaw with one palm.

The embrace was so casual and unplanned, so free of complications, that Leigh was not involved on any sexual level. That was why she glimpsed the slight movement of the man who was kissing her. Peter's glance darted upward for one preoccupied fragment of time. With a reaction much like that of twisting toward a sudden noise, she, too, caught the dark movement of a tall shadow outside the car window.

There was really no time to think about anything. Peter's arms were suddenly about her with an embrace she couldn't break. Her head was snapping back against his arm. As his lips slanted hard across hers she was paralyzed, and those fingers which had, only seconds before, snapped a simple bracelet about her wrist now buried themselves with ravaging mastery into the mass of her streaming black hair.

Leigh cried in protest and struggled against Peter's amazingly powerful arms. Dazed, quivering all over with confused shock, she wriggled and shoved and wrested. Her knee, kicking him in a terribly exposing manner, only succeeded in placing her more than half beneath the sensual sprawl of his big body.

"Peter!" she strangled as she wrenched her mouth from his long enough to gasp a breath of air.

"Kiss me," he demanded quickly and trapped her head between the pinioning fingers of one hand and her striking arm with the other.

The entire affair was as blistering a display of savage passion as any which had graced a movie screen. Only when the car door jerked viciously open behind her and the howling wind swallowed up Shostakovich and the purr of the engine and the warm comfort of the heater did Leigh even begin to fathom what madness was transpiring.

This was insane! A memory of Becky hunched over the telephone, deep in conspiracy with Peter, flashed vividly into her mind.

"It's cold out tonight," came Padgett's grinding voice from behind her head, dangerously tight with anger.

As if the producer's words were the cutting bite of a whip across his back, Peter jerked upright and released Leigh. She fell away from the actor and crumpled into a mass of disarrayed embarrassment upon her seat.

The ignition died immediately. Shostakovich was rudely silenced.

Leigh didn't even have to look at Peter. She knew exactly what had happened. This was a premeditated advance, deliberately planned to do exactly what it had done: drive a thorn deep into Padgett's sensitive jealousy. This was a plan devised by Becky Fisk and her very own client.

"Are you coming in?" Padgett demanded curtly.

Shifting about in his seat in a flurry which Leigh was positive was pretended, Peter ducked his head in chagrin.

"We were just getting out, sir," Peter explained with more sincerity than Leigh thought he was capable of. He would be wise to take care; Padgett could ruin the actor if he were a vindictive man. Peter had to know that, and she wished she could laughingly explain everything to Padgett and tell Peter she appreciated what he and Becky were trying to do. If Padgett's harsh, chiseled features were a barometer of anything, Leigh guessed explanations wouldn't accomplish much just now.

She found herself stupidly saying, "I didn't really expect you to be here, Padgett."

"So I noticed," he clipped, one side of his mouth curling with an effort to harness his temper.

"There's no need to be rude," she threw at him

and glared as he swung the door wide and gestured for her to get out of the car.

He countered sarcastically. "Forgive me. I didn't know about all the benefits your agency offered. It caught me a little off guard."

"Sir—" began Peter.

Padgett stooped slightly and measured the actor with a narrow-eyed warning. "If you touch her again I'll break you," he said with startling sincerity.

Leigh had to admire Peter's courage in standing up to a man as powerful as Padgett. The younger man moistened his lips, and she knew he trembled, but he held his ground and made no apologies.

Padgett hardly gave Leigh room enough to straighten herself upright as she climbed out of the TransAm. Her eyes darted upward to see the tiny muscle in his temple flexing tightly. He loomed like an outraged prince whose favored province had just risen in rebellion. His leather fleece-lined jacket was buttoned high, and his hair tumbled majestically about his head, making his gray eyes almost colorless in the deepening night.

Her long cape caught in the wind and whipped wildly against him, swirling between his parted legs and about his hips. In the billowing flurry Padgett's hand slipped easily inside its soft folds and settled possessively at the base of her spine.

When Peter's door slammed loudly, Padgett flinched but didn't release his piercing glare at Leigh.

"You're playing with nitro, my darling," he muttered between gritted teeth. With the insight of a lover who truly loves, she knew he was remembering the times she was beneath him and above him and accepting him and learning every part of him. If he had asked for it all again, right then, she didn't think she could have told him no.

"Repair your lipstick before you go in," he said and released her so abruptly that she stumbled.

Throwing out her hand to catch her balance, she stood gaping at the sight of his tall, proud back. Peter, after moving beside her, presently turned with an oddly pleased look on his face.

"I think we got his attention," he said with a short laugh.

She gaped at him in staggering wonder. Her words sounded as if she had been heavily drugged. "I'm going to fire Becky and break your contract," she choked.

"Damned if you will," he said and shook a finger at her nose. "If you had half the foxiness as you have brains, you'd be married now. Damned if you do anything but what I tell you, Mrs. Padgett Williams."

Freezing, the wind catching her hair and tossing it magnificently in all directions, she let him lead her to the door like a child who is lost and has just discovered it.

# Chapter Twelve

*W*ith Peter behaving like some pseudovillain out of a prewar novel and Padgett making noises like an offended Bedouin sheik, Leigh was hardly aware of entering Ben Harrod's Carmel retreat.

A blast of loud music and warm air greeted them as she and Peter stepped into the foyer. A vivacious redhead, extremely pretty and very pregnant, instructed them where to put their wraps and where the bar was located. Leigh followed Stella Harrod out into a sparsely furnished carpeted area of several levels. Except for nooks where luxurious plants defied it and fireplaces where crackling flames discouraged it, every inch was crowded with people—dancing, ordering refills at a lavishly appointed bar, or folded down into huddles to consider more intellectual things.

Like water invariably seeking the lowest level, Leigh's eyes searched for, and found, Padgett's. He would have to wear that black turtleneck sweater which set off his silver hair so splendidly! And she wasn't the only woman who noticed. He stood in a small group of men who wore the look of the upper echelon, one foot propped on a low stool and one forearm braced across his knee. She could spot at least half a dozen women who pretended interest in something else but whose gazes turned with amazing frequency to try to catch his eye.

But his riveting eyes drilled straight into her as she ambled into the room with Peter.

"He could kill me," she murmured from the side of her mouth. Peter was all smiles for his public.

"Don't you dare go over there and make peace," the actor warned her. "Let him stew. It's good for him."

She didn't believe a word of it, but she remained beside him as several co-stars called toasts and slightly obscene greetings across the room. He signaled back and leaned to whisper in her ear.

"Leigh girl, I probably blew a contract renewal for this. If you let me down I'll break your face."

Padgett was still staring, and he caught the edge of his upper lip in an insolent refusal to yield one inch.

Since the party consisted of dance, talk, and flirtation, when a perfectly strange man walked up and asked her to dance without even introducing himself, Leigh was obliged to choose dance. Dancing to Mitch West, fortunately, didn't require more than a square foot of floor space. So Leigh did her rhythmic steps with finesse, remembered to smile at her partner, who gave her a military salute in return, and grew hotly aware of Padgett's unrelenting crusade to unravel her.

"Stop that." She glaringly mimed the words at him and tossed her head, determined to not look at the arrogant man again.

But she did look again, like a helpless moth bedazzled back into the consuming flame of the candle—and he still had not lessened his critical study of her. If people spoke to him he answered civilly but without looking at them and persisted in drilling through her.

A sultry Polynesian glamour girl dressed in a strapless sarong of brilliant tangerine print, laid her hand upon Padgett's braced knee. It was obvious that she asked him to dance. Perhaps even more, mused Leigh. Finally, placing his drink upon a nearby table, Padgett relinquished his observation of Leigh long enough to maneuver both of them into the glittering cluster of couples.

Leigh wasn't certain if she appreciated the benefits of modern dance or not. When the music changed she suddenly found herself turned by a hand placed not too discreetly upon her waist. Her partner noticed that his place had been usurped by a tall, authoritative man who could wither him with a set of his jaw and migrated to greener and much more willing pastures.

Without a comment Padgett whirled Leigh into his arms and drew her securely against the familiar movements of his body. The music mellowed and grew dreamily intimate, suggestive, made for close dancing. She tilted her face upward beneath his.

"I thought you were dancing with someone" was all she could think of to say.

The sternness of his features did not lessen. "And I thought you were kissing someone."

"Oh, Padgett," she sighed into the curve of his shoulder. She was hardly able to think, because it was heaven being in his arms again, feeling his jaw braced against the side of her head, breathing his subtle musky scent.

"Peter didn't mean anything by it," she whispered. Wisps of hair about his ears brushed gently against her temple. "Forget about it."

"I don't forget men who kiss my wife."

Amazed then, leaning back in the circle of his arms, for they hadn't discussed marriage in months, she arched her brows high ahd hoped her woman's exhilaration wasn't too obvious. Perhaps Peter's mad strategy wasn't so mad, after all.

Padgett's mouth, though not as grim as it had been the last half hour, remained unsmiling. Lines cut craggily down his face on both sides of his mouth. *He's tired*, she thought and wished she could kiss them away.

"I'm not your wife, Padgett." She forced herself to sound detached, when what she wanted to say was that she would marry him whether he said he loved her or not. Everything was a risk; she would take it.

"Are you staying home for the holidays, Paddy, old man?"

Ben Harrod danced agilely up beside them, which was an accomplishment, considering the magnitude of Stella's extended abdomen. "If you stay in town, I have something to show you. Box office," he said with a contented shake of his curly head. His admiration for his producer brightened his eyes and make him wink at Leigh. "Might not be as pretty as she is, but *good* box office."

"Well," drawled Padgett, "I'm not sure I'll be in L.A., Ben."

"Big plans, huh?"

Padgett squinted at Leigh's pensively pursed

mouth. He replied without glancing at Ben. "Maybe."

Stella Harrod tossed back a red wave from about her face. "Leigh, precious, that dress is just . . . well, it's really great."

"What she's trying to say," her husband threw in as people began to crowd in on both sides of them, "is that any dress is great, as long as you can get into it."

Leigh almost laughed and said that she knew exactly what Stella meant. But she caught herself in time and only smiled. "Thank you. But I don't think you have much longer to wait."

Dropping a hand to her middle, Stella stopped dancing. Both she and her husband laughed at the rounded tummy, as if it and they were the most wonderfully clever things in the world. Seeing them so proudly satisfied with themselves reminded Leigh of what it had been like for her to have Margie alone. She wished she could find her way from all these people and have a good old-fashioned cry of self-pity.

Since her thoughts were focused on her own troubles, she didn't see the devastating wave of compassion that swept over Padgett's features, smoothing away some of the weary tension. With an adept turn he moved them nearer the panels of sliding glass opening out onto the dark catwalks which hovered high above the roar of the Pacific Ocean.

"She's right," he said more gently than he had spoken all evening. "That really is a great dress." Her eyes flicked suspiciously to his, wondering what line of attack he was planning now. As if he read her distrust, he shrugged. "It really is."

Floor-length black crepe, long-sleeved and sheer, it was a dress she had bought with him in mind, but she would never give him the satisfaction of hearing her say it. The design was elegantly simple, yet at the same time daring. The deep plunge of its neckline fell almost to her waist. A soft, wide collar lay over the swell of her bosom, in perfect taste unless someone placed her in awkward position, which Padgett did now.

As Ben Harrod drew his wife toward other host-and-hostess duties, Padgett deliberately fitted Leigh further into the seductive hollow of his arm. With a shrewd shift of the other arm he nudged the deep collar upward from its black pearl button. It yielded easily and allowed his eyes to see, delightfully unimpeded, her naked, pink-tipped breasts.

Of course, he was the only one who was privy to the intimacy except Leigh herself, and her eyes were drawn like a magnet to the silky valley between her breasts, to their paleness. In that lightning moment, before logic reminded her where they were, she grew achingly pleased that he found her so lovely. He had once settled her upon his stomach and arranged her hands behind her head in a bewitching pose and had lain back again, fascinated with every part of her.

"Beauty is such a small part of it," he had told her, "but I'm glad you are."

He had touched her and kissed her and tantalized her with his tongue which drew such leisurely, skillful patterns. She had arched her back like a cat and tangled her fingers in his hair because it was all utterly unbearable.

"A really great dress," he repeated now with a hoarse break in his voice.

Leigh blushed furiously, not that he would look at her, but that he could arouse her in this public place.

She quickly attempted to step into his body and prevent him from embarrassing her. An immodest grin slashed across his face.

Moistening his lips, flicking his eyes to hers only for the seconds he needed to read what she was thinking, he winced at the accusation he found. Slowly he let out his breath. His desire reached across the inches which separated them. Without a touch, without a word, Leigh felt her breasts tighten and respond to his man's need to touch them. That one reaction denied any protest she could have raged at him.

She knew he saw the urgency which rippled through her, even in the unnerving distraction of people moving around them. They found themselved strangely unable to keep up the aloof pretenses of the last months. She wanted to collapse in relief that he understood how she felt without her clumsy attempts to explain. And she was positive—in spite of his anger this evening, and his jealousy—that he would take her anywhere and make love to her if she would only say yes.

"What do you want?" he said thickly.

"What do I want? I want you to apologize for mistrusting me with Peter."

"I apologize. I apologize," he murmured, moving his gaze longingly over and around as his color darkened with fascination. "If you'll get out of here with me, I'll get down on my knees and apologize."

One of the knees in question leaned heavily against hers; then the long muscles of his thigh pressed into hers. In a moment of lapsed control he moved to touch what his eyes had been adoring.

A voice spoke his name from behind them, and Padgett started. He gave the casual impression of turning as he pulled Leigh into his own body, crushing her curves into his chest. He breathed a soft and infinitely satisfying obscenity into her ear.

She couldn't prevent her gentle laughter.

"There's a long-distance call for you, Mr. Williams," the bartender said. "Do you want to take it in Mr. Harrod's study?"

"Ah . . . yes, thank you," Padgett replied with the most extraordinary difficulty in talking. "Thank you. I'll come."

Leigh felt as if she had drunk too much wine. Blinking, she drew herself tall. Involuntarily her fingers buried themselves in Padgett's sleeve. He closed a large hand over them.

"Stay put," he said. "I'll be right back."

As Padgett left her—and she reminded herself they weren't parting, only separating by a few board feet—she suffered a depressing sense of loss common to a special class of lovers. Part of her vanished with him; she was instantly lonely.

Stepping nearer the glass doors, she strained to see through the December blackness outside.

"Can't I trust you for five minutes?" snapped a familiarly playful voice.

Leigh whirled to find Peter Joshua pretending to twist his beautiful features into a scowl. "You're supposed to be circulating, my lady," he scolded. "Putting your best foot forward and all that rot. How do you think you're going to inflame the Old Man by standing around and pining away? I simply don't know how you can be so unsophisticated. Come on."

"The Old Man is inflamed too much already," she objected with a narrow-eyed smirk. "Butt out, Peter."

"Nonsense. He can't come back and find you

waiting for him like a ninny. And don't give me that garbage about he said he was sorry and all is forgiven."

"Well, he did."

But the actor drew her behind him, much against her will, and she wondered if he were determined to send Padgett's jealousy clear into orbit. They paused at the bedroom where everyone's coats were piled in several unlikely heaps.

"What are you doing?" she demanded.

For a moment Peter burrowed through the wraps, discovered her cape on the bottom of one of the piles, and slung it about her shoulders. He retrieved his own jacket before he answered.

"I'm going to take you out on the catwalks. Breathtaking view. You wouldn't want to miss it."

"Breathtaking? I guess so, in weather like this."

She followed behind him, grumbling with every step. After satisfying herself that Padgett wasn't bearing down upon them in one of his smoldering tempers, she yielded and ducked her head against the bite of the wind.

Leigh clutched the handrail with a passion; even though the walkway was lighted, she didn't trust it. The roar of the surf crashed furiously below them, hurling itself on rocks which she couldn't make out in the darkness. Its violence was surpassed only by the howling savagery of the wind. Her cape swirled out like some Draculean symbol in a supernatural thunderstorm.

"What do you think?" he yelled above the power of the breakers.

She laughed at the wildness of it. "It's wonderful!"

The actor stepped forward and bent over the rail.

"Don't do that!" she cried.

Realizing that he had frightened her, Peter stepped back to wrap a reassuring arm about her. Their hair was torn in all directions, and hers was as much about his head as her own. When Padgett appeared from nowhere, her choked surprise was swallowed up in the fury of the ocean.

The older man clapped a meaningful hand upon Peter's shoulder. Leigh guessed it must have taken all Pete's skill to appear calm. But he did release her with prudent haste.

"We were looking at the sea!" he yelled.

"You're going to be looking at an unemployment line if you don't get one thing straight," Padgett shot back. "Hands off!"

"Exactly." Peter laughed. "Are you going to need a best man, sir?"

"No!" Padgett thundered.

Leigh began to get the impression that the two men were actually enjoying this outlandish charade. Peter grabbed Padgett's hand as if he were presenting him with a Nobel prize and pumped it up and down vigorously. Over Padgett's shoulder he sent Leigh a triumphant wink. She wanted to roll her eyes to heaven and plead, *Why me?*

"Congratulations, sir."

"Stop calling me sir."

"Yes, sir. She's a fine woman, sir."

"I know that. Now get out of here!"

Padgett's glare would have incapacitated someone with less insight than Peter. Giving the man a slap on the back that sent a shadow of discomfort flickering across Padgett's face, the actor planted a healthy kiss upon Leigh's cheek. Obviously considering his work finished, he vanished with amazing swiftness.

Hiking at the collar of his jacket, Padgett pulled

Leigh close into the curve of his big body. "Do you actually like it out here?"

"Yes." She laughed up at him. "Padgett, I want to go down to the beach."

"It's freezing, woman."

Caught up in her desire to do something wonderful and wildly illogical, she stepped forward and bent over the rail as Peter had done.

Padgett caught her cape and yanked her back. "Idiot!"

"Is there a way down the cliff?"

He shook his head. "There's a way through about a mile on up the coast. Are you sure you want to see the ocean? Let me take you to Palm Beach. It's much more pleasant."

"Padgett, where's your spirit of romance?"

"Somewhere down the front of your dress, I think," he shouted back and pulled her back toward the glass doors. "Come on, infant, I'll drive you in the van. But if you freeze that gorgeous little fanny off, I'm going to make you pay."

Leigh had to admit that it took no small amount of courage to leave the cozy interior of Padgett's customized van. Stepping out onto the deserted coastline of Big Sur in the dead of winter was not an ordeal for the fainthearted.

It was a turbulent night. The moon, when it peeped through the scudding clouds, only made the sea appear more temperamental than ever. Above them, far into the distance, twinkled the merry pinpoints of lights strung around Ben Harrod's catwalks.

Leigh grabbed one of Padgett's hands and pulled him forward like some Lorelei intent on having her way. Then, running ahead, she twirled and coaxed him, scampering along the edge of wet sand amid scattered beach clutter—seashells and agates and fragments of driftwood that weren't splintered upon the rocky coast.

"Listen!" she cried. She was silhouetted against a glittering spray of water which reached high into the sky like a million brave and falling jewels. "The Sirens are calling us, Padgett! Hear the goddesses singing in the wind?"

If Padgett cherished any hopes of remaining warm, he finally abandoned them. In a number of limber strides he caught the impish sprite in a demanding embrace which more than matched the daring of her mood. She arched back against the bones of his thighs, her hair billowing, and was conscious of her cape lashing about their entwined legs.

He laughed. "I'm deaf and blind already. Bewitched, by heaven, by another temptress."

"I have you under a spell?" Her merriment rippled deliciously. "Never fear, I shall turn you into a charming prince."

"And what does that make me now?" he growled with mock ferocity. "A frog?"

For that moment he was as lighthearted as she, but his gray eyes probed too deeply for that. Buried within them smoldered a primitive humanity groping to find the permanence of its counterpart. She glimpsed his intensity; it was the same driving need which had kept her faithful to him. She recognized it instantly.

"It makes you Padgett Williams," she said lovingly, and her breath came with warm misty curls. "Wonderful, wonderful Padgett."

His lips were icy when he kissed her. As the

savagery of the elements raged about them the inside of his mouth was warmly sweet. Leigh met his searching tongue eagerly, willingly, as if she were starving for the smallest taste of him. She drew the warmth of his breath down into her own lungs and clung to the rugged strength of his body.

He released her quickly and they began to run to keep from freezing. Monuments of black rock jutted upward beyond them, and in the capricious moonlight the foam swirled in about them like a virginal bride begging the favors of an unapproachable husband.

"Seen enough of nature?" Padgett called as she clutched at him with freezing fingers.

"Yes! Race you back if I can live that long."

Darting from him, she ran as hard as she could toward the promised haven of the waiting van. Its parking lights glowed an inviting amber, and she kept her eyes riveted to them.

Wet sand squooshed beneath her feet, and the high crest of an incoming wave caught her by surprise. It swirled greedily over the tops of her shoes and soaked the hem of her cape. In a flash she scooped up the hem of her cape and gown, bending slightly forward and wondering why she didn't try to outrun the wave.

"Oh!" she squeaked.

"You are truly mad," Padgett teased as he paused beside her for as long as it took to sweep her up into his arms.

For a single captured moment of eternity—that rare landmark which a person knows that he will look back on and remember for the rest of his life—their eyes met. Leigh watched the moon cast his features into golden prominence for a brief second. She tingled, partly from the cold and partly from the impression that time was being kind; it was standing still for them.

"Do you love me, Leigh?" he asked with husky urgency.

Her answer was poignantly simple. "Yes. Do you love me?"

"More than I can ever tell you."

"Will you please marry me?" she asked. "Tomorrow?"

"You couldn't stop me."

As quickly as they had separated, the clouds moved shut to hide the moon. When Padgett swung open the doors of the idling van, the night was very dark. Leigh felt, held tightly in his arms, that she was sheltered from the sea. He was a bold pirate who took what no man dared to deny him, and she was a princess from a faraway land who would be his forever.

The van beckoned them into the intriguing plushness of its interior: an island of sensual promises and soft cozy carpet, a hideaway shut off from everything except what they wanted to make of it.

She almost hated to begin the ritual of removing her wet shoes and stockings and the soggy cape and gown. When she was a naked portrait, bent, her cheek resting on her knee and her arms draped about her legs, Padgett swiftly folded her into a blanket.

The minutes on the beach had been crazy and beautiful. Now she leaned her head forward and let her hair curtain her face. She didn't want to be kissed just yet; she wanted to hold herself intact for a few more seconds and realize who and what they were. It was coming true, that dream which she had refused to relinquish for all those years.

Padgett stood over her, barefooted and bare-chested. She looked up at him then, at how splendid and desirable he was.

"I do love you," she told him, as if she must repeat the words lest there be a mistake.

Not replying, he leaned across her and rummaged in a compartment beside a swivel chair. He withdrew a bottle of red wine.

"You came prepared for this?" she chided gently.

"I wish I could say yes, but it was a gift. If I had planned it, little one, I would have done a much better job, believe me. I want to drink a toast."

"Well, we can do it the old-fashioned way," she said, "straight out of the bottle. It's obvious you're not adept at keeping assignations. Which suits me perfectly."

Using a pocketknife and chewing on his lower lip, Padgett negotiated the cork. He flicked on the stereo and dropped down beside her, Indian fashion. He was as limber and flexible as a boy, and it dawned on her that that was what they were: children, beautiful children doing things for the first time that most people had long since grown weary of.

Her eyes mellowed, and she cupped the virile plane of his jaw in her palm.

Turning, he said, "Yes, sweet lady?"

"We've done this all backward, haven't we? According to the rules, I mean?"

He chuckled. "I suppose. Having our daughter first, then making love, then courting, then getting married. Yes, I'd call that backward."

"But good. Right?"

"Yes." He brushed her lips delicately with his. "Definitely good."

For long moments they did not move; they didn't talk or smile or appear restless. They listened to the soft music and were grateful that life had not allowed them to lose each other.

"What shall we drink to?" she asked him finally.

"Why do you have all the blanket?" He countered her question with his.

"You gave it to me, silly."

He eyed her reproachfully and began unfastening the corner of blanket draped about her shoulders. "I was a fool, then."

He bared her shoulder, her arm, and then the pale softness of her side. Her back tapered into a tiny waist; his eyes moved along its curve as he increased his pull on the blanket. It played into his hands until she was a slender statuette of such gentle, gentle beauty that he couldn't speak.

No coyness sparked in her eyes when she met his. She was his woman; he was her man; and—backward or not—they belonged together for all time. With a flick of his wrist, he swirled the blanket about them both. Still, he didn't touch her, as if the moment should be spun out until every second counted for something unique.

He offered her a sip from the bottle. "It'll make you warm," he said.

Her smile curved. "Warm?"

"Hot, then." Lifting the bottle in a toast, he said, "To what we've found, darling. After so long."

As Leigh sipped and then returned the long-necked bottle he talked in slow, husky whispers. "You're everything I've ever wanted, Leigh." He touched her lips with his fingertips, as if he were a blind man. "Your kiss, the way you smell." His words came muffled against the rounded curve of her shoulder. "Sometimes I think wanting you will kill me."

She leaned back against the chair as the inadequacy of one blanket became more and more obvious. Padgett forced himself to stop nibbling tiny morsels of her and took a quick swallow of wine as most men would throw down a shot of burning whiskey.

"I've never really cared for this stuff," he said and wiped his mouth. "Drinking wine in December beside an ocean is good luck, you know."

He placed the bottle out of reach. Giggling, Leigh inched backward and folded her arms across her bosom. "You made that up this very minute."

In the near darkness he smiled back. "Yes, I did. Do you believe it?" With a slow gesture, he pulled aside one of her protecting arms. Then the other.

"Ab-absolutely," she whispered. She let him arrange her in the waiting circle of his arm. She felt herself trembling and knew it didn't matter; he was trembling, too.

"I wasn't sure you loved me," he admitted in a disjointed exploration over the satiny curve of her stomach. "If I had been in your place, I'm not sure I could have loved me."

Lifting his hand from her belly, she placed it over the frenetic throb of her heart. Gradually Padgett shaped his fingers around the perfectly fashioned little nipple.

"Oh, Leigh," he muttered as his head dipped low. "Don't ever leave me."

Leigh's throat stretched smoothly as her head fell back against the chair. She hated to seem utterly overcome, but her fingernails buried themselves in the tense muscles spreading the width of his shoulders.

"I would never hurt you," she groaned. "That night"—she paused to flick her tongue over dry lips, and his mouth moved into the inward dip of her waist—"that night at the dance . . . who would have thought it would end here?"

After a few moments of kicking his pants into a negligent crumple, Padgett drew his weight upon her. He shook his head and grinned down at her. "Not ending, sweetheart. Beginning."

She tried to lift her head. "You'll help me tell Margie about us getting married? Then, later, about the other?"

He stilled her movements by clasping her jaws in one palm. "Don't worry about anything, Leigh. It's only when people don't love each other that one should worry. It'll work out, I promise."

She trusted him for no other reason than that she wanted to. She wanted his love so badly that when he slipped his knee between hers, placing his hands beneath her and filling them with her hips, she made it very easy. She was, he discovered, like a blossom which had never quite opened to its fullest. Part of her had still been hidden away, waiting to be told she was loved. There seemed no end to her womanly depth, to her ability to please him.

"Thank you," he said after a very long time.

Leigh nestled deeper into the hollow of his side. "For what?"

"For being who you are. For giving me Margie."

"I didn't give her to you. You gave her to me."

He contentedly pulled himself up onto an elbow. "We have it all, see? Each other, Margie, the ocean, and wine in December."

She agreed drowsily without opening her eyes. "You're an incredibly lucky man, Padgett Williams."

He bent to kiss the silky furl of her lashes. "Yes," he said tenderly, "I know."

## Chapter Thirteen

The drive to the airport the next morning seemed to be a crystallization of several things. Padgett was at the wheel of Elizabeth's car, while Margie and her grandmother were exchanging looks in the back seat over the quiet plans for the wedding and honeymoon. Legal approval would stamp itself upon a relationship which had existed for many years. The two families would converge neatly into a close-knit structure. But where did one small girl fit into all these interlocking facets?

Leigh found herself smiling constantly during the drive, and that only made her daughter's childlike withdrawal more noticeable. Margie felt left out of everything which was happening, Leigh thought, and she wondered if parental love would be enough to keep the young life from jarring, from unsettling.

Even though Leigh and Elizabeth had reassured Margie in every way they knew how that their lives would not be changed by this marriage, the girl remained politely but unusually quiet. All the way to the small airport outside Los Angeles she had kept her solemn little face pressed against the window, turning only when forced to and speaking in well-mannered monosyllables, if at all.

"We will live at the ranch, sweetheart," Leigh promised her daughter. "And you'll see your grandmother almost as much as you do now." She smiled, hoping this reassurance would help. "Where would I find such a good baby-sitter as Grandma?"

Margie returned her bleak smile and said nothing.

Cajoling, Elizabeth made several futile attempts to distract the girl. "You and I will have to drive Gunther in to see the vet," Elizabeth suggested. "It's time he was vaccinated, you know."

But even the beloved Gunther couldn't turn up the corners of Margie's mouth into a cheery smile. Over her shining head the two women's eyes met. Suddenly Leigh began to worry that her marriage would throw a whole new set of problems into her lap.

As they stepped out of the car at the terminal, blinking into the blinding sunlight even though it was cold, Leigh tightened the belt of her long suede coat. In smart knee boots and wide-brimmed hat which she quickly clapped to her head, she looked more like an executive than a bride. But her green eyes sparkled like a girl's as Padgett caught her fingers tightly in his.

"Happy?" He grinned down at her, the crinkling about his eyes drawing the tanned flesh taut over the bones of his cheeks.

There was little they hadn't said to each other the

night before. "Yes," she said and threaded her fingers through his. "But Margie's crying inside, Padgett. I don't know quite what to do."

Over his shoulder, Padgett studied his small daughter as she carried a leather bag which she had insisted was not too heavy. The Learjet he had chartered was all ready for takeoff, and in the outlying terminal arrangements were swiftly completed. Elizabeth and Margie trailed behind the bride and groom out the glass doors, hugged and said their goodbyes, then waited in the chilly wind with Margie standing bravely at attention beside her grandmother.

Halfway to the plane, as Leigh turned to wave a final goodbye, Padgett set down the two pieces of luggage. The copilot was waiting at the door of the plane, but Padgett ignored him.

Leigh hesitantly followed the path of Padgett's eyes as Margie lifted one gloved hand almost to her jaw. Her fingers fluttered in the faintest imitation of a wave, and she crinkled up her face in an effort to hold back the tears.

When Padgett gestured for her to come to him, her face smoothed, then widened with open anticipation. The smile they had all been waiting for spread across her lips, and her booted feet sped across the asphalt.

Leigh's heart filled as she watched the darting form of her daughter. An awkward knot lodged somewhere deep in her throat. Inside, she felt herself growing, becoming a larger woman, with the maternal capacity to share more and more love from a source which had no end. She swallowed hard as Padgett stooped to one knee and Margie threw herself into his open, waiting arms. She stepped nearer as he spun a slow circle and held her close.

Padgett slowly lifted his head from the curve of Margie's shoulder, and she braced her hands against his chest. The girlish words were half laughter and half crying. "You won't change your mind, will you?" she asked in a high voice. "You're coming back, aren't you?"

The eyes of the father met the eyes of the mother, and they knew then what troubled their daughter. Leigh saw the compassion which had made Padgett care for his men who had died with the same tenderness as those who lived. She didn't think it was possible to love a man so much.

"Oh, my dear," Padgett groaned as his large shoulders slumped. "Of course I'll come back." He kissed her cheeks, then blotted the shining tears which glistened on her face. "You have a daddy now, little one. Daddies have a way of insisting that their daughters be right with them. Do you understand that?"

After a second's pause, Margie laughed a bit. "Will you call me from Las Vegas, Mother?"

With maternal habit Leigh pulled at the zipper on Margie's boot, then smoothed the rumpled hair. "The minute we land. I promise."

"Will you call up Dad for me?" Padgett asked with the same seriousness he would use in addressing an adult. "I didn't like to leave him alone."

Margie's reply was filled with self-importance. "Of course. He told me he's going to give me a horse."

Wailing a small shriek of dismay, Leigh stamped her foot, bent her head, and gave it a vigorous shake. Padgett laughed. "I think I'm going to have a long talk with that man," she promised. "You Williams men are far too generous with your possessions."

They watched Margie scamper back to her grand-mother. Padgett grasped both bags in one hand and took Leigh's hand with the other. Wordless intimacies telegraphed between them in that private language only husbands and wives understand.

"I'd give you the world if you had a place to keep it," he teased.

The copilot, giving Leigh an admiring glance which she missed entirely, extended a hand and assisted her up the steps. At the door, for the last brief moment, Leigh looked at Margie, who waved frantically. She threw her daughter a kiss and thought, *We're all beginning a new life, Margie. Be happy, my darling.*

"I don't need the world," she told Padgett breathlessly.

From the step below her, he lifted his silver head. His brows arched in a question, his lips half smiling.

"I don't need the world, Padgett," she said again as a different kind of happiness sent its warmth over her. "I already have it."

# Silhouette Special Edition

## MORE ROMANCE FOR
## A SPECIAL WAY TO RELAX

### $1.95 each

| | | | |
|---|---|---|---|
| 2 ☐ Hastings | 21 ☐ Hastings | 41 ☐ Halston | 60 ☐ Thorne |
| 3 ☐ Dixon | 22 ☐ Howard | 42 ☐ Drummond | 61 ☐ Beckman |
| 4 ☐ Vitek | 23 ☐ Charles | 43 ☐ Shaw | 62 ☐ Bright |
| 5 ☐ Converse | 24 ☐ Dixon | 44 ☐ Eden | 63 ☐ Wallace |
| 6 ☐ Douglass | 25 ☐ Hardy | 45 ☐ Charles | 64 ☐ Converse |
| 7 ☐ Stanford | 26 ☐ Scott | 46 ☐ Howard | 65 ☐ Cates |
| 8 ☐ Halston | 27 ☐ Wisdom | 47 ☐ Stephens | 66 ☐ Mikels |
| 9 ☐ Baxter | 28 ☐ Ripy | 48 ☐ Ferrell | 67 ☐ Shaw |
| 10 ☐ Thiels | 29 ☐ Bergen | 49 ☐ Hastings | 68 ☐ Sinclair |
| 11 ☐ Thornton | 30 ☐ Stephens | 50 ☐ Browning | 69 ☐ Dalton |
| 12 ☐ Sinclair | 31 ☐ Baxter | 51 ☐ Trent | 70 ☐ Clare |
| 13 ☐ Beckman | 32 ☐ Douglass | 52 ☐ Sinclair | 71 ☐ Skillern |
| 14 ☐ Keene | 33 ☐ Palmer | 53 ☐ Thomas | 72 ☐ Belmont |
| 15 ☐ James | 35 ☐ James | 54 ☐ Hohl | 73 ☐ Taylor |
| 16 ☐ Carr | 36 ☐ Dailey | 55 ☐ Stanford | 74 ☐ Wisdom |
| 17 ☐ John | 37 ☐ Stanford | 56 ☐ Wallace | 75 ☐ John |
| 18 ☐ Hamilton | 38 ☐ John | 57 ☐ Thornton | 76 ☐ Ripy |
| 19 ☐ Shaw | 39 ☐ Milan | 58 ☐ Douglass | 77 ☐ Bergen |
| 20 ☐ Musgrave | 40 ☐ Converse | 59 ☐ Roberts | 78 ☐ Gladstone |

### $2.25 each

| | | | |
|---|---|---|---|
| 79 ☐ Hastings | 87 ☐ Dixon | 95 ☐ Doyle | 103 ☐ Taylor |
| 80 ☐ Douglass | 88 ☐ Saxon | 96 ☐ Baxter | 104 ☐ Wallace |
| 81 ☐ Thornton | 89 ☐ Meriwether | 97 ☐ Shaw | 105 ☐ Sinclair |
| 82 ☐ McKenna | 90 ☐ Justin | 98 ☐ Hurley | 106 ☐ John |
| 83 ☐ Major | 91 ☐ Stanford | 99 ☐ Dixon | 107 ☐ Ross |
| 84 ☐ Stephens | 92 ☐ Hamilton | 100 ☐ Roberts | 108 ☐ Stephens |
| 85 ☐ Beckman | 93 ☐ Lacey | 101 ☐ Bergen | 109 ☐ Beckman |
| 86 ☐ Halston | 94 ☐ Barrie | 102 ☐ Wallace | 110 ☐ Browning |

# Silhouette Special Edition

## $2.25 each

| | | | |
|---|---|---|---|
| 111 ☐ Thorne | 133 ☐ Douglass | 155 ☐ Lacey | 177 ☐ Howard |
| 112 ☐ Belmont | 134 ☐ Ripy | 156 ☐ Hastings | 178 ☐ Bishop |
| 113 ☐ Camp | 135 ☐ Seger | 157 ☐ Taylor | 179 ☐ Meriwether |
| 114 ☐ Ripy | 136 ☐ Scott | 158 ☐ Charles | 180 ☐ Jackson |
| 115 ☐ Halston | 137 ☐ Parker | 159 ☐ Camp | 181 ☐ Browning |
| 116 ☐ Roberts | 138 ☐ Thornton | 160 ☐ Wisdom | 182 ☐ Thornton |
| 117 ☐ Converse | 139 ☐ Halston | 161 ☐ Stanford | 183 ☐ Sinclair |
| 118 ☐ Jackson | 140 ☐ Sinclair | 162 ☐ Roberts | 184 ☐ Daniels |
| 119 ☐ Langan | 141 ☐ Saxon | 163 ☐ Halston | 185 ☐ Gordon |
| 120 ☐ Dixon | 142 ☐ Bergen | 164 ☐ Ripy | 186 ☐ Scott |
| 121 ☐ Shaw | 143 ☐ Bright | 165 ☐ Lee | |
| 122 ☐ Walker | 144 ☐ Meriwether | 166 ☐ John | |
| 123 ☐ Douglass | 145 ☐ Wallace | 167 ☐ Hurley | |
| 124 ☐ Mikels | 146 ☐ Thornton | 168 ☐ Thornton | |
| 125 ☐ Cates | 147 ☐ Dalton | 169 ☐ Beckman | |
| 126 ☐ Wildman | 148 ☐ Gordon | 170 ☐ Paige | |
| 127 ☐ Taylor | 149 ☐ Claire | 171 ☐ Gray | |
| 128 ☐ Macomber | 150 ☐ Dailey | 172 ☐ Hamilton | |
| 129 ☐ Rowe | 151 ☐ Shaw | 173 ☐ Belmont | |
| 130 ☐ Carr | 152 ☐ Adams | 174 ☐ Dixon | |
| 131 ☐ Lee | 153 ☐ Sinclair | 175 ☐ Roberts | |
| 132 ☐ Dailey | 154 ☐ Malek | 176 ☐ Walker | |

------------------------------------------

**SILHOUETTE SPECIAL EDITION,** Department SE/2
1230 Avenue of the Americas
New York, NY 10020

Please send me the books I have checked above. I am enclosing $_____
(please add 75¢ to cover postage and handling. NYS and NYC residents please
add appropriate sales tax). Send check or money order—no cash or C.O.D.
please. Allow six weeks for delivery.

NAME _____

ADDRESS _____

CITY _____ STATE/ZIP _____